A SHARPER, MORE MORE LASTING PAIN

ALEX HARVEY-RIVAS

OTHER WORKS

Short Stories

Collections

AUTHOR'S NOTE

Thank you for taking the time to pick up this novel. I cannot say enough how much I appreciate it. If you liked what you read, please consider reviewing it. Word of mouth helps authors out a *lot* and I'd love to see what you think! I am also working on having new projects out in 2025, and they're all set in the same universe as this novel, so consider keeping an eye out for them.

Reader discretion is advised. This is a book with darker subject matter and themes within it. As such, this book will include content which may make readers uncomfortable, including the following:

Body horror

Death

Drug use

Illness

Sex and mild kink

Suicidal ideation

Terminal illness

Violence

Vomiting

To those of us whose bodies have been our harshest battlegrounds, and to those of us whom the institutions over us ultimately failed.

PROLOGUE

The following are the last recordings of Dr. Chloe Duval, provided in accordance with the applicable sections of the Laws for Miasmic Interaction. Copies of the transcribed vocite distributed with permission by the Academic Coalition for Arcane Study (A.C.A.S.)

Recording #1

Today marks the first day of the newest A.C.A.S.-funded expedition into Idune to reclaim it for archaeological use. Gods willing, we will be up-river and studying the ruins by the end of the fortnight. There's a wealth of miasma there, ripe for the sampling.

[A long stretch of static broken by the snapping of twigs, the stamping of boots, and unintelligible murmurs.]

I'm hoping these new preservatives prove useful.

As am I, Professor Blanc. The samples we collected during our last expedition proved too volatile to give more than a cursory scan. Without something to test the preservatives on, it's difficult to determine their success... but I maintain faith, regardless.

Professor Duval, do you think we'll find success out here?

Time will tell. At the very least, our new group of Abjurors should make our current trek leagues safer than the last one.

The Gods willing.

The Gods willing, indeed.

Recording #2

The forests in Elrick are trickier than I gave them credit for.

The first day, I found myself trampling a circular path around the same set of bushes. [A soft chuckle.] How many times did we do that, Professor Blanc?

Four or five, I think.

That sounds right. [A cough, followed by a sniffle.]

We've been walking for a couple of days now with the map Doctor Guérin provided for us. It seems the path has seen some changes since their last expedition. That's nature for you. Still, I have ensured the appropriate updates get made as we go.

[Papers rustle. Twigs snap in the background.]

Professor Duval?

Yes, Dominique?

It... I feel like we're being followed.

Ah, yes. [The rustling of papers continues.] Nature, for all its beauty has a way of making you feel paranoid. This is your first expedition, is it not, Dominique?

Well... yes.

As I thought. The feeling will pass.

[Footfalls trail off in the background. Moments later, heavy crunching.]

I'd be remiss if I did not confess to you I felt similar, Professor Duval.

It gets easier to ignore. The wildlife gets curious, takes to poking around a bit. So long as we ignore them and keep our wards in place, we will be fine.

It feels different this time.

[A sigh.] Go speak to Professor Kontos, then. Perhaps between them and Agnis, some extra preventative measures can be taken.

[Stomping and snapping twigs fade into the distance. A long pause punctuated by static.]

I must confess to feeling the same... but the Gods would not allow us to let their most holy of sites remain in corruption. Though the trek is long and full of brambles, I am not so eager to retire from it.

Besides, the chairwoman would have my head for wasting funds.

[Another sigh.] Laur—Professor Blanc's paranoia is getting to me. That's all this is.

Recording #3

I've updated the map to an incomprehensible degree at this point. Professor Blanc has had to make copies for the sake of legibility. Keeping the interns at bay, though, has proved to be a challenge most unique.

Dominique continues with her insistence on there being something in the woods. Our zoologist, Professor Kontos, assures me they'll remain out of our path. [Harsh metal jangling.] As a precaution, they've distributed clackers to keep us from stumbling upon things we shouldn't.

Still, our fumbles have delayed the timeline considerably. Alas... where the Gods give, they also take away.

[Distant jangling stops.] *Professor?*

What is it now?

Look.

[Clanking continues.]

Ah. It seems you've come across the remains of something's dinner. A deer, I think. Laurent, get a look at this.

[A long pause, filled with crackling static and jangling clackers.]

Seems too neat to be a prey-kill. And it's still intact.

I thought similar. It's unsettling. Dominique?

Yes, Professor?

Take some blood samples and a few photos, if you please. Professor Kontos is still a ways behind and I'm sure they wouldn't want to miss this.

Recording #4

I submitted Dominique's sample to Professor Kontos and found the deer carcass had been covered in miasma, not blood. This struck me as odd, given every miasma sample I've recovered from Idune looks the same: it's viscous and black and inky. These new samples seemed more like a halfway stage, something in between. Does this mean blood can turn miasmic? Can blood be so easily corrupted?

Enlightening and troublesome in equal measure.

Another interesting discovery is the sample collected appears to have limited activity. It was practically alive when we rested for the night, straining against the glass. I've never seen a sample behave this way.

There's been slime molds that look like this before. *Lindbladia tabulina* comes to mind, known for its dark color and dense clusters. Still, slime mold wouldn't kill a larger organism. Not by itself, anyway.

[Glass clinks together.]

Looking at it now, this sample has lost much of its animated properties, but I'm unsure if that's due to decay or something else. Gods willing, I can keep it preserved enough to compare to samples in Idune once we arrive.

Recording #5

[The recording opens with shuddered breathing and stifled gasps, followed by silence lasting several seconds.]

Dominique was right.

[Shuffling and more gasping.]

We had made camp for the night, as usual. I had Professor Blanc and the group do chores while I continued my (unsuccessful) port-mortem observations of the material we collected. It was while doing so Dominique herself came to visit me.

"I've felt it again," she told me. I told her it was the paranoia of an amateur explorer.

And yet, she was right.

Not long after her visit to my tent, I heard them. I don't even know what to call them. Monsters is as apt an approximation as any. Creatures reminiscent of humans, wearing what looked like insect carapaces and dripping with pitch. It's easy to describe them in retrospect, I suppose. In the moment, I could only focus on how absolutely *wrong* they looked.

The hunt was already on when I emerged from my tent. Dominique's blank expression focused on me across the clearing. A mix of blood and black slime seeped from the wound in her side. Dead before she hit the ground. I pray the Gods were merciful and took her swiftly.

Most of the research team was killed in the attack.

It's just three of us left. Myself, Professor Kontos, and Laur—Professor Blanc. I still don't know how to describe the full depths of what happened.

[A long pause. Low, pained groaning in the background.]

I will stop my recollection here. It appears Laurent is coming back to.

Recording #6

Laurent, my dearest friend, my loyal partner in science, is dying.

The wounds they sustained during the attack have festered in a way I've never seen before. Each time they're leeched, the fluid is brackish and putrid. The scent that rolls off them is equally as foul.

"Leave me here," they said last night. [Shuddered breathing.] I had half a mind to comply.

But... I can't. Professor Kontos succumbed to their own wounds a couple of days ago. If Laurent dies, I'm alone. I can't bear to try to continue this journey on my own.

[More shuddered breathing, accompanied by sniffling.]

In a sick twist of fate, Laurent's injuries have allowed me another look at the fluid we recovered from the deer corpse last week. It appears this fluid surging through Laurent's system now is like what we sampled and recovered before. It's behaving in a similar fashion, animated and reaching. I have no doubts now as to what caused it. There are monsters stalking these woods. Are they related to the miasma we've studied in Idune?

By my new counts, we will be in Idune within a couple of days. I have to keep us moving.

Recording #7

Idune, once a massive and holy gravesite, has become naught less than an overgrown hovel in the years since its formation. Nature in Elrick, it seems, is aggressive and quick to reclaim any stolen land. The statues here look more like poorly-trimmed hedges.

But, at last, I've found it.

I don't know how I'm getting out, if I'm being honest. The exploration team has been reduced to... me. Can I truly brave the wilderness all by myself?

Ah, well. I am wasting time thinking of my own mortality. For now, it is just me and the wealth of miasma bubbling around me. I should get to studying.

[A long pause punctuated by static.]

Laurent should have been here for this. It was their department that backed the expedition, not mine. I'm just the woman with the vocite clusters and the knowledge of miasma. I've been at this for longer than I've had any right to.

It's just... it's just not fair.

Recording #8

The pools of miasma here have grown considerably since our last expedition two years ago. I tried to take measurements to compare to the old notes and ran out of tape for most of the sites. The smallest mass of it I've found thus far is an impressive five feet wide. It swallowed the stick I used to try to measure depth, however. For now, the notes just say "very deep". An unscientific approximation as any.

Another feature of note is the activity. Much like the small samples I've obtained from corpses along the way, the pools here gurgle constantly. If I turn my back for too long, I find they've shifted position, like they're reaching for something.

It's difficult to quantify their makeup, but it's reminiscent of slime mold. Only... more sentient. I set traps and fed a couple of the sites what small vermin I managed to catch. They consumed the offerings. Or perhaps, like the stick I lost, the animals drowned in their depths and are fermenting somewhere below.

A final, strange observation I've had: the whole of Idune—miasma and all—becomes incredibly active whenever I cast a spell. Being the byproduct of said magic, I cannot say I'm fully surprised, but it feels different than the notes I've made previously. It's not that more miasma forms when I cast a spell. For example...

[The crackle of magic being cast.]

Here, I have produced a wink of Evocation magic, a simple ball of flame. Despite the weakness of the spell, the puddles around me have reacted in an instant.

[Another hiss.]

I've tested this theory with all the avenues of magic available to me. The result is the same. Somehow, this is all connected. I just hope I have time to decipher it all.

[Distant groaning.]

I'll have to pick this up la—

[Growling in the background. The sound of a pistol cocking.]

[A single gunshot, followed by an astonished shout. Static slowly builds to a crescendo before the audio suddenly cuts.]

ONE

Simone Allard || After

Across the desk, Simone's Intro to Glyph Design professor reads their thesis proposal with a thoughtful furrow in his brows. In the silence that follows, the standing clock in the corner of the room ticks in time to Simone's heartbeats.

Then, with a soft chuckle, he says, "This is quite ambitious."

He sets their proposal down with a slap, sending his small army of pens scattering. Their title stares back at them, *An Investigation of Sanguina Malefica and Possible Causes.* They won't have to worry about their thesis—or the accompanying spell tome—for another year at least, but they like to be prepared.

Clearing their throat, Simone says, "Perhaps, but you'll find it relates well to my Casting major and abilities."

Professor Darzi gives another soft laugh. He is a graying man, strong in the jaw and wearing his age the way one might a favored coat. Many of the students in his class swoon when they see him, their affection painfully obvious. Simone can admire the smattering of white in his goatee and the brown patches on his elbows. However, it is his earthy lecturing voice and his perspective on glyph design they appreciate the most.

Design in general, it seems, is his strong suit. Hints of his aesthetic pepper the office: a seventh century map of the world, color-coded with political relations of the time; books along every shelf, wrapped in leather and wrinkled with age; an incense burner which exhales a soft stream of lemon-tinged smoke.

Professor Darzi clasps his hands over their thesis. "I'm impressed, Mx. Allard. It's all too often we have floundering third-years still trying to get themselves together, so I find your eagerness refreshing."

The pause after his words is a knife at their neck. "But?" Simone prods with a swallow.

"I must admit concern. Relations with Elrick are quite tenuous as it is. I wouldn't want to send a student into more than they could handle."

His point is valid, of course. Elrick in particular is a country riddled with monstrosity, its Casters fighting a losing battle against miasma in an attempt to keep it from enclosing on the rest of the world. Even Simone's enbei had urged caution in them when they first brought the proposal up to them, citing the travel required into the heart of the warzone to conduct their research, but Simone didn't care. Sanguina Malefica as a disease has ravaged Casters as harshly as monsters have.

Simone shoots up, spine rod-straight, and jabs a finger into the desk. "It wouldn't be, though." Their whole body rattles. "See my records, Professor, and the recommendation letters. I'm quite capable."

With a soft smile, Professor Darzi shifts their thesis to regard a brown folder underneath. He lifts a corner and thumbs through, expression never changing. "You are," he says as the folder closes with a whisper. Then, hands again clasped, "I just want you aware of your options. You are not yet into your third year. Sometimes, interests change."

Simone's stomach clenches. Sucking on their cheeks, they shift focus to the window. Outside, the midday sun casts shards of golden light across the campus. Casters mill about in the expansive courtyard in small groups, wearing the capelets of their grade and specialization. Simone adjusts their own capelet, cobalt for second year Abjurors. In a few months, they'll don the powder blue capelet signifying entry into their third year—if they can keep their classes and thesis in order.

"We'll start with this."

Their attention flicks back to Professor Darzi. He pulls a stamp pad closer, flips open their folder, and presses a stamp into the top page, hard enough to make it crinkle. Simone reads the words as he pulls away: Discussion Needed. Their breath catches.

"The idea of it," he says, replacing the stamp, "is a fine one. But…" His words lack the soft, baritone lilt they've carried the whole conversation. Hesitance makes itself known in the crinkle of his thick brows.

"But?"

"Mx. Allard, I will be frank: the concept you're presenting is dangerous. The last students we sent into Idune did not return."

Simone bows their head. One year ago, Professor Chloe Duval and her group of scientists traveled to Idune to investigate the wealth of miasma there. Monsters had slaughtered most of the group along the way, and even Chloe herself hadn't lived long after recording the last of her findings. Simone remembers the vigils Voterique College had held when word came back, and how lost in the sea of sorrow and disparaged shrieking they'd become, though they hadn't known anyone who had gone on the voyage.

Now here they are, proposing a mission which could grant them the same fate.

"I'm aware of the risks, Professor," Simone says. "They do not sway me."

The soft smile he wears tightens around the edges. "Very well. Do keep an alternative or two in mind, just in case." He slides their thesis forward, mouth a thin line, before leaning back with a sigh. His leather chair squeaks with the movement. "For now, I believe we're out of time to discuss."

Simone takes their folder back with the faintest tremble in their hands. With it planted against their chest, they rise on doe-like legs and offer bow. Anxiety hums in their blood. "Thank you very much, Professor," they say before nudging the chair back in and stepping away. It takes unearthly restraint to keep from bolting out of the room.

In the hall, Simone's stoic composure buckles with the rest of them. They slump against the wall, blood roaring in their ears. Their thesis proposal crinkles when they clutch it closer, sure the moment they let go it will disappear.

Despite their overwhelming nerves, though, there are pinpricks of relief. After months of planning and writing and rewriting, and though there is still some debate to be had, they've been accepted.

***

The plaza is active with students milling about in the afternoon sun. Capelets of various colors and shades snap in the soft breeze, distracting Simone from their notes.

With a sigh, they set their stylus down and read the single sentence they've written all afternoon. *Alternative proposal ideas.* Below it, a bullet list devoid of actual points. The rest of the page remains woefully blank, dribbles of enchanted ink clinging to the edges.

They could come up with alternatives, given more time. Abjuration is a realm as diverse as the other seven and they have a whole year to consider. Alas, nothing at this moment fascinates them as much as their desire to find the source of Sanguina Malefica and destroy it.

Still, as frustrating as Professor Darzi's feedback is, Simone's determination burns all the brighter for it. What was science if not a—often dangerous—pursuit for answers?

Nadia will know what to do.

Mouth quirking, they shove their notes into their bag. She had already left when they woke up this morning, much to their chagrin. They still had plenty to discuss with her after... whatever last night had been, but this is more important right now.

The eight dormitory towers loom in the distance as they begin their trek for the dorms. They recognize a few of the students heading the same way—there's Didier, assistant to the library workers of Voterique, his face hidden behind a mountain of books. Simone would've missed him were it not for the telltale cloud of brown hair. Moments later, they pass Alienor, recognizable by her shock of pale blonde hair and ebony cane. She's the head of the graduating Abjuror class this year, which makes her Simone's—and all the other Abjuration Casters—advisor. The smile she offers is all sunlight, enough to warm Simone from the inside out.

After a moment to fawn, they keep moving.

The dormitory towers are arranged in a tight octagon, each three stories tall. Simone eyes their apartment building as they walk past, blue Abjuration banners flapping in the wind.

As they approach Nadia's building—purple banners signifying Divination—the lamps along the courtyard flare to life. *Is it already close to sundown?* Simone surveys the sky with narrowed eyes, watching as blue shifted to gold, with tinges of pink creeping through. Before long, summer will be upon them, and Simone for one is grateful. Mertish winters are milder than the rest of the world, but any chill in the air is enough to make Simone long for the comfort of their room.

Inside the Diviner's tower, soft plum carpets make each step uneven. Portraits along the walls gaze down at Simone with eyes of charcoal and acrylic, their minor animations fighting for Simone's attention. They hobble up the stairs to the third floor, on the verge of gasping at the top of the landing. A dull throbbing keeps their knee in an uncomfortable grip.

But it can wait. Their thesis is more important.

They scan the hallway before them as they struggle to regain their breath. Twice, Simone has seen the frenzy students whip themselves into as they decorate their dorms. Walls, carpets, doors... nothing is spared from exorbitance, undone at the end with the flourish of a spell tome. While Simone has never longed to waste time on such frivolities, Nadia's door illustrates her passions to the fullest. Her name is printed in bold silver letters against a dark purple background. White and gold clouds border the corners.

Simone nudges the door open with a couple harsh bumps of their hip—she *really* should talk to the administrators about getting the latch fixed—and stumbles into the darkness beyond.

"Nadia?"

No response. Simone eases the door shut behind them and taps the magicite lamp to their side. Golden light floods the room, illuminating the worn purple upholstered couch and scratched-up table. The rug beneath them is grayed with dirt.

"Nadia? It's me." They set their notes down on the table, wincing at its creak. Everything about Nadia's apartment is as fragile as she is.

Still no answer, they note with a frown. *She must still be out.* A soft sigh slips free at the thought. *I'll wait for her.*

A horizontal half-wall separates the main room and the kitchen. A jar of herbs sitting on top catches Simone's eye. They can't decipher the scrawl, aside from a line at the bottom highlighting its purpose. *Nausea and pain relief.* Their stomach twists in sympathy. Nadia's symptoms have been worsening for weeks now.

I'll revisit the notes this weekend. There's some answer we're not seeing.

Simone's jaws part in a yawn. Nadia won't be offended if they nap while they wait, will she?

They consider sleeping on the couch, but the high rise of the armrests promise a sore neck. Instead, they tiptoe for her bedroom. A canopied bed is pushed to one wall, gauze framing it the color of a winter sunrise and riddled with moth holes. Beside it, a modest desk is losing a battle with the army of papers stacked atop it. A water and food bowl are tucked underneath, each half-empty. The pile of clothes at the foot of the bed has grown since Simone last noticed it.

With a frown, they gather the clothes up. The items with more of a smell drift back to the floor. Everything else they sort further: a corduroy skirt; a button-up blouse with a faded brown stain; a yellow turtleneck she wore on their first official date. Once everything is sorted, they set to work putting it all away.

As the last drawer shuts, they give Nadia's room another slow spiral. Rays of setting sunlight illuminate the dust drifting in the air. *I'll need to talk to her again.*

Had she mentioned being somewhere after classes? They can't recall, but it's possible they'd forgotten. Lately, their memories have been hazier than normal.

"Well," they say, gaze landing on the threadbare cat doll resting on Nadia's pillows, "she'll come back when she comes back. In the meantime..." A sudden yawn overtakes them. Rubbing their eyes,

Simone slides under the blankets, holding Nadia's doll close. It smells of sweat and Serenity and dust, a bouquet all Nadia's own.

***

The screech of the wall phone tears Simone from their dreamless sleep. Eyes wide, they shoot upright at the sound, stuffed cat tumbling away. Their heart beats wild in their chest.

Perhaps it's Nadia, they think, seconds before it dawns on them how foolish the notion is. Still groggy, they stand, the ground swaying underneath them. The pits of their stomach coil tight. Despite their optimism, something feels off in the too-still air. They take a step for the living room and falter as the phone cuts out mid-ring, replaced by crackling static.

Then, after a moment of silence, it rings again.

The rattle of the receiver jerks Simone from their stupor. After a breath to collect themself, they approach. The receiver is leaden in their hand.

"Hello?"

"Nadia, what the fuck?"

They recoil from the lash-sharp voice on the other end, struggling to identify the speaker. "I... don't know," they say between yawns. "She isn't here."

"Where the fuck is she, then?"

Simone searches their thoughts for a name matching the harried voice. "I don't know," they say again. "I've been waiting for her to return. Is everything all right?"

The caller's next words chase the remainders of drowsiness from Simone's mind.

"Wherever she is, tell her to come to the hospital ward. It's about Etienne. He's..."

The receiver twirls and slams against the wall. They don't give themself time to hang up. Trembling anew, Simone bolts for the exit.

TWO

Nadia Dupont || Before

The week begins as many of them have recently: with violent vomiting.

Pregnancy is out of the question—she hasn't touched a dick since the awkward handjobs in undergrad, and she isn't fond of them besides—and she's spent one too many mornings hunched over porcelain to blame her problems on an ill-cooked meal. A lesser person could attribute it to her frequent misuse of Serenity, but such opinions aren't worth listening to.

Nadia's stomach churns as she dares a glance at what she's expelled. The liquid is as dark as mashed licorice candies, a maelstrom of ink. Staring at it makes her want to vomit again. Instead, she clings to the porcelain with leaden limbs.

If she's being honest, there is no real cause to blame. This is part of the pattern she's found herself in for months, each day rolling into the next in a burning ball of agony. Between her stomach's inability to settle and the constant creaking of her joints, she can't remember the last time she's been well and truly healthy.

The medics really need to get their shit together.

She's still hunched over when the front door slams. Seconds later, the click of Etienne's heels fills the apartment.

"Nat, are you home?" As he speaks, she hears his jacket drop, buttons clacking against the wood.

As she opens her mouth to speak, a new wave of bile churns and threatens to spill. With a deep breath, she calls, "Yeah."

The slap of his bare feet draws closer. Nadia reaches for the toilet lid, hands shaking, before reconsidering. Etienne has seen her in worse states before. He's *been* in worse states before with her.

"Class is gonna star— oh."

She doesn't look behind her—not that she can, given her sudden lack of strength. Instead, she raises a trembling hand and flashes what she hopes is a wave before slumping back down.

"Too much Serenity last night?"

Another wave of bile curdles her stomach. "I would've preferred that."

He drops down beside her. "You look like shit," he says as he reaches over her and hits the lever. She shrinks back as the water swirls and gurgles. Bracing herself against the wall, she throws her head back and examines the flickering lamps overhead.

"Is this...?" Etienne starts before falling silent. Then, after a beat, he finds his courage. "Are you sick again?"

Nadia folds her arms, wincing as her muscles tense. *I've* been *sick and didn't get better*, she wants to say. *I can't remember when I last woke up without nausea, or without my joints flaring with such intensity I would rather die than experience it again.*

Instead, with a resigned sigh, she says, "I don't know."

"Do you want me to copy today's notes? Have you stay home again? I can brew you some tea and get you settled in bed."

She hates that she considers it. The truancy notices are piling high on her nightstand, though, and sleeping all day will do nothing but give her a headache and a worsening sense of worthlessness.

"No." Nadia shakes her head. Her stomach takes a hard dip when she stands and, just for a second, she again reconsiders. Still, as she meets Etienne's widened eyes, she says, "I think I will be okay for now." She hopes he can't hear the undercurrent of doubt in her own words.

She flinches when she catches her face in the mirror. Thick black rings frame her sunken eyes. Greyness has sucked the vibrancy from her light brown skin, giving her a sickly hue. Once, she'd maintained a respectful amount of softness in her thighs and hips, but illness has since deflated her.

Etienne meets her gaze through the reflective glass. "You're starting to worry me."

A harsh laugh spills free before she can stop it. "I'll be fine, Etienne. Nothing can hold me under for long."

"Stubbornness will not sustain you forever."

Nadia continues her half-hearted preening, washing her face before reaching without looking for the jars balanced on the sink. With two fingers, she swipes soft powder under her eyes. An enchanted balm seeps into the cracks of her lips and fills them. Her reflection livens in an instant.

She is still working cream into her cheeks when Etienne draws closer and takes her wrist.

"Nadia."

She stills, cheeks tightening with the unworked product.

"I'm serious," he says.

"I'm serious, too." She shrugs Etienne off with a snort. "Soon enough, the medical ward will know what ails me." *And if I could, I would make them tell me faster.* As she pinches her cheeks to redden them, she gives him a pointed stare. "Do not grab me like that again."

His mouth opens, releasing a soft sigh and a fraction of a word before closing once more. "My apologies." Then, collecting her jars into a neat pile, he says, "Your field trip is today, right?"

Nadia doesn't remove her gaze from her reflection. Truth be told, she had all but forgotten about the trip, a venture to some museum with a small-scale model of a historical sight she was supposed to know but couldn't find within her to care about. For a third, final time, she considers taking Etienne up on his offer. The tram ride into town aside, a field trip promises more mobility than she thinks herself capable of handling. Not without assistance, anyway. Perhaps she can get an aid out of him.

"It is." One by one, she collects the jars from Etienne and replaces them. "So I don't suppose you have time to draft me up a pain sigil?"

***

She thinks their name is Simone, but it's hard to remember with their fingers deep inside her.

They have her propped against a pillar, her favorite black skirt bunched around her hips and their mouth locked on hers. Nadia clenches around them as they thrust soft fingers into the deepest parts of her. The vanilla and orange musk drifting from their skin sends any rational part of her brain scrambling.

For the first time in weeks, someone livens her in a way Serenity never can.

She's known they wanted her from the moment they shared looks in the waiting line for the tram into town. While their professor of the day was busy droning on about historical sites in Elrick, Nadia had worked every subtlety she could think of into their brief glances to show her interest. Soft scratching of her neck. A coquettish smirk. Though her stomach is still a raging sea, the ache in her joints is dull today, and she has the sigil Etienne crafted for her in case the pain makes an unwanted return. She can afford to be adventurous.

Besides, sex always beats out a lecture.

Nadia nibbles the stranger's neck, a rare sensible thought coming to her as they continue to work her. "If we get caught, we're fucked."

"Best hurry, then." As they speak, the stranger's fingers spread apart, rubbing her in a way that sends stars skittering across her vision. Head thrown back, she arches into them and moans again, low and keening.

It's such a shame this encounter is a one-off.

Their thumb circles her, decimating her capacity for lucid thought. Then, as she approaches the precipice, their hand slows. "Do you know the history of this place?"

Their words slice sudden, violent clarity through her. Tight around them, she feels the heat dissipating. "I..." She fights the urge to smash her mouth against theirs and help them coax her over the edge, though she bucks her hips with a soft whine. "What?"

Their sly expression doesn't change. "Not the ground we're standing on, obviously, but the place they've modeled it after. Idune."

"N-No, I can't say I have." Nadia rolls her hips again, breath fluttering. "Is this the best moment for—"

"It's fascinating, really." Just like that, they resume their pace inside her. Nadia loses herself in the sudden swell of heat, so consumed she almost doesn't catch their next words.

"This was once the final resting place of the original Gods, before miasma consumed it. Did you know that?"

Between soft moans, Nadia chokes out, "If I wanted a lecture, I'd have stayed back." Still, as she speaks, there is something about them that makes her heart skip.

They hum, eyes narrowed and dark like over-brewed coffee. "But you're here." With quick flicks, the stranger returns her to her delicate dance on the edge of orgasm. "With me. Getting fucked within an inch of your life. You should still learn something."

What kind of person talks like this during sex?

"When the new Gods ascended, They were made to exhume the graves of their predecessors and carry them to a new gravesite," they continue. "For obvious reasons, the model we've been taken to is just an approximation of what Idune once looked like. Quite fascinating, don't you think?"

Nadia doesn't have time to think of a rebuttal as, legs quaking, the world falls out beneath her. She bites their lip, hard enough to draw blood, to muffle the scream as her orgasm crests over her. They're better than her hand or any toy she has half a mind to conjure, and for a heart-stopping second she fears she'll be caught in this state of bliss forever.

Then, as the hum in her ears starts to fade, they withdraw.

"It was nice to meet you." As gentle as possible, the stranger lowers her to the ground, arranging her skirt just so and smoothing back her hair. Light frames them from behind, reminiscent of a painting Nadia saw once, *Dakota Encounters the Goddess Maka.*

Soft murmurs escape her mouth as she gazes up at them. She can only watch, dumbfounded, as they wipe their hand against their slacks.

"My name's Simone, by the way. Not sure if I told you that."

"Pleasure," she replies, chuckling at the pun. "I'm Nadia."

"I'll see you around, Nadia."

Then they're gone, leaving her a heap of twitching limbs and shaking breaths.

Gods, it really is a shame she'll never see them again.

***

That evening, Nadia finds herself in a darkened apartment thick with foliage, the ache in her joints having crescendoed throughout the day to a feverish pitch. The ceiling spins overhead, painted to depict a mural from the Coven Era several centuries ago.

"Let me be sure I understand," Etienne says as he passes a goblet on. "You fucked someone during a field trip?"

Chantal laughs beside him. "I've done that before," she says, taking the goblet with a shake of her cloud-like hair. A soft, silken headband keeps her cluster of curls out of her face. Nadia watches her take a slow sip, grey liquid clinging to her lips, and hates herself for the twinge in her gut that makes her want to suck the liquid free.

"Same," says Luc, taking the goblet next. "The thrill of it all is more than enough, even if the sex itself is bad." Mouth grey, they pass the goblet along next. Their eyes turn dark, pupils consuming the iris whole, and they throw their head back with a low growl. "*Fuck*, that's strong."

Chantal's smile is wicked, teeth like a predator's. "I have a contact in Elrick, up the Foxtrot. A hefty price for certain, but this is as pure as it gets."

Nadia conjures a vague map of the far-away country as her head dips in respect. During summer break, a professor had launched an expedition to Idune—the same sight she saw a model of today, she recalls. Whether it was monster attacks or the Elrish militia, everyone on the expedition had been killed. Regardless, all Nadia knows is it's now a bitch and a half to get mail to and from the country.

The goblet continues its rotation when the moment of mournful silence has passed. "I can feel the universe," Etienne says, quiet enough only Nadia hears. She gives his thigh a soft squeeze in response.

Her thoughts flick back to the stranger she met earlier in the afternoon, but she clears them with a stiff shake of her head. What is she doing, pondering over someone she doesn't know? This campus is one of the larger institutions in Mertaln. Chances are they'll never see each other again.

Before she knows it, the goblet is back in her hands and she dares a look into its inky depths. This batch of Serenity is thick and sluggish, leaving a slime trail in its wake. She doesn't have to sip it to know Luc is right about its potency. It reminds her of her disjointed morning hunched over the toilet, though, and with that revelation, she hesitates.

"Don't drink all of it, Nat," Etienne says beside her. He reaches for the goblet with trembling hands, the veins in his eyes dark. She sees her reflection in his blown-out pupils, uncertain and haggard.

"S-Sorry." She passes it along without drinking, for once unnerved. As Etienne sinks deeper into the drug's thrall, she gives the group another appraisal. Chantal is lying on her back now, tracing shapes into the ceiling. Sparks of magic dance off her gloved hands. Luc is curled around her, stroking her hair and purring.

On a normal day, she's deep in the throes of ecstasy with them. It's so strange, then, to be a sudden outsider.

"Nat."

His voice comes from inside her skull now, another benefit to Serenity. If they're both inducted, they can share *much* more between themselves. Flickers of their combined memories fill the back of her mind at the thought.

She looks at Etienne from the corner of her eye. "Hmm?"

"You didn't drink." He holds the goblet up in offering, leaning hard against her. Her skin ripples where he touches her. "I can't drop alone." Through the channel he's burrowed into her brain, she feels the traces of his apprehension.

"Everyone else is with you," she says, eyeing the cup with a tight throat.

His pulse beats through their joined fingers, slow but strong. He doesn't need to speak, mentally or otherwise, to make his retort known. *I can't without you.*

She takes the goblet back from him and gives it a sniff, stomach curling. Normally, she's the first to drop in these blissed-out moments. When was the last time she was able to observe?

As she struggles to recall, she swipes at the dregs around the rim with her tongue.

Dropping into Serenity is like stepping into a blizzard, she thinks—one of her last lucid thoughts as the room spins away. She takes another sip as the room darkens before setting the goblet somewhere behind her.

Etienne's presence brushes against her mind again, slow enough to catch this time. "Ready?"

Nadia blinks. The world is black, then white, then a kaleidoscope of colors she cannot possibly decipher. It converges in a swirling vortex inches from her nose, so cold her skin pimples. With a soft swallow, she takes one last look at Etienne before the vortex swallows her whole.

THREE

Simone Allard || After

As Simone folds over on themself, heart a pinned butterfly within their chest and their breath coming out in wheezes, it occurs to them how nonathletic they are. Matters of the body have oft been relegated to their younger sister, a warrior in her own right. Meanwhile, much of Simone's own childhood had found them within their enbei's study, poring over tomes until their eyes burned and their mother collected them for dinner. Not that they had minded, of course. History fascinated them more than sportsmanship.

Still, the ability to run without getting winded would suit *quite* well right about now.

They focus on the thud of the cobblestones beneath their boots as they run. For a few minutes, it's enough to silence the questions bubbling to life in the back of their mind.

The medical ward attaches to the administrative offices like an unwanted growth. It juts out on its own at an awkward angle, an amalgamation of crooked shingles and rotting wood and sickness. Twice the building has burned down in the college's recent history, and both times it has regrown with a vengeance.

White walls form a dizzying maw around them as the medic ward swallows them whole. The ward blurs around them as a nurse takes their hands and says, "Are you hurt?"

Simone's gaze latches on the nametag pinned at her breast—Doctor Hanae Aiza, she/her—before taking in her bloodstained smock and the grey ring framing her irises. Gods-touched—if the rumors are to be believed of anyone with such a feature. A nurse like this, granted powers from beings far beyond, means they're in good hands.

"Why don't we sit down?" she says. She must have picked up on the panicked flicking of their eyes and unstable breathing. Or perhaps she can see the waves of pain radiating from them. Simone can't say for certain; it is difficult to tell without asking where a Gods-touched one's powers lie.

"Etienne." The name comes out in a froggish croak. "I'm here for Etienne LaChance."

Her gaze is quizzical, then serious. She pulls back, mouth twisted in a poorly-repressed grimace, before exhaling. "Come with me."

Without pausing to let them process, the doctor's grip on their hand tightens and she pulls them deeper into the building. Stark white hallways whirl by them, one after another, before they are deposited into a larger waiting area. They look for Nadia in the crowd outside of Etienne's room, desperate for at least one familiar face, but she isn't there. Instead, they face a sea of strangers. Some are sobbing, while others are clustered in tight circles and wringing each other's hands. Thankfully, none give Simone any mind as they approach.

"You'll have to wait out here," the doctor says, as if it wasn't obvious. Then, by the time they've turned around, she's gone.

Their gaze rakes over the crowd once again. Chantal is the closest to them, hair pulled back in a tight puff. She's chewing on the nails on one hand and pacing as best as the people cloistered around her will allow. After a beat, she catches sight of Simone and darts over.

"Still no sign of Nadia?" she asks by way of greeting.

Simone's stomach sinks. "No. Have you heard anything?"

"No."

Before Simone can ask more, someone claps Chantal's shoulder and pulls her away. They lose themself to the dull hum of voices, skin prickling with irritation at the commotion.

"Monsters? On campus?" says a trembling girl nearby. A man holds her close to his chest, fingers tangled in her blonde hair. With wide eyes and pupils the size of tea saucers, she trembles, reminding Simone of a small hunter dog.

Simone's breath catches. "Monsters?"

The dull hum dissipates. Every head turns their way. The sudden onslaught of attention on them makes them want to turn their skin inside out.

"You didn't hear?" asks Luc, now visible over Chantal's head.

Chantal covers their hand with her own. "I... didn't have time to tell them."

"Tell me what?"

"Etienne... he..."

At once, Chantal's composure crumples. She turns into Luc's chest, whole body heaving as she sobs. How strange it is to watch her shatter. Her eyes had been the driest in the room—until now.

Luc rubs circles into her back as they meet Simone's stare. "Etienne was attacked," they say, wincing all the while.

Any moment now, they will open their eyes and find this a strange dream. And yet, after a few blinks, they don't. "By a monster?" they ask, the words heavy on their tongue. "On campus?"

The silence that follows speaks louder than anything else.

Monsters as a phenomenon had first appeared in history texts some two hundred years ago, creatures of all forms and shapes twisted by the miasma consuming Idune. While true that their influence has spread world-wide, Simone knows the wards wrapping the campus like the back of their hands. How did a monster slip through?

Their fist clenches. "How did this happen?"

"We don't know." Luc's voice is a broken whisper.

"And where did it go?"

Luc opens their mouth, fractured syllables tumbling forth, but they can't get the words out. Beside them, Chantal's gaze has gone glassy and vacant. Simone closes the distance and helps guide her trembling form to a chair.

"W-We're taking watch i-in shifts," she at last says between harsh hiccups. "When they let us, anyway. Oh, Gods. What if he—"

"He won't." The lie is a bitter lump on their tongue. Simone can't remember the last time they've heard of a monster attack with survivors, but if Etienne is still alive, that's the best they can hope for. "Most attacks," they continue, voice soft, "end before they even get this far. He'll be okay. He has to be."

As they wordlessly smooth back Chantal's hair, they can't tell if they are trying to convince her or themself. At the end of the day, they suppose it doesn't matter. As they said, the odds are in Etienne's favor.

Or, at least, Simone hopes they are.

***

Hours pass. Some students get tired of waiting and return to their dorms, mumbling to each other as they leave. Simone sits in the same chair they've been in since their arrival, rear end numb and spine tingling. Across the waiting room, Chantal and Luc lean into each other with matching tear-tracked faces, hands tangled together.

And Nadia still isn't here.

Simone has asked for her every time a member of faculty passes by, but they each give a sad shake of their head, nose buried in their clipboards, before walking away. It's enough to make Simone spit.

Where the fuck is she? Concern and frustration war within them. Etienne is supposed to be Nadia's best friend, but she can't be bothered to be here?

They chew on their bottom lip, relishing the taste of their own blood and how it distracts them. "Still no word?" they ask in Chantal's direction, if only to wrench them from their swirling thoughts.

She gives them a glassy stare, brown eyes rimmed with red, and shakes her head.

She could be strung out somewhere, a faint voice goads. *You've seen her that way, more than once. You've* been *that way with her.*

But wouldn't Etienne have been with her, in that case?

The thought gives them pause. Etienne and Nadia have been all but attached since Simone has known them. Perhaps they'd been together during the attack. Perhaps what got to him had—

Simone grinds their palms into their eyes and groans. It's bad enough Etienne is so badly hurt. If Nadia had been with him...

No. It'll do them no good to consider the worst.

Lost in their thoughts, Simone almost misses the distinct rattle of a door sliding open. They lift their head and look towards the source. A nurse steps out of Etienne's room—the doctor who escorted them hours ago, they realize—clipboard pressed to her chest as she clears her throat.

"He's stable," she says. "Badly wounded, but stable."

The relief that fills the waiting room is thick enough to choke on. Simone slumps forward with a sigh. Finally, some good news.

"You'll have to go one at a time, but you're allowed to see him if you would like."

Simone and Chantal meet eyes. She starts to open her mouth, but Simone is quicker.

"You should go."

Chantal's face pinches, but she doesn't argue. Nudging Luc, she settles their hands in their lap and follows the nurse inside. Seconds later, her sudden sobs are cut off as the door slides shut.

He'll live. The nurse suggested as much. He'll live, he'll live, he'll live.

"It was kind of you to come," Luc says in the silence that follows, "considering you and Etienne get on like wet cats."

They nod. Simone doesn't know why they're waiting in the medical ward, but they don't have it in them now to leave. Instead, they take in Luc's unruly pompadour and stained lapels. The hems of their sleeves have been worried to an unironable wrinkle. Etienne's state has worsened them, too, it seems. He has this sort of effect on everyone.

"It was the least I can do," they say at last.

Simone counts along to the ticking of the clock over their head. Before long, several minutes have passed and there is nothing to distract them from the question burning holes in their mind: Could Nadia have been attacked, too?

***

Chantal leaves Etienne's room an hour later, knees knocking together, and gestures for Luc to go.

"Be prepared," she says in a choked whisper. "He's... Be prepared."

As they depart, Chantal gestures to the seat beside Simone in askance. Her mouth opens, closes, opens again. Then, eyes wet with tears, she sits down.

"He's..." She takes a deep, shuddering breath. "Oh, Gods."

Simone pats her knee, discomfort wringing their guts. "You don't have to talk about it if you don't want to." And, truth be told, they aren't sure they want her to.

"Thank you." Then, sniffling, "I can't believe Nadia isn't here."

"Neither can I."

"You haven't been with her?"

Simone shakes their head.

Chantal picks up a pamphlet from the table and thumbs through before setting it back down. "To be honest with you, I'm starting to think she was involved. Doesn't it make sense?"

It does. Simone bites the words back, hesitant to add to Chantal's raving. Though her words have the jilted cadence of fear, they can't decide if she's declaring Nadia the monster or a fellow victim.

They manage a dry swallow, heart skipping. "Oh?"

"Etienne is found half-dead. Nadia is nowhere to be seen. You don't think the two are related?"

"They... could be," they admit after a long pause. Their palms bead with sweat. Chest tight, they take the pamphlet Chantal glanced at, *The Signs and Symptoms of Sanguina Malefica*, and pray it's enough to end the conversation.

"They're going to find her body next, you know."

Simone's vision blurs. Apparently, it's not. "Don't say that."

"My apologies. I forgot—" Chantal sighs before trying again. "I should have thought more."

Their attention returns to the pamphlet—barely. Her words are needles in their side. As much as Simone is loath to admit it, there's a strong chance she's right.

With a stiff lip, they stare at the pamphlet until the words swim and force themself to focus.

Sanguina Malifica's cause and cure are currently unknown. Ask your physician if you experience the following symptoms: lethargy, nausea, joint pain, chest pains, unsteady pulse, headaches, change in blood color or texture (especially in menstruating folk), and disorientation.

Simone wraps a cluster of braided hair around their finger. They keep a copy of the brochure with the rest of their research materials on Sanguina Malefica, but this is the first time they've read through so deeply. Nadia's first-hand experience is enough for them to understand the gist. The two of them have spent the last few months—at least, when they haven't been working to improve Nadia's academics—discussing the disease, but all of their work has so far led to the same dead ends. Where did Sanguina Malefica come from? Why has no cure for it been found? The uncertainty of it all had been enough for Simone to change their thesis prospect.

With a heavy sigh, they set the pamphlet down once again. Their skull is fit to burst with the amount of questions flooding it. They need to take a walk. "I'll come back."

"You're leaving?"

"I left my notes for our Practical Defenses course at Nadia's. It's... It's possible she's come back by now and isn't aware of what happened. She could have not heard the news, or... and, besides, I need to make sure Dio is fed."

Chantal lunges for their hand, brown cheeks dusted with pink. Her voice is faint as she says, "You *will* return, though?"

"Of course I will." Their lip stiffens as they swallow the urge to cry. "I wouldn't let you and Luc watch him alone."

"I appreciate that." Though hesitant, she releases them. "Try to return soon."

The lump in their throat thickens. They don't trust themself to talk, so they nod instead.

On their way out, they pass the front desk. Simone recognizes the woman from earlier, the one who had mentioned Etienne's attack to begin with. Her pale skin borders on translucent under the harsh lights. The variety of flower arrangements on the desk and in her hands are enough to dwarf her.

The moment she sees Simone, her mournful expression dissipates. "You're one of Etienne's friends, right?"

They read the card on the nearest floral arrangement. The paper is wrinkled, the handwriting reminiscent of a child's. Simone is unable to tell who it is from.

"I didn't mean to startle you," the woman continues. The dark green cape over her shoulders advertises her introduction to the realm of Enchantment. Perhaps Etienne was a tutor to her?

"I'm a friend of his, sure." Not an entire lie. Him and Nadia were thick as thieves, after all... but he had never taken a liking to them for reasons they still don't understand.

"How is he?"

Her doe-brown eyes glimmer with hope, and Simone almost wants to lie to preserve it. The moment their expression falters, however, she seems to catch on. Tears spill freely down her cheeks.

"He won't survive," she says in a voice like broken glass, "will he?"

"Nothing is certain yet." Over and over, they repeat in their mind their own words to Chantal earlier. *He'll be okay. He has to be.*

"But monster attacks are..."

"He's beaten the odds thus far. Most victims don't make it to the hospital."

At once, the tears rolling down the woman's cheeks thin. "You're right. He'll be okay." She stops to fumble through her bag, making an attempt to wipe her cheek as she does so. "He has to be."

Poor thing. She wouldn't last a day on the battle field, allowing herself to openly cry like this.

"Here."

When they look up, she's offered them a wrapped package. The bow on top is lopsided, one side twice the size of the other.

"I made this for him, since he was—is—my mentor and all. I'm still so new to magic, but it might help. I would bring it myself, but..." Red washes over her face and she looks away. "I don't... do good with gore."

Simone takes the package from her with a sad smile. "I understand."

"Please send him my regards. If he wakes up, that is."

With this, the girl spins on her heel and is gone.

Simone's fingers dig divots into the package as they emerge into the courtyard once more. Cold night air kisses their cheek, freezing the tears that well to the surface without their bidding. A single lamp flickers over their head, the magicite within buzzing with bee-like intensity.

Then, with a noticeable *pop*, the lamp overhead flickers a final time and is dead. Simone's sobs bounce off the bricks and are lost in the darkness beyond.

FOUR

Nadia DuPont || Before

The sharp ring of the bell cleaves through Nadia's pain-addled, hungover haze. She jumps in her seat at the sound, hand to her chest as she surveys the classroom. Everyone else has already stuffed their satchels and are in the midst of leaving. Her notepad is woefully blank.

As per usual, she is the last one in the room.

Professor Favreau looks up from her desk as she packs up her lecture materials. She's a monochrome woman: grey coat, black scarf, white hair. The brightest things about her are the chunky rings she wears, a rainbow of gems gleaming in the watery sunlight coming through the window behind her. Divination focuses, the lot of them, though Nadia isn't sure how anyone can use such flashy pieces to divine through.

She clears her throat as Nadia shoves by, the way a stern parent does to start a lecture. On instinct, Nadia freezes, heart thudding as she regards the coin-sized ruby perched on Professor Favreau's extended finger.

"Ms. DuPont, are you well?"

No, she wants to say. Everything in her body has screamed to go home since she opened her eyes this morning. No amount of willow bark tea or pain patches Etienne has crafted for her are enough to curb the sting. On the way to lunch, she debated the logistics of diving off the side of the mesa, if the fall would be enough to kill her or only disable her further. She's so tired, she wants to say. So tired of having to consume Serenity to cope and ending up hungover. So tired of waiting for answers. So tired of the pathetic, pitying looks people give her, the same kind of pitying look Professor Favreau gives her now.

Admitting any of this would be enough to send her to the psychiatric wing, though, and going there means kissing graduation goodbye, so she bites the sharp words back. Instead, thumbing through the books in her satchel to avoid meeting the professor's gaze, she says, "I didn't get enough sleep last night. That's all."

Professor Favreau gestures to the empty chair before her as she reorganizes the stack of books on her desk. "Was there something on your mind? Would you like to talk about it?"

If I sit down, I might not get up again. "Thank you for the offer, Professor. Really, though, I stayed up later than I meant to."

Professor Favreau's smile tightens. "And that's all?"

"That's all."

She hums, lips turning slit-thin, and returns to her books. "Very well. In the future, it would behoove you to make a greater effort to pay attention, sleep-deprived or not."

Nadia nods, thinking back through the course of the class and conjuring nothing. Pain has obscured her memory in a dense, dissociative fog.

"You are dismissed, Ms. DuPont."

Hard lumps fill her throat at the admonishment. She leaves the classroom as fast as she can without limping, and rushes down the hall. The sooner she can return home and numb herself, the better.

Soft autumn wind catches her hair as she steps outside. Twin sycamore maples, trimmed to keep errant branches at bay, form a natural arbor over the class hall entrance. Stray leaves tinged with yellow spiral on the breeze, catching in her hair. In the blink of an eye, the first semester of her final year has been whirling by her. Has it been a month since it began?

Her knee, already tender, is throbbing by the time she reaches the bottom of the staircase. It will be a miracle if she can make it to her room, elevators or not.

With a sigh, she adjusts her capelet and begins the trek back. The signature clicking of Etienne's heels is the sole warning she gets before he falls into place beside her.

"Nat."

Warmth blooms under her collar at the concerned lilt in his voice. She hopes he can't see the wet gleam of unshed tears. "Don't," she says, flicking the word off her tongue like a whip lash. With a subtle swipe around her eyes, she maintains her offset stare and continues her awkward hobble.

"Okay." Then, after a pause, "You really should go home."

"That was the plan."

Etienne's steps falter. Then, "Good."

He means well, she knows, but that doesn't stop the irritation bubbling under her skin, seeking a way free. She focuses on the sting of her nails against her palms to keep her tongue at bay.

"What did Professor Favreau want?"

"What does it matter to you, anyhow?"

The heat of dozens of stares prickles along her back. So much for maintaining control. Instead, chin tipped in what she hopes is defiance, she stares Etienne down until he shrinks.

"Nat..." He holds both palms out in a placating gesture. "I'm trying to—"

Her jaw sets. "I *know* what you're trying to do, Etienne, and I don't need the lecture."

"I'm not trying to lecture! I just wanted—"

"I-Is everything okay?"

Nadia stills. The voice is low and soft and, somehow, familiar in a way that makes her stomach warm. It cuts through the overwhelming irritation running rampant in her veins. After a beat to glower at Etienne some more, she turns.

The person before her knocks the wind from her lungs with a single look. Their hair is pulled into numerous small braids, all tied back with a leather cord. The capelet around their shoulders is cerulean—an Abjuration Major, then, and a second-year at that—and is spread open enough to reveal their buttoned sweater underneath. With a slight pout to their full lips, they look her over.

"Do I know you from somewhere?" they ask.

Despite the aching in her knees, despite Etienne, despite *everything*, Nadia feels another wave of warmth consume her. The ghostly remains of their hand on her thigh comes to mind. She bites her lip, scanning her scattered brain for a name she can match to them.

"We met a week or so ago," she says as she thinks. "On a field trip."

The ring on their thumb rattles as they snap their fingers. "Right! When we saw the diorama of Idune, right?"

For half a second, she thinks they'll continue, that they'll remind her of how they had fucked her against the trees while their escort had droned on in the distance. But they don't. Instead, they arch a thick brow, head cocked as they wait for her response.

All the while, she can't decide if the thought of being potentially exposed embarrasses her or not.

"Right," she says as she latches back onto the conversation.

Etienne presses so close to her, his subtle cologne is suffocating. "A friend of yours?" he asks.

"More like a wayward ship," the stranger replies. "Two stars crossing in the night."

The quote is familiar to her, from one of those prophet prose writers she studied in undergrad, but she can't recall the source. "Right," she says again instead.

"Is everything okay?"

The crowd around them has continued to Nadia's relief. The three of them are once again at the center of an ever-moving whirlwind. No matter her response, it's unlikely anyone will eavesdrop on her. "An unruly conversation," she says, running a hand down Etienne's front to try to grasp his wrist. "Nothing more."

"Fair enough," the Caster replies. Before they can say more, the stranger's stare shifts past her. The chime of the clock tower sounds in the distance. "Ah, I should get going," they say when the chiming stops, tossing a cluster of their braids over their shoulder. "I'm glad to see you again, though. Nadia, was it?"

Flinching, her cheeks turn warm again. How did they remember her name? Better yet, why can't she remember theirs?

"Yes. And you were...?"

They chuckle, smothering the sound behind a sepia-toned hand. "Simone. Until we next meet."

She can't help but admire the sway of their hips as they walk away, no matter how badly her joints ache. What she wouldn't give to have their legs wrapped around her head, to have them pulling her hair and telling her—

"Are you even listening?"

She snaps back to reality with a gasp. Etienne waves a hand over her eyes, forehead wrinkled in a way she knows he'll complain about later. Shaking herself free of her lust-addled daze, she sighs. "I'm sorry, Etienne. What were you saying?"

"Nothing."

Now it's her turn to frown. "Are you sure?"

"Yes." The sigh he gives deflates him. Eyes downcast, he takes her hand, thumb rubbing circles into her knuckles, and starts for the dorms. "Let's get you home."

***

"You know, you didn't answer my question earlier."

Nadia bundles up tighter in her star-patterned blankets while Etienne shuffles about in the other room. "Which one?" she calls.

"About Professor Favreau. After class, you were, well…"

She waits for him to continue, but he doesn't. Her irritation resumes its scuttling, so deep-seated she doesn't think she'll ever be able to claw it out. "She wanted to talk about my attendance."

The roar of a dust sweeper in the plaza outside fills the silence. Undisturbed, her thoughts flick back to Simone. Why had she never seen them before now?

And why, after a single, sweaty afternoon, are they all she can think about?

"Somehow, I doubt that's the whole truth."

Her jaw sets. She strains an ear to the sound of ceramic clinking together. So he's preparing them tea. With every last shred of her control, she chokes down a bitter response.

"I think our professors would understand your predicament," he continues before the sputter of her sink faucet drowns him out.

Nadia waits for the noise to die before speaking. "You would be surprised."

Etienne says nothing. The silence between them stretches impossibly thin, snapped by their shuffling before knitting itself back together. She's almost convinced he's left her to stew in her own toxicity.

But then, as her eyelids begin to shutter closed, he enters her room with two steaming cups. He balances one on her knee, keeping the other close to his chest.

"Thank you," she says as she brings her cup closer. Etienne remains silent save for his soft breaths and a soft grunt of acknowledgment.

It's not until he's halfway through his cup that he speaks.

"Are we okay?"

He's the most uncertain she's ever heard him, like a cornered mouse. Nadia thinks his words over. A mouthful of tea, bitter and floral, swishes between her teeth and goes down with a harsh gulp.

"Of course we are," she says at last.

"Then why..." He stops to set his cup aside. Raking through his mop of brown curls, he tries again. "Why were you so at my throat this afternoon?"

Is that all this is about? Nadia would laugh if he were anyone else. The two of them have been attached at the hip for years, though. She knows him better than anyone else. Better, perhaps, than even herself.

"I didn't mean to," she says.

"And what about with that person? In the courtyard?"

The tea scalds her throat as she swallows a too-large gulp. She should have guessed the conversation would lead here. Squirming with the sudden, uncomfortable heat in her stomach, she says, "We've met before."

His green eyes are hardened chips of emerald. He says nothing, but his brow quirks.

"Shards, Etienne." Nadia's face is blistering hot. She sets her cup aside. "That's the person I was talking about."

"From the field trip?"

"From the field trip."

Etienne throws his head back with a sharp, hawkish laugh. "Ah, no wonder."

Just like that, the wall of ice between them melts. How stupid of him to believe anything could come between them.

"I'm sorry," she says, and she mostly means it, despite her annoyance.

"I'm sorry, too." His brows furrow. "We've had a rough couple of days, so I was beginning to worry and—"

"Favreau reprimanded me for being sick."

His mouth remains open. The lump at his throat bobs.

"Rather," Nadia continues, "she was upset I wasn't paying attention. Because I've been feeling so sick."

"And because you won't do coursework," Etienne adds under his breath.

Her gaze flicks to the satchel she abandoned at the base of her bed. She debates grabbing the bag, just to prove a point to the both of them. Then her foot touches the floor and a surge of pain rolls through her and she decides against it.

"Perhaps you are right," she says.

"But it was cruel of her to point out."

"It was." Her body trembles as she sighs. "And I guess I then took it out on you, so... I'm sorry."

Etienne takes her hand again. "It's already forgiven."

With a low hum, Nadia sets her cup aside and rests her temple against his. She holds onto him until her fingers are numb, and she keeps her hold on him still for a while afterwards.

***

They're leaving from Harding Hall when she sees them.

"Simone!" Nadia calls before she can stop herself. In this moment, it matters little how dozens of their peers are glaring at her, or how Simone freezes like a deer at the sound of their name. She crosses the courtyard in the blink of an eye. Simone's shocked gaze melts into something tender.

"Hey, Nadia."

The way they say her name makes her want to stuff their tongue down her throat, but she refrains. Even their first meeting had started with manners.

"It's nice to see you again," she says. At once, she wants to kick herself. What kind of intro is that?

Their smile is all sunlight. "Of course!" Then, motioning for the door. "Were you coming in?"

She can't stop staring at their mouth, at the delicate bow of their top lip. More than anything, she wants to suck on the soft flesh like an orange slice. A blush creeps onto her cheeks at the thought.

"No," she says after a moment to recollect herself. "I, um... I was looking for you."

Which isn't a lie. Between pacing by the phone and attending classes (or pretending to), she's found herself drifting through the courtyard like a wayward ghost. Perhaps it is by divine design she has found them today, after several days of trying.

Simone stills. This close, their wide eyes are two disks of red obsidian. "You were?"

Her throat is too dry, so she nods instead. Her stomach flutters at the slight smile on their face.

They step out of the doorway and lean against the railing. "Sure. What did you need?"

Make me taste stars again, she wants to say, but the words are caught between her teeth. She hadn't thought this far ahead. Instead, a clumsy collection of sounds tumbles free. Simone laughs at her sputtering, the sound like the ringing of a dozen bells. They flip a cluster of braided hair over their shoulder before running their fingers through it.

Nadia forces the words out in a flurry. "Go out with me?"

Their hand stops. A soft gust of wind blows through them both, carrying with it the scent of Simone's skin—orange and pine and a soft vanilla undercurrent.

Still they say nothing.

Fuck. Nadia's skin crawls under the heat of their gaze. "I'm sorry," she says. "I don't know why I—"

"When?"

Their cheeks are as bright as Nadia's feel, their smile overwhelmingly radiant. Nadia eyes the leagues of distance between their hands and fights the urge to close the gap.

"I..." *Didn't think I would get this far.* "What are you doing tonight?"

A softer, deeper chuckle. Simone sweeps closer and brushes against her hand. "With any luck, you."

By the Gods. Her legs turn to gelatin.

"Your apartment," they continue, seemingly unaware of her shock. "Right?"

"Third floor of the Diviner's tower," she replies, voice dropping to a whisper. "Purple door. Can't miss it. Before dusk?"

"Sure. See you then."

She follows them across the courtyard with her eyes. Her breath comes out in fluttering gasps. With a hand on the railing to support herself, she slumps down as they round the corner and disappear.

FIVE

Simone Allard || After

Simone has never considered themself a religious person. Not in a "priest in the temple" sense. True, the Gods walk the earth still, and they've seen enough Gods-touched people in their life to know the hand of the Divine in everyday places. Still, Simone has never had reason to pray to them. Their eyes have always been devoted to the realm of academics, not the Divine.

Until now, that is.

"Please let him live. Please let her be safe."

And on and on it goes. On the walk back to the dormitories, the names of Gods they half-remember stumble from their lips, earning Simone a fair amount of glances for their troubles. If a Divine ear is among the listeners, all the better, they think.

The harried recitation stops only when they reach the Diviner's tower. Their resolve carries them forward, though it rattles with their ragged breathing at the third floor landing.

And yet, when they enter Nadia's apartment, it is as empty and untouched as the last time Simone stepped inside it. The name of

Tifar turns to ash on their tongue. All their prayers have amounted to nothing.

Simone buries their face in their hands and screams.

Tears, sudden and hot, spill down their cheeks. Warmth wraps around their ankles. Hiccuping, they meet eyes with the all-white cat nuzzling them. Dio's eyes are a brilliant gold, like divine ichor. Nadia had told them once she named him for a minor Parish God of wine and frenzy. This cat is the closest Simone will get, they think, to a divine presence.

"Hey there." Simone sniffles, wiping their face with a sleeve and dropping to their knees. Dio rubs against them with more fervor now, leaving a cloud of fur in his wake. After a beat, they scratch him behind the ears.

"Have you seen Nadia?"

Dio's eyes remain wide and unblinking. How foolish of them to expect a cat to talk, no matter how many stories they've read. Their fingers tangle in his snow-white fur as they give a sad sigh.

"Of course you haven't."

They stop their gentle ministrations. What if Nadia never returns?

Dio chirrups and twists between their legs the moment they start crying again. With a soft gasp, they thread their fingers in his fur. Their chest is tight—tighter than binders normally make it.

The cat grows tired at last of the attention. Tail fluffed, Dio marches into the bedroom, but they don't follow him. Instead, they sway back and forth on their feet, a wayward ghost in living skin.

They slump onto the couch, gaze drifting over Nadia's spotted carpet and cluttered table. A bundle of pamphlets sits on top of a wobbling tower of books, all focusing on Sanguina Malefica.

The bundle hits the floor with a slap. Simone shifts focus to the books underneath. A tattered leather book greets them, devoid of decoration. A quick flip through tells them it's a textbook from her Divination and Mysticism class. This too, they set aside.

The book beneath is one wrong spine-tug away from disintegrating. The pages inside are scattered, comprised of various mediums; receipts and shredded envelopes and old book pages now repurposed. Each of these haphazard pages are covered in sigils. Some of them Simone understands. Their time studying Divination has been brief thus far; they can translate some of the spirals and lines they see, though many of them are intermingled with other sigils or twisted in an indecipherable way. If only they hadn't left their Casting glove at home, they could attempt to channel the sigils to decode them.

They turn the page. The sigils become more advanced. Deep-seated pencil grooves retain their shape despite the shreds of eraser that tried to sweep them away. In places, Nadia has drawn the same line over and over again with minimal change. Some sigils are still half-formed, Nadia's tiny scrawl crawling in the spaces around them to denote their use. *Communion?* says one. *Have to ask Etienne about memories for this one,* says another.

Simone shuts the tome with as much care as they can muster. Nadia's spellbook is as tattered and inconsistent as she is. She'll have to come back for it, right?

With a sigh, they press the book to their chest.

The clock on the wall chimes to signify the hour. Simone shrinks when they see the position of the hands. It's three AM? They have classes in the morning and—

Etienne. They still have their watch over Etienne.

They rub the back of her spellbook before setting it back down. They should leave before it gets any later. But the moment they turn away, the book creeps into their nest of thoughts and settles there, a constant weight.

The spell tome slides into their bag and settles against their hip. Nadia shouldn't mind, especially when she isn't here to use it. Perhaps it will do them good.

***

Etienne, already one with a penchant for avoiding the sun, is the palest Simone has ever seen him. The blue of his veins form a garish roadmap up his arms, disappearing into the cuffs of his sleeves.

And the blood. There's so much blood. Though it's dried and all open wounds have been sealed shut by now, the rust-colored streaks cover much of his torso and arms.

"It's too dangerous to move him, let alone touch him," the nurse says when she escorts them into the room. "So he's going to be... messy."

An understatement. A polite one, but an understatement nonetheless.

Now Simone sits at his side, his limp hand in theirs. His Casting glove is sleek against their skin.

Sigils crisscross his skin in varying shades of green and gold, moving in time to his breaths. Though Simone doesn't understand the specifics, they know the sigils are related to the way his body is being forced to knit itself back together.

"I don't know how this could have happened," they say, though they know he can't respond. "What were you two doing? And where is Nadia?"

They fall silent as the door slides open. It takes a beat to recognize the grey-eyed woman who enters. Doctor Aiza.

"Everything okay in here?" she asks.

Her phrasing is poor, but they can't fault her for it. "As... good as it can be."

"Right." Her cheeks brighten. Then, more solemn, "He's going to be asleep for a long while."

"I understand." Their gaze rakes over his features. His Enchantment cloak has been shredded to ribbons, splotches of blood turning the green the color of rust. His stomach and chest have been tightly bandaged, but even now specks of red bleed through.

"It took a while to stabilize him," the Gods-touched doctor says as she steps to the foot of Etienne's bed.

"I didn't think he would make it," Simone replies. "Once I heard it was a monster attack..."

"He may still not. Time will tell." The nurse's eyes reflect in the low light like a cat's. "I didn't tell the others this, but you seem to have a decent head on you. There's still a sizable chance he will die in this room... but we are doing all we can."

Simone tightens their grip on Etienne's hand. "That's all we can ask for."

She hums, gaze unfocused. After several moments staring into an empty corner, she speaks again. "Perhaps the Gods will show this one mercy yet."

It is the closest thing to good news Simone can hope for. While most Gods-touched remain within temple walls, spending their hours studying or praying, some still drift through the wider world. No matter where they find themselves, the voices of the Gods reach them all the same.

"Whichever God has chosen you," Simone begins, the words coming one jumbled syllable at a time, "I pray they guide your hands in his favor."

She nods, the sole acknowledgment they receive before she leaves the room again. Beside them, Etienne's sigils continue to glow.

"As soon as you wake up," they say under their breath, "you're going to tell me everything you know."

***

Simone wants more than anything to focus on Professor Favreau's lecture, but their mind continues to drift.

All their life, they've prided themself on their steel-clad attention span. It has aided them in everything from reading to homework to the grueling entrance exam to Voterique they endured six years ago. But now, Professor Favreau's voice is a garbled whine at the back of their skull they cannot get to clear.

Lost to their thoughts, they don't register the class has ended until someone shoves past them in their attempts to leave. Simone snaps back to with a start. The page before them is woefully blank. Stomach sinking, they realize they'll have to consult their study group for notes.

Professor Favreau is at the front of the room still, wiping away her lecture from the blackboard. Clouds of chalk dust hover around her and drift away. The rings on her fingers are covered in a fine film she rubs clear one by one.

"Ah, Mx. Allard," she says when their eyes lock. "Is there something you need?"

They sling their bag over their shoulder and approach her desk. A tower of ungraded papers sits to one side, an emptied mug on the other. In the ocean of space between the two, her desk is bare of decoration save for the splotches of ink. It's these splotches they focus on, trailing a path around them with a finger, as they ask, "Do you ever do sigil translation work?"

Professor Favreau quirks a brow. "Sometimes, yes. If it's not Divination or Necromation, however, I am afraid my expertise is limited." She sets her chalkboard eraser down and pins Simone down with the full weight of her stare. "Why do you ask?"

"Well..." After a beat, they lift Nadia's spell tome from their bag, placing it on the desk with a sheepish grin. "I have some of these designs a friend showed me and I wanted some help decoding their meaning."

Professor Favreau's Caster's mark, an inter-connected circle of squares, glows a brilliant orange as she presses it to one of the sigils on the page. Then, after a beat, the glow fades.

"This is someone else's handiwork, then?"

"It is."

They flip to the next page. Professor Favreau studies it without a word, pulling the tome closer and running her hands along the pages.

"I see elements of Illusion and Enchantment in these," she says, lips pursed. "They seem more minor elements, however. This one, for example." She points to one, waiting until Simone is studying it to continue, "This is a sigil for some kind of recollection." She flips a page. "Meanwhile this one, despite its crude shape, seems to be the beginnings of creating an avatar for communion. It's incomplete, however."

Simone absorbs this with a wrinkle in their brow. "I see."

Professor Favreau closes the spellbook with great care. "They're impressive works, for sure... if whoever wrote them could get them to a functional state, they would be a force to contend with."

Simone trails their fingers over Nadia's spellbook, chest aching. "I see," they say again, swallowing the lump in their throat.

"But that's for them to solve." With this, she slides the book back across the desk. "Is there anything else I can help you with?"

They hold the tome to their chest, sure it will crumble into dust if they let go. With great hesitance, they say, "Do you know anything about Nadia?"

"Who?"

"She was a student of yours last semester." They've found themself subjected to her rants about their Professor from time to time, too. Professor Favreau is a raging bitch—her words, not Simone's—but that doesn't stop them from admiring her strictness and collected air. She is the perfect Professor for certain sorts of minds, Simone's included.

"Oh, Ms. DuPont. I can't say I've heard of or from her since the semester change. She should be doing mostly independent study now, I would think. Why?"

They swallow the growing lake of saliva in their mouth. "I just... haven't seen her lately is all," they say at last.

"I wouldn't be too concerned on that front, dear." Now, Professor Favreau leans close, silver bells around her neck clinking. "Not the most... reliable sort."

Simone bristles, thankful they have at least enough restraint to keep from snapping back. What does she know about Nadia, anyway? True, she is often capricious, built more on whims than discipline, but that doesn't give a Professor the right to profane her.

After a beat, they straighten, running anxious fingers through their cluster of braids. "I'll... keep that in mind, thank you."

With this, they turn to leave, but a sudden inhale makes them pause.

"I heard there's a student in the hospital." Professor Favreau sets a wrinkled, ring-laden hand on their shoulder. "An acquaintance of yours. For that, I do apologize."

Throat thick, they nod. "Thank you."

"I pray he is granted mercy soon."

They give a wordless nod before scurrying away.

SIX

Nadia DuPont || Before

The moment Nadia enters her apartment, her heart is a butterfly pinned within her chest. A date. With Simone. What was she thinking?

She's never been one for dating. In primary school, no one was enough to catch her interest. It wasn't until the gap years she found a need for romance and sex at all. Casual affairs only, though. She'd seen how her mothers, in love and destined for each other, had been torn apart in the end.

Even now, entering her third year in the Diviner's program and her seventh year at Voterique overall, she hasn't gone beyond a date or two, let alone anything more than a meaningless hook-up.

With a groan, she regards herself in the mirror hanging from her bedroom door. The surface is smudged enough to give her a sort of warped aura around the edges. Still, it suits its purpose as she holds up shirt after shirt, dress after dress, determined to find just the right outfit.

She's getting ahead of herself, though.

In a huff, she calls Etienne.

Minutes later, he's perched on the edge of her bed. She stares at him through the mirror, a floral-print dress pressed to her chest. After several seconds of frowning, she decides she can't imagine wearing it.

His lips purse as he inspects the fabric. Finally, "Too busy."

"You're right." She tosses the dress aside and scours the mountain of clothes surrounding her for a new one.

"You're putting... quite some effort into this one."

Nadia straightens with goldenrod fabric in her grasp. "Am I?" she asks as she unfurls the turtleneck—when did she get this one? Where?—and examines herself in the mirror. "I think this might work with that one dress I have."

Before Etienne can reply, she's stripping to her undergarments. Even this she has agonized over—not that she'll ever admit such to Etienne—and had finally settled on a simple sheer slip. There is a chance, however slim, Simone won't get to see it, so Nadia picks something comfortable and hopes for the best.

"Besides, you—Are you even listening to me?"

She stiffens. Perhaps she's putting too much thought into her garment options. "I'm sorry, Etienne. What did you say?"

An unusual darkness flits across his features. "Nothing."

"Doesn't *sound* like nothing." Nadia positions the neckline just so and twists back and forth. Though she wants to focus on how the fabric falls along her body, Etienne's glower distracts her.

She stops twirling. "What."

He chews on the inside of his cheek. "I don't know what you're talking about."

"Don't try to bullshit me. This." She gestures up and down at him. "Why are you being so sour?"

He leans forward so his hair obscures most of his face. "I thought you didn't like dating."

"I don't." The words come out clipped. Harsh. "But that doesn't mean I won't go on one—just to see what all the fuss is for."

"And..." His knee bounces, a tell-tale sign of his anxiety. Thin fingers rake through his mud-brown hair. "What if you decide you like it?"

"Then who cares?" She throws the sweater on, just to have something to wear. She feels too naked without it. "It's not like we need to write the campus newspaper. Look out, everyone, Nadia got good sex for once. This might be the one to settle her down!" Then, turning back and forth to scrutinize her sweater, "Don't be ridiculous."

Etienne's cheeks brighten. "That's not what I'm saying at all."

"Then what *are* you saying?"

"What if... you decide you like being with them more than with me?"

A snort escapes before she can stop it. "We've never been romantic."

"Of course not!" Then, quieter, "I just mean... what if you stop being friends with me?"

Sighing, Nadia crosses to the bed and slings an arm around his shoulder. "Why would that ever happen?"

He remains stiff against her. "It's happened before."

"Not between us." She squeezes tighter. "Not everyone is Aleksi."

"I know that."

"Then don't worry. Be happy for me! I'm seeing someone for the first time in..." She stops to count and, failing to conjure a number to mind, says, "I guess it's been a while."

Nadia (finally) settles on her date ensemble—goldenrod turtleneck, a soft black dress with thin straps, and a pair of earrings made to represent orbiting stars—and Etienne takes his leave. For once, she is all the more glad when her front door clicks shut. She's still staring at herself, haggard and exhausted but nevertheless trembling with excitement, when there's a knock at her door.

Nadia meets eyes with Dio, settled as he is on the edge of her tub. "Well, wish me luck."

Dio offers her a soft mewl before tucking his head into his paws and falling back asleep.

Another knock. Nadia gives herself a final look in the mirror. Thick dark circles rim her eyes and her bangs are a roughly chopped curtain over her eyes. It'll have to do.

Whatever expectations she's set in herself of Simone are immediately blown away. Blue beads cap the ends of their braided hair. Beneath their soft blue capelet, they've changed into a yellow button-up with narrow sleeves that billow before tightening at the cuffs. Their teeth gleam like fresh-farmed pearls, so bright Nadia is dazzled as she regards them.

Their smile widens at the sight of her. "May I come in?"

A dozen half-baked syllables sputter forth before Nadia can recollect herself. Then, "Of course."

They sweep past her, a wave of orange and vanilla musk trailing behind them as they take a slow circle around her apartment. Too late, she notes the dishes half-cleaned in the sink and the blanket pooling on the ground in front of the couch.

"I, um..." Nadia's cheeks grow warm. "I haven't had much time to clean lately."

Simone lowers onto her couch cushions with a smile. "I've seen worse."

Her sharp exhale rattles her choppy bangs. With a bump of her hip, she forces the front door closed.

"Stuck door?"

Her cheeks fill with heat. "It's picky."

"You should talk to the groundskeep about that."

She shrugs, failing to conjure a better response. Crossing to the kitchen, she allows her gaze to leave Simone at last. "Would you care for a drink?"

"Something warm, I hope. Isa's Godly breath is warmer than the campus is right now."

Nadia chuckles. "Tea it is."

***

The stove won't light. The water in her sink comes out grey and refuses to clear. Finally, when the lamps flicker in unison and burn out with a hiss, Nadia buries her head in her hands and, from her spot on the couch, says, "Maybe you should leave."

"Nonsense." Simone rubs warm circles into her back. "We'll go somewhere together."

Minutes later, she finds her hand in theirs as they trek across campus. Though her joints voice their protest, Nadia shoves the discomfort down and carries on. Casters-to-be pass them by in a blur. Though their gazes burrow into her skin, Nadia can't help but get a thrill from the stares.

That's right. She clings tighter to Simone's arm. *Nadia DuPont is capable of a date.*

The thought surprises her. Since when has she cared what others thought of her? Half of the Majors programs have scored themselves on her bedposts. At the very least, they should think her a good lay.

Before long, they're waiting in line for the trams down to the city. With a harsh swallow, she recalls the last ride she took. The feeling of weightlessness—even the memory of it—makes her stomach drop.

For a moment, she considers telling Simone to find them somewhere on campus, but then she decides against it. What's another risk when they're already going so far?

They flash their amulets in unison to the faculty running the trams, who nod before gesturing them into an open car. At once, she is assaulted by the smell of other people—the sweat, the mismatched cologne—and her gut lurches. *It's a good thing I didn't eat yet.* The thought dawns on her as the tram begins its descent. *Otherwise I would have vomited twice by now.*

In the midst of her panic, she's faintly aware when Simone wraps an arm around her and pulls her close. The jittering of her knee (which she hadn't been conscious of) stills at once.

When it's over, Nadia waddles out of the tram like a sailor, legs bowed at awkward angles. The pain in her ankles worsens as she finds a spare wall to lean against and catch her fluttering breath.

"You don't leave the campus much, do you?" Simone asks.

"Can't say I do." And it's the truth. Aside from the field trip a few weeks prior, Nadia can't remember the last time she was in the city of her own free will. Most days, it is consumed in soft mist, so when she can brave a glance off the mesa there isn't much to see. Now, she admires the intricacies in the brick roadways. Large vehicles drive past, hunched like animals ready to pounce. Magicite in a rainbow of colors illuminate their path as Simone leads her through a maze of streets, hands soft in hers, and at last pulls her into a small cafe.

"My enbei and I used to come here when I was younger," they say as a bell tinkles overhead.

Nadia doesn't have the heart to mention how the smell of coffee makes her stomach curdle. Instead, she offers a mildly-enthusiastic, "Oh?"

They hum in agreement. "Even now, it's one of my favorite places."

Minutes later, they sit across from each other in a quieter corner, warm cups of tea before them.

"You've been in school for seven years now." Simone stirs their drink as they talk, gaze dark and unreadable. "And, clearly, you're a Diviner-to-be. Why?"

Nadia chokes on the last dredges of her cup. She didn't realize how thirsty she was until they arrived. "That's quite abrupt of you." And in truth, she can't remember the last time anyone was willing to jump straight to scrutinizing her. Perhaps during her entrance exam, when the likes of people such as Professor Favreau had seen fit to quiz her to the point of frustration. That was nearly eight years ago, though. Most of the flings she's had have wasted time first on pointless small talk.

After setting her cup down, she fingers the hem of her Diviner's capelet and says, "For plenty of reasons. I aim to specialize in oneiromancy. There's much exploration to be done within the realms we turn to in sleep, wouldn't you say?"

Their expression remains unchanged. Nadia's skin prickles under the heat of their stare.

"For example," she continues in a softer tone, anxiety turning her fingers to gelatin, "there are studies now to suggest dreams are how we process the events of the waking world. And, I think, it can be the safest place for people to dissect more... traumatic events."

Their brow gives the faintest quirk. "As a means to recover from them?"

"Of course." Nadia coughs to clear the dryness in the back of her throat—and the remains of her tea. "Sitting across from you right now does not have me inclined to dive into your innermost secrets—or to allow you to view mine. However, the dreamspace is..." Here she pauses, chewing on her lip as she thinks of how to continue.

"I think I understand." Simone's soft smile widens. "It's a neutral ground of sorts, right?"

"Yes! Exactly."

"How fascinating."

Nadia leans forward, legs crossed. "There's plenty of interesting sides to me, I think you will find." Then, dragging her spoon along the rim of her cup, she says, "And what about you?"

"Pardon?"

"Abjuration." She points to the soft blue capelet wrapped around Simone's shoulders. "It's not flashy like Evocation. You don't get the *fun* reputation of the Diviners, or the strictness and danger of being an Enchanter. Some might even say that Abjuration is the most boring realm to become a Caster of. And yet, after acquiring your general degree, you selected this realm to major in. What about it appealed to you?"

After a couple of beats to collect themself, Simone leans in closer. Their mouth curls into a soft smile.

"Are you familiar with Candide Allard?"

She scans her mind for a face to match the name and, conjuring nothing, shakes her head. "Can't say I am."

"Fascinating." Their dark eyes flash again. "They're one of my parents and a prominent member of the A.C.A.S. It is through their work I've seen the true havoc that monsters are having on humanity across the world. As such, I want to do something about it."

"The same can be said for many here."

Simone shakes their head, the beads capping their braids clacking together. "Not the way I wish to. Even now, as we struggle to grow more connected as a world, there are many pitfalls that separate us." After a pause to sip their tea, they say, "Take Hadorae, for example."

Nadia shivers. The northern country had sent its pleas for help a few months ago after losing too much ground in their fight against such a monstrous threat. She remembers the Hadoraec spokespeople who had visited the college. The vacant horror in their eyes as they stood before the students of Voterique and begged for aid had been enough to disturb her sleep for weeks.

"They've begun to receive the aid they need, but did it need to get that far?" Simone continues. "There are ways to streamline communications worldwide, especially in the realm of Abjuration. In doing so, it is my hope we can quell this threat once and for all."

Nadia mulls their words over, impressed and shocked in equal measure. Their aspirations are so... noble. Selfless. So unlike her in every way.

What is she doing? She stares into the dregs of her teacup, hoping it will provide some kind of answer, but there's nothing.

"Quite ambitious," she says at last.

"That's the truth of it, though." Simone sets their spoon down and straightens in their chair. Gone is the flirtatious air and gentle smile. They examine her the way the deans had all those years ago, with a hawkish stare and a firm set to their jaw. What is it they seek from her?

"I don't waste time, Nadia."

Clearly. Her thoughts drift to their first encounter: how they had pinned her against the tree before either of them had exchanged more than a sentence, how they had dragged her to the precipice of orgasm within—

She forces herself back to the present, cheeks aflame.

"Before we go further," Simone continues, unaware of her drift into fantasy, "I would like to know there won't be any... complications."

How abrupt. "All...right."

"What are your aspirations after you graduate?" Their gaze rakes again over the lilac purple of her capelet. "You've mentioned oneiromancy, but I find that answer to be lacking."

"It's the honest truth."

"Part of it, I'm sure, but not the whole of it."

She's had these kinds of dates before, had her fill of arrogant partners-to-be who wanted nothing more than to make her a trophy for themselves. At this point, she normally tells whoever she's with to go fuck themselves and leaves the date at that, but something about Simone's no-nonsense air makes the pit of her stomach grow warm. Dampness settles between her thighs. They aren't aiming to make her a trophy—she knows without needing to ask. No, their direct manner of speaking to her is born out of a sense of concern.

"It... It depends on my final grades, I suppose," she says at last, hating how all-encompassing the heat in her face has become. "Ultimately, I think it would be nice to use what I learn in a therapist's setting."

"Through dream work?"

"Through dream work." A strange giddiness bubbles to life inside of her. Bouncing in her seat, she continues, "Because where you see a monster epidemic and the potential to forge new communication avenues, I am seeing all of the hunters who come home afterwards. They're tired. They're in pain. They're traumatized." Again, the haunted faces of the Hadoraec spokespeople come to mind. "And what is being done about their trauma? Nothing."

It's close enough to the truth, she thinks. Of course her methods could be expanded to the monster hunters set abroad—in due time. Her thoughts are more local, though. And, with shame rolling down her back, she realizes she's thinking of herself most of all. She can't compare herself to the wealth of monster hunters, certainly, but she has her own traumas to sort through all the same.

Simone's eyes narrow to slivers. Panting, Nadia waits for them to say something, *anything*.

Then, "A fair answer."

They rise from their seat and extend a hand to her. She examines it with a dry swallow.

"We're leaving?"

"Our drinks are done, are they not?" Then, with a wink, "I have the perfect dessert in mind to round out our day."

She can't help herself. With a wicked grin, Nadia takes Simone's hand in hers and drags them towards the exit.

There's no urgency when they re-enter Nadia's apartment later. Instead, a comfortable sort of quiet wreaths them as they slide their hands under each other's clothes. Their capelets tangle together in a pile on the floor, blue over purple. Though Simone won't let her remove their shirt, she redeems herself when she undoes the buttons to their pants with her teeth. Having exhausted themselves of words, they instead explore each other in the quiet of Nadia's dusty apartment.

Afterwards, for the first time in a while, sleep claims Nadia swiftly and without mercy.

***

Awareness comes to her in snatches. Her chest aches when she reaches across the mattress and finds nothing but fleeting warmth. The remains of her dream vanish in a puff of smoke. She had made sure to memorialize her and Simone's date in sigils, reliving it every time she put herself to sleep.

The final ring of the phone from the other room registers at last.

Sighing, she pulls the blanket tighter around her. Whoever is calling can leave a message—or else, call again. Otherwise, they have no reason to disturb her peace.

Seconds pass. Then, as if it read her mind, the phone rings anew. The shrill peals are enough to make her ears ache. *Who is calling me? Perhaps it's Simone.*

It's been days since their date, long enough Nadia is half-convinced she scared them away. Sure, they called her earlier today, intending to set up a follow-up date. But, as the peals of the phone stab into her ears, she considers the possibility they've changed their mind.

When she stands, Dio winds around her legs, white tail fluffed up, and chirrups in greeting.

"Hello, sweet boy."

A deep meow rumbles in his throat. Wide golden eyes regard her. His body trembles as he rubs against her.

"I've missed you too."

Seemingly satisfied with the attention, Dio scurries away. The telephone resumes its piercing refrain. This time, finally, she's quick to grab it.

"Hello?"

"Is this Nadia DuPont?"

Her stomach flips. Not Simone, then. "May I ask who is calling?"

"Ms. DuPont, this is Doctor Aiza of the Voterique medical ward. If you have some time today, could you please visit our office? Your test results came in."

"O-Of course." After a dry swallow, she says, "Is everything okay?"

"We just need to discuss your results is all."

At this, she tenses. What did they find that must be said in person? Did they notice the elevated levels of Serenity lingering in her blood?

"Ms. DuPont?"

"Understood." She forces calm into her voice even as the swirl of possibilities makes her tremble. "I will come by within the hour."

It's only once she's hung up the phone that Nadia remembers the follow-up date with Simone. She eyes the clock on the wall. With any luck, her discussion will be brief and she'll return before they arrive. They'll never have to know.

Or, at least, she hopes.

SEVEN

Simone Allard || After

Etienne's skin glistens with the dozens of sigils the nurses have drawn, each one pulsing with dull light. Simone watches the slow rise and fall of his chest from their chair in the corner of the room. It's their turn to keep vigil again and they brought their thesis notes with, intent to get *some* work done, but the second they tear their gaze away from Etienne, the letters swim and refuse to still.

At last, they give up, tossing the notepad to some forgotten corner of the room. Professor Darzi will forgive them, they hope.

Their gaze flicks back to Etienne. If not for the tattered clothes and thick scab along his forearm, they could fool themself into thinking he's asleep. They can't imagine sleeping for an entire week, though.

A mountain of coursework looms from his bedside table, enough to make Simone blanch. They're already feeling the stressful pinch of trying to focus on their coursework in the wake of the attack. Their studies will stop for no one, though, the half-dead included. If it were them on the gurney, they're sure Etienne would feel the same.

In all of this, there's still no sign of Nadia.

The realization makes their guts curdle. They've been on the receiving end of her mood shifts, as violent and unpredictable as the weather in the Isles d'Emireau, enough times to know. Still, they thought she would be done with whatever fancy has crazed her now. Especially where her best friend was concerned.

The more they think on her disappearance, the more irritated they get.

Etienne's face twitches. They catch the movement at the last second, half-convinced they imagined it. Breath fluttering, they stare at him until their eyes burn and wait with something akin to hope.

After a moment, he settles.

It's possible he'll never wake up. The thought turns their flickering hope to ash. The nurses have mentioned this fact more than once during their visits. Still, it's a painful thing to consider, no matter how tenuous their relationship.

His face scrunches again.

Perhaps he is dreaming, they reason. A better sign than most. Nadia had told them once everyone dreams, even the comatose and unconscious. A specialized set of sigils would allow them into his brain, they know, if only they had the knowledge.

If Simone spoke to him, would it reach him, wherever he mentally was?

They almost convince themself it was a fluke. Etienne could have felt something, even in his unconscious state, and had a minute reaction to it. The nurses have reminded them such activities are normal.

But as they decide to return to their work, they freeze. Etienne's eyes are wide open, staring at something far beyond them.

They grip the arms of their chair. *This is a dream. Some sad, pathetic, messed up dream.* And yet, underneath their words, the glimmer of hope rekindles.

The machine beside him beeps faster now. With rapid blinks, Etienne begins to shift.

"Etienne." Their notepad slaps the ground as they stand.

His eyes rake the room in an unfocused arc, settling at last on Simone. Thin brows draw together. His nose wrinkles.

"What are you doing here?"

It's not quite a question—at least, not one asked because he's curious about the answer. Despite the croak in his voice, Etienne's words come out steeped in venom.

Simone's skin prickles. They want to convince themself he's upset because he was nearly killed just days ago, or because he's tired. Neither of these things are true, though. Deep down, they know it's because, for reasons they've never understood, Etienne LaChance hates them. He's hated them from the moment they and Nadia met on the field trip, and will likely hate them still when he dies.

And yet, here they are, the two of them in a cold hospital room. Simone has stayed by his side in the hopes he'd awaken, even if his time asleep fails to provide a change of heart. He needs kindness right now, they tell themself. It's the only way they can brush off his hostility.

And yet, they can't hide from the question burning holes in their throat.

"Etienne, where is Nadia?"

The look in his eyes turns to something colder. One of the machines at his side beeps at a rapid pace. After a glance to the wires in his skin—likely to assess the source of the noise—he turns away and picks at something in his lap.

"You need to leave."

Their jaw sets. "I'm not going anywhere."

His hand, thin and gnarled after his week unconscious, grips the bed frame. "Get out of here, Simone."

Irritation ripples through them. How ungrateful, after they've spent every waking moment this week ensuring he didn't die in his sleep. They've forgone their study group to see him, spent nights half awake sick with worry, and this is what they get?

"You're ridiculous." The words come out with more bite than intended, but they don't have it in them to be sorry for it. A week's worth of turmoil bubbles over. They don't have the time for Etienne's prissy behavior.

They turn to shout for attention. "Nu—"

Their lips fuse together, voice dying in their throat. Sweat beads on Etienne's face as he glowers at them, a piece of paper clenched in his gloved fist. The Caster's Mark shimmers, magic fading away as Simone watches it in disbelief.

"Don't say a fucking word," he spits with eerie calm.

They've never seen the kind of grim resolution Etienne has on his face before. As they start to slowly nod, he lets the paper free. They both watch its erratic spiral as it settles in his lap.

"Listen very carefully, Simone." His throat bobs as he speaks. He makes a harsh, gagged noise before continuing. "This is not a safe place to talk." He casts a quick glance to the door. "You have to get me out of here somehow. Not now, but soon."

A million questions swarm their brain like bees, but they don't trust themself to speak. Shock has made the world fuzzy around the edges. Did he just use magic on them? Offensively?

"You're going to pretend this never happened for now." The resolve in his eyes hardens. "If a doctor comes in, I am still comatose and you haven't seen any changes. Do you understand?"

Before they can respond, he throws himself back against the bed, eyes squeezed shut. The thud of shoes on marble echoes from the hallway.

"Etienne."

Eyes still closed, he pats his front and clasps the sigiled slip of paper once more. Simone winces as the Casting glove again brightens.

"Please." They hate the desperate crack of their voice, but they press on. "What happened to—"

They fight against the lump at their throat when the door opens.

"Everything okay in here?" Doctor Aiza, the grey-eyed nurse who has visited them so often this week, balances the door against her hip as she surveys the room.

The lump in their throat eases a touch. The heat of his stare burns them through his closed eyelids. *Don't say a fucking word.*

He knows what happened to Nadia. He has to. They would never forgive themself if they squandered the opportunity.

And so, as much as they want to tell the truth, Simone steels themself and forces a falsehood out.

"Just fine," they say through a set jaw. "No real changes here."

Their throat fills with bile, but it's too late to take the lie back. Doctor Aiza nods as if she expected nothing less and ducks out of the room.

The instant the door is shut, Etienne peeks at them through half-open eyes. It takes all of Simone's restraint to avoid rattling the bars framing his bed and shaking him for all he is worth. Instead, teeth grinding together, they swallow hard. "What the fuck, Etienne?" A thousand questions form a sandstorm in their mind, but they're unable to decide on what to ask first.

"Get me out of here and I'll tell you."

They both freeze at the sound of footsteps in the hall, relaxing only when it passes. Then, leaning closer, Simone says, "And how do you propose I do such a thing?"

"That's for you to figure out."

They entertain the notion—just for a second, they swear—of grabbing Etienne by the throat and squeezing until his eyes pop out. But they know it won't help matters. Nothing they can think to do will.

"Etienne…" Their voice cracks again, betraying the turmoil boiling underneath. "Just tell me where she is."

His gaze is molten metal. "Get me out of here. Then I'll tell you whatever you want to know. I can't… I can't risk them finding me awake yet."

"Who?"

For a second, they swear they see tears beginning to roll down his face, but then he's turned away and they aren't sure anymore. Perhaps it was an illusion, a trick of the light. If he really cared about Nadia, he would tell them where she is.

And yet he doesn't reply.

"Fine." The chair rattles as they rise, trembling with the force of their fury. "Have it your way." With this, they gather their books and pens and hug them close.

Then, as they reach for the doorknob, a thought comes to mind.

"You could help us find her, Etienne." The lump in their throat swells, but they press on. "If anything happens to her… if anything happens to her, and you are preventing us from being able to stop it? There's no force in the world that will be able to stop me killing you."

With this, they step out into the hall, making sure to slam the door on the way out.

***

Other Casters blur by Simone as they march for the dormitory towers. Normally, they lose themself in the waves of conversations surging from all sides, but not today. Not when so much remains unanswered.

After all, he's their only lead back to Nadia.

Their jaw sets. Over the last nine months, there's been plenty for her to apologize for. Lying about her studies. Stealing from the campus marketplace. All of the times they've found her half-catatonic state, pupils the size of dinner platters…

But not this. Disappearing in such a suspicious fashion, right after her best friend is found half-dead? Simone doesn't think they can forgive her for this.

By the time they bound up the steps of the Diviner tower, their vision is framed in red. They almost don't catch what's so different about Nadia's apartment until they've barreled through the door, but then the difference dawns on them with startling clarity.

Tape criss-crosses the entryway, held firm by sigils. Across the surface, written in everything from Elrish to Mertalc, is some variation of, "Restricted."

"No," they whisper, fingers ghosting over the words.

Then they catch the paper flapping against the door itself.

ATTENTION STUDENTS: ACCESS TO THIS DORMITORY IS HENCEFORTH FORBIDDEN. IF ANYONE ATTEMPTS TO ENTER THE PREMISES, OR IF STUDENT RESIDENT NADIA DUPONT IS SEEN, PLEASE ALERT FACULTY IMMEDIATELY.

THANK YOU,

VOTERIQUE COLLEGE FACULTY

"No, no, no." Their heart is a lion's roar in their skull. Simone's hands twitch. A strange hollowness blooms within them.

"Looking for her, too?"

They almost miss the words through the low static buzzing in their ears.

"I overheard some of the professors recently—she's gone missing," the stranger continues.

"I-I know that," Simone manages. Now they dare a glance at the speaker. A lilac cape flutters around them, long enough to obscure most of their form. They have the high cheekbones and plum-flower patch on their capelet denoting them as a Ximuchi transfer student. A pair of wire-frame glasses balances on the end of their upturned nose.

"*Ohh*," they say, nose scrunching. "I've seen you around here before. You're her partner."

"Yes."

"Right." Their gaze shifts to Nadia's door. "And you have no idea what happened to her? Truly?"

Simone shakes their head.

"A shame." They suck on their bottom lip, a careful and pensive expression . "If I were you, I would distance myself from her situation entirely. Rumor has it she's the reason that Enchanter is hospitalized."

Their throat dries. "Impossible. It was a monster." *At least, that's what everyone keeps saying.*

"Perhaps... and perhaps not.. They were prone to nasty arguments, you know."

Nadia's and Etienne's relationship tended to be as mercurial as they were, but that didn't mean they didn't care for each other. No matter how many times she may threaten to harm him, Simone knows she would never harm him.

They shake their head. "They were closer than siblings."

"Love turns to hate all too swiftly."

They have heard that line before, somewhere in a book of poems. When they scour their brain for the title, it dissipates before they can recall it.

The stranger's stare becomes distant. Chewing on their lip, they do nothing as Simone turns to leave. Then, as they walk away, the stranger clears their throat.

"Did the faculty even announce capturing the monster that attacked that Enchanter, do you know?"

Simone stills. "They haven't said it's still loose," they say slowly. "And... and if they recovered Etienne without issue, then..."

The stranger makes a noncommittal grunt. Then, "I might be able to get you in."

Simone turns.

"You'll have to be quick, of course. Once the sigils break, I'm sure faculty will be coming along to investigate." After a short pause, gaze locked on the doorframe, they nod. "They'll *definitely* be coming to investigate."

Simone joins them in examining the doorframe, brow furrowed. At once, the meaning is clear. Framing the sigil meant to bind material together—in this case, the ends of the tape to the door—is the makings of an alarm sigil. Their knees quake. The moment the seal on the tape is broken, faculty will be alerted to the intrusion. Though the punishment is unclear, getting caught in any capacity could spell difficulty to Simone's career.

"You're not going to have time to stop and examine things—but this isn't your first venture, is it?"

The words drag them back to. At the forefront, with stunning clarity, comes a single name. Nadia. It's all the incentive they need.

"What do I have to do?"

The stranger snorts. "You'll need a bag. I said you wouldn't get to stop and examine, didn't I?"

Simone's frown deepens. "Why would you help me?"

The stranger waves a hand as if making to swat a fly. "I was once in a situation similar to yours," they say at last. "Now, are you going to get a bag or do you feel inclined to stand here until someone catches us?"

"You'll be here when I come back?"

"If you're quick enough."

By the time they've returned to the third floor of the Diviner's tower, they're panting hard with exertion. Sweat prickles along their brow and seeps down the back of their neck. As exhausted as they are, though, they don't dare stop. Not even as their knees begin to throb.

True to their word, the stranger is still waiting for them, looking up from their pocket watch at Simone's approach.

"I hoped you would be inspired," they say, clicking the watch closed. They flip their ink-dark hair over one shoulder. "Now. I'll get you in, and I hope what I do will get you back out."

"Thank—"

"But if I find you back here again, I'll turn you into the Headmaster myself."

Simone swallows and gives a sharp nod.

From deep within their clothes, the stranger produces a small jar of paint and a narrow brush. Then comes the chill of the paint, not unlike slime, as the stranger draws a complex series of swirls and lines on any bare skin of Simone's they can find.

"I am unsure how long the effects will last. That said, it should help."

With this, they enclose Simone's hand in their own. The Caster's mark on their glove glows a dim gold.

"I'm Shae, by the way. Not that you bothered to ask."

"Shae. Thank you."

With this, the glove emits a final, eye-piercing flash before dimming once more. Simone's skin turns translucent, a faint outline giving away their general shape.

"I hope I need not repeat my warning," Shae says as they turn on their heel. "Don't let me find you here again."

Then they are gone, the faint smell of ozone following in their wake.

The tape doesn't resist when Simone barges into the apartment. Though there's no audible alarm, there's a second, fainter puff of ozone, the tell-tale sign of a spell being cast.

The race is on.

Everything appears to be as Simone remembers it, complete now with a thin veneer of dust. Perhaps there's something of worth they can grab; some sort of clue.

At least, they hope so, but their search proves futile when they realize it's the same Sanguina Malefica pamphlets and tattered dream journals that litter Nadia's apartment. How naive of them to think a clue would manifest itself now.

They move to the near-bare bookshelf against the wall. Many of the books are ones Simone gifted her: devotional poetry, chintzy romances, the occasional textbook. Small glass-and-enamel statues glare from their perches. Nothing they can scan for clues, though.

They've moved on to a book about ancient health remedies when Dio's sharp meow startles them. He's at their feet when they look up. They don't remember seeing him enter.

The moment their fingers brush his snowy fur, he lunges away from them.

"What are you doing?"

A second, quieter meow. Simone follows the noise. The cat weaves a path through Nadia's furniture, thick tail swishing, and bounds for the bedroom.

They find Dio under her bed, sharpening his claws on one of Nadia's blouses. Scraps of yellow fabric form a dizzying vortex around him. Simone sweeps an arm in his direction to distract him.

"Stop that, Dio."

As beams of light illuminate his fur, he stills. His gentle purrs rumble the carpet beneath. When he shifts, the light moves with him. Between his paws is a small black vial.

"What do you have there?"

Dio grows statue-still, vial still nestled between his paws. With shallow breaths, Simone reaches for him. His spine bristles when they make contact, but he doesn't stop them from pulling the vial free and examining it.

Inky liquid bubbles with a life of its own within the slim glass tube. Simone doesn't have to uncork it to know it contains Serenity. Though their encounter with the drug had been brief, they'll never forget the way the liquid moved as they drank it, like it was alive. Worse still had been the foreign feeling of stepping outside of themself, of filling a space much larger than they were capable of comprehending when sober. And the sensation of their mind coalescing with Nadia's...

The sample trembles, liquid sloshing around before settling.

With startling clarity, a solution forms itself in the back of their mind. Without a second look at the vial, they shove it into their bag.

EIGHT

Nadia DuPont || Before

She can't have heard right, so she leans forward in her chair and asks Doctor Aiza to repeat herself.

"The news is shocking. I understand." Before her, the doctor caps her pen and tucks it through her red-blonde tresses. "Sanguina Malefica is not a... kind diagnosis to contend with. We have some options, though, which will help make you more comfortable for the time being."

"No." She leans forward to look at the file, but the doctor snatches it back. "That can't be right."

"My apologies, Miss DuPont... but I'm afraid it is."

If only she could burn her to cinders with her stare, or bend her body inside out. Alas, she majored in the wrong realm of magic. Instead, Nadia gives Doctor Aiza the fiercest glare she can muster, chin tipped with the force of her defiance. Undoubtedly, the doctor has delivered this sort of diagnosis before to hapless, tired students with unknown illnesses. Perhaps some had acted the way she is now, armored with the scathing looks. Still, she's nothing like them. She can't be.

"I'm not dying," Nadia says at last.

The folder in the doctor's hand tips. "The results are quite clear."

She unclips her capelet and throws it to the floor. As it forms a sad puddle at her feet, she gives her bruising forearm a harsh smack. "So check again. Do more tests. Make your salary fucking worth something."

"Miss DuPont."

Now, her name is uttered without any warmth to it. She stills, heartbeat too loud in her ears. The pity remains in Doctor Aiza's grey-rimmed gaze, so intense it makes Nadia want to smother her.

"I truly am sorry," Doctor Aiza says, voice soft like she expects Nadia to shatter.

But she doesn't. Nadia is stronger than this. She has to be, she tells herself as she shoves the maelstrom of emotions within down. If not for the tears burning her eyes, it would be easy for her to dismiss the emotional breakdown she feels herself teetering on the edge of.

She focuses on the mole between Doctor Aiza's eyes to distract herself. "So," she says, "what now?"

The doctor blinks once, then again. The faint twitch of her brows betrays her surprise. "Would you like a moment to process?"

"I can process and act at the same time." Nadia is almost proud at the briskness of her own words, of how she has wrangled the turmoil curdling her insides. "Again I ask: what now?"

Doctor Aiza leans back, eyes wider now. She sets her clipboard aside. "Well... Sanguina Malefica works in stages." She pauses to flip through the pages on her clipboard before continuing. "You are in an early stage still, so we would like to keep an eye on the progression."

"Progression." Nadia rolls the word around on her tongue and tries to not think of her mother. "Does not sound like there's a cure in mind."

"I am afraid not, Miss DuPont. The disease can be monitored—blood tests and checkups, primarily—and when you become too ill for normal function, we can reassess. There are centers we can send you to at that point. A sort of hospice."

"So, for now, what *can* we do?"

Doctor Aiza drums well-manicured nails on her thighs. "We have done trial runs with doses of Serenamine for pain management. While not the most ideal solution, the results have been promising."

Serenamine. The legally-prescribed version of the drug Nadia keeps festering in vials under her bed. When the pain in her bones had first reared its head, she had acquired as much of the medication as the medical ward would allow her to. While it had dulled the edge, she had still been aware of the pain lingering on the fringes of her consciousness. Serenity was a more concentrated—and unregulated—version.

She chews on the inside of her cheek and breaks her gaze. "Is that all?"

Doctor Aiza frowns. "It... we have little else at this juncture. I can schedule meetings with one of the Evocators on-staff to help further mitigate the pain, if you would like."

Her words dangle in the fragile silence. With a soft hum, Nadia turns the conversation over the way a child might an Akalese puzzle toy. As of yet, she knows one detail has not been broached.

"How long do I have?"

Doctor Aiza's frown deepens. "That, we are unable to determine. For now, I would advise you get your affairs in order. Ensure there's no loose ends when the time comes."

Nadia's chest tightens. The same sentiment had escorted her mother to an early grave. "So then, I don't have long."

"I cannot say for certain."

"Do I have weeks? Months? A couple of years?"

Doctor Aiza's grey-rimmed eyes flash like sun-warmed metal. "To be frank, Ms. DuPont, you would be lucky to see graduation."

She can't help the sharp inhale she gives. Nine months. Nadia's life, already so insignificant in the grand scheme of it all, reduced to nine months.

"I see." The two words tremble under the weight of emotions she struggles to contain. Then, breath rattling, she stands. An all-too-familiar pain traps her knee in a vice-grip, one she now knows the cause of.

"Do you have any questions?"

Nadia shakes her head. "Thank you for your time."

As she turns to leave, Doctor Aiza grabs her hand. Her skin is as cold and smooth as wind-carved stone. Nadia pauses mid-step.

"Even in our darkest nights," Doctor Aiza's voice is a whisper now, "There is light available. Remember that, if nothing else."

How strange of her to offer a parable after delivering fatal news. Nadia would laugh, had the words not come from one so obviously Gods-touched. Her heart twinges, and she again feels the budding heat behind her eyelids.

"I'll keep it in mind, thank you."

With this, she snatches her hand away.

***

Chantal answers on the second ring. She's barely gotten a syllable out when Nadia cuts her off.

"Do you have those notes from your friend in Elrick?"

She's never been so overt, she thinks. All the phones are monitored by the operators who connect the lines. Having witnessed the expulsion of her peers, Nadia has learned to speak in code. This is the most daring she's ever been.

Chantal's breath catches over the line. "Yeah, I think so," she replies after several seconds.

"Can you bring them by in, say, twenty minutes?"

The moment Chantal affirms, Nadia hangs the phone back on the cradle. She's being abrupt, she knows, but she doesn't have it in her to care. Her heart beats at the pace of a hummingbird's wings.

After a pause, she picks up the phone once again.

"Etienne LaChance, please," she says into the mouthpiece. After a click, his soft hum crackles across the line.

"Nat?"

Her mouth opens, but nothing comes out. She should have planned what to say. Curse her over-active instincts. How do you tell someone you're dying?

"Etienne." Her voice cracks, betraying her.

"I'll be right there."

He hangs up before she can argue. She guesses, in a way, she deserves it after her brusque discussion with Chantal. Replacing the phone, she steps away.

The door trembles on its hinges with the force of his arrival. He doesn't knock. He doesn't have to. Before she can speak, he has her enveloped.

It's in his warmth she lets her first tears of the afternoon slip free.

He detaches from her only when Chantal shows up, but then he's back again with a small paper bag. After he sets it between them, he takes her hand. Neither of them speak for a long while.

The ticking of the clock in the corner of the room digs its way under her skin.

"So." Tick, tock, tick, tock. Nadia's free hand tangles in her skirt. "I got some news today."

Etienne adjusts his glasses as he looks up. "I knew something happened."

"I'm…" Her breath catches, the words forming a dam at the base of her throat. Where to even begin?

"We don't have to talk about it." He takes her hands in his, grasp limp in case she decides to pull away. How does he know her so well?

It would be easy to bury the truth. After a good, private cry, she could go on with the knowledge held close to her chest, and in nine months she'd be gone and none of it would matter.

She thinks about it, briefly, but the concern in Etienne's gaze fractures her resolve. He deserves the truth more than anyone else.

"Etienne, I'm dying."

His hands tighten around hers, knuckles paling. When she tries to meet his gaze, he's staring off into the distance. A chasm opens in the pit of her stomach.

In a voice entirely too small, she says, "Etienne?"

"Are… Are you sure?"

"That's what the doctors told me today. They—" She swallows down the growing lump in her throat. Death is a part of life, she knows. If the Gods see fit to end her story here, who is she to stop it?

After a deep breath, Nadia tries again. "They said I will be lucky to see graduation."

Etienne's breath hitches. "That's—"

"I know."

His eyes squeeze shut. Nadia cups his face, desperate to wipe the pain from his face.

"Etienne… I'm sorry."

Thick sobs tear from him as he howls like an animal wounded. Despite the way her throat closes, though, Nadia refuses to let her own tears fall.

Her mind drifts to when her mother had shared similar news with her, the stony quiet that had enveloped them. Neither of them had been much for words or emotions. Nadia's mom had cried harder than either of them. She was losing her wife, after all.

It's that way now. She's Etienne's closest friend. Now, in a twist of fate neither of them had seen, she'll soon enough leave him.

"Hey," she says, tipping his chin. Water-logged green eyes consume her vision. She swipes a thumb over his cheekbone. "We still have time. Not as much as I would like, but we have time."

He lunges into her arms with a choked sound, head pressed into her ribs. She rubs slow circles into the ridges of his spine. The sound of his sobs turns to unrelenting static.

This is not how the conversation should be going, she thinks. She should be the one breaking down, right? She is the one whose life is coming to a close. Why is Etienne crying instead of her?

She shoves him back, perhaps a bit too roughly, and hates the mix of hurt and confusion swimming in his eyes.

"I... I need to be alone right now, Etienne."

She might as well have slammed a door in his face, the way tears well up and roll down his cheeks. His brows crinkle together as another, harsher emotion flickers across his face. Indignation.

"I'm sorry." A fist clenches in her lap, the most she'll allow her anger to show. "This is a lot for me to have to take in right now. You understand, don't you?"

He gives a dry swallow. "Of course," he says, the syllables sticking together.

She guides him to the door, every bone in her body aching. More than anything, she needs to slip into the oblivion Serenity can give her. Perhaps, wrapped in its inky tendrils, she can find an answer to her plight.

Or perhaps not. Perhaps she'll just be high. In her last moments of sobriety, Nadia isn't sure which outcome she prefers.

***

The world becomes a haze of the past and the present and the possible. As Nadia swims through her blankets and stares at her swirling ceiling, any thought she conjures quickly vanishes.

A far-off knock disturbs her trance.

The room around her distorts, like she's viewing it through a scrying spell, but she knows her room from any in the tower. Perhaps on the entire campus. Unless she spontaneously managed to master teleportation. Ha.

Getting upright is like swimming through stone. The effort has her gasping, each breath rattling her hollow lungs.

The knocking sounds again. Nadia rises, stumbles, and tries again.

Who is bothering me at... She glances at the clock on her living room wall and squints to keep the object still. *Seven in the evening? Fuck.* Each mental word is punctuated by an uneven step. One could mistake her for a drunkard, perhaps, but her movements lack the discomfort that often clings to them. This is blessing enough.

She plants herself against the door, the wood bending under her weight and threatening to cave. Standing on her tiptoes, she peeks one bleary eye through the peephole and flinches at the distorted figure standing on the other side.

"Nadia?" Simone raises a hand and knocks again. "Are you in there?"

The Serenity has twisted every sense she has, but she gets the feeling they're talking loud enough to attract attention.

With a hiss, she yanks the door open. They've changed since she saw them last—or perhaps the Serenity makes it so their clothes are more vibrant. Gone is the Abjuror's capelet, letting the soft cream of their button-up shirt breathe.

"Simone," she whispers. At least, she thinks she does.

"Nadia? Are you okay?" Their voice bounces around in her skull. Though she doesn't feel the usual tug of nausea, she thinks she might puke.

"Fuck. I..."

Their brows knit together. She feels their aura in the space between them. It guides her back, a sturdy wall keeping either of them from making contact.

As soon as they're in her living room, they shut the door with a soft sigh. Irritation and concern seeps from them like ink into water. The click of the lock makes her bones vibrate.

"What happened to you?"

If she was more sober, she could attempt to pull herself together and lie. The moment she has the thought, the ground sways. She couldn't fake it if she tried.

"I..." Her tongue is coated in fuzz. In a rare moment of lucidity, she says, "You shouldn't see me like this." She lumbers forward to shove them out, to get them to leave, to do *something*, but the wall comes up between them again and she falls back.

And then, with a gentleness that threatens to shatter her, they say, "Let's get you in bed."

"I'm fine." Her words come out seconds too slow. "I can handle myself." And yet, she knows the way her words stick together like melted sugar.

Their face is a mask, all smooth curves and thick dark lips. With the faintest twitch of their eyebrow, they hook her arm through theirs and guide her deeper into the apartment. Great, uncomfortable heat forms where they touch her. Images flash behind her eyes in an instant: open books with words she can't decipher; a burly figure's pressed suit and leather elbow patches; Nadia herself, brown skin gray-tinged.

Is that how they really see her?

She yanks back, desperate to sever the connection between them, but the images keep coming. A figure, so like Simone and yet so different, scowling at her from across a yawning chasm. Sparks of magic. The sharp, fresh scent of ozone.

With a grunt, Simone's arm curls tighter around her.

"That way." She weakly gestures with her chin. If they won't let her go, they can at least put her to bed. "To my room, I mean."

She must black out. One moment, she's in their arms still; the next, she finds herself falling back against the mattress. The stars on her ceiling dance to the tune of her twisting vision. A true, vicious wave of nausea roils her stomach and it takes everything within her to not pitch over the side of the bed and vomit.

Her gaze falls on the bedside table. A black smudge mars the rim of her cup. She has half a mind to be panicked; she and Simone have barely interacted before now. Will they know what she's consumed?

Her fear is swept away in the next moments as Simone smooths the sweat-slicked strands of hair sticking to her forehead. Each movement vibrates through her body like a lake disturbed. This close, their fingers against her brow, dozens of images flicker in their dark brown eyes, so fast she can't comprehend them.

Nadia whips her head to the side, desperate to break the mental link between them, and her stomach lurches at the motion. Too fast, she thinks as she takes a deep breath to keep the bile at bay.

"Sorry." Their voice bounces around in her skull. "I should have asked before touching you."

Slower this time, she tilts her head to gaze at them from the corner of her eye.

"I... um..." Simone's cheeks pinken a touch. Their aura is so murky now Nadia is incapable of reading it. "I wasn't expecting this."

Some primal part of Nadia screams is the back of her skull. *You fucking idiot. You're so devoid of compassion and empathy you'd allow them to waste their time on you? You stupid, stupid little girl.*

She squeezes her eyes shut. Deep breaths do little to calm her. At any second, the dam will burst and she will be a sea of pain.

"You should go," she forces out between clenched teeth. Then, "I'm sorry to have wasted your time."

The silence is tangible, thick and waving and enough to make her dizzy. It's in this silence she waits, straining an ear for the sound of Simone's shoes on the floor. *Leave me,* she pleads from inside herself.

There's nothing. Her gaze latches to the ceiling. Her mouth opens, but her thoughts linger at the end of yawning tunnels and she finds herself incapable of speaking.

And then, mercifully, the squeak of their shoes fills the silence. Nadia knows without checking that she is alone. So utterly, terribly alone.

Nine

Simone Allard || After

O f all the hare-brained activities Simone has found themself involved in, they're sure this is the worst. The thought cements itself into their brain as they scurry out of the Diviner's tower, bag an anchor at their hip. And then, as soon as they look up, a cluster of people are marching towards them. Faculty members.

Shit, shit, shit.

They stiffen against the stair railing as several pairs of eyes rake through them, focusing instead on the entrance to the tower.

Simone glances down. Their body remains a faint, watery outline. True to Shae's words, the spell holds firm.

One by one, the faculty members surge up the stairs and through the doors. None of them spare Simone a glance, though an older professor of Illusion sweeps close enough to breathe on. Simone presses themself to the rail, breath held and body stiff. The doors of the tower slam closed.

Dio squirms in their bag, dragging them back from their paralyzing panic. It's been through the miracle of a minor Enchantment sigil they had in the back of their notes they were able to soothe him at all, but there's no telling how long it'll last. Simone needs to get him into their apartment before he escapes or causes a stir. They break into a sprint, heart roaring like a train in their chest.

Finally, shrouded in darkness of their room, they think they've evaded discovery.

Dio looks up from his curled up spot on the bed as they approach him later. Grabbing him had been an act of impulse, but how could they leave him behind? The two of them had never been on the friend-liest of terms, though they had been at least amicable. Even now, he pulls away from their touch, but relents at last with a slow blink of his golden eyes.

They'll have to ask Chantal for advice on pet care. While her expertise tends to lie in horticulture, her love of pets means she should know a thing or two about cat care that Simone doesn't. Scratching him behind the ears, they wiggle their satchel free from underneath him. As they undo the buckles, it dawns on them they've never had a pet before.

They sift through their findings. A medical textbook on the thinner side of informative and brochures on Sanguina Malefica join the small collection of reading materials they've gathered over the last few weeks. And then, beneath it all, the vial of Serenity taunts them from the bottom of their bag.

They've been under the drug's influence once before—a desperate attempt to comprehend Nadia better—but they preferred to leave such proclivities to Nadia. The feeling of being of multiple minds was something they weren't able to come to terms with.

Flashes of her memories bubble beneath the surface. The face of a jubilant brother. The sudden alleviating of weight with the snip of hair shears. Pieces of her linger within their skin even now. How can one willingly subject themself to such an alienating sensation?

Simone picks the vial up without looking at it and turns for the bookshelf against the wall. While most of the books on the floor-to-ceiling shelves are legitimate copies, they find the one decoy hidden amongst them. A holiday gift from their enbei, with sigils overtop only they know how to decipher. The spine claims it's a collection of maps from the Coven Age, and true to the illusion is a map of eastern Elrick on the front cover. Most of the map is shrouded in trees. A single, skinny river snakes its way from the sea into the mainland. The Foxtrot River.

They turn the book on its side and push a loose bump on the spine. The cover flips open, revealing the box within.

Their collection has grown over the years. Cuff links procured from their enbei. A pocket watch from one of their first professors. A pair of six-sided dice cut from agate from Nadia. All of these cherished trinkets, hidden in plain sight.

Simone regards the vial one last time. The liquid rolls around, straining for the cork stopper. They don't want to sully their prized possessions with such contraband, but the alternatives are limited for now.

This will be a last resort.

With this, they set the vial in the box and slam the lid closed. The weight in their chest lifts with the click of the lock.

***

For hours that night, Simone stares at the ceiling and grips their blanket with paling knuckles. They half-expect faculty members to swarm them for their entry into Nadia's apartment—it wouldn't be the first time they have done such a thing, after all. And yet, at long last, sunlight begins its gentle creep along their ceiling.

A soft sigh escapes, the last acknowledgment they're willing to give of the day before. The stretch they give pops their vertebrae, one after another. Time to begin their morning routine.

It's the same every day. It has to be in order for Simone to function. As a child, their enbei said a chaotic routine would lead to a chaotic personality and Simone had never thought to question it. Now that their school life has grown so hectic, though, they aren't so sure, but they don't have it in them to break from tradition. It's this strict adherence that has often drove Nadia to chew her nails in frustration.

They spend five minutes stretching their body. First their toes, then their legs, up the valley of their stomach, ending with the soft pop of their shoulders. Then they strip their nightclothes and set them in the basket in the closet. The faint salty smell emanating from their laundry heap reminds them they have yet to wash clothes this week.

Breakfast is a serving of yogurt topped with lemon curd and blue-berries still cold from the refrigerator. They pick at it as they wait for the coffee to finish steeping and have moved on to a piece of bread toasted over the stovetop burner when a sudden, sharp pain rakes through them.

Pain is not part of the routine.

Simone stumbles with a soundless gasp. It's as though someone is attempting to pull the cap of one knee free of its socket. For several seconds, all they can do is let out a low whine and pray for the moment to pass, eyes rolling.

The timer for their coffee dings, a knife of clarity. Clenching the counter, they hobble towards the machine and at last collapse into one of their stools, stretching their aching leg. Already, the pain has abated some, but is still strong enough it keeps Simone's thoughts in a vice-grip. And yet, when they pull up the cuffs of their under-shorts, there's nothing. No swollen flesh. The skin isn't blushed like it would if they had struck it against something. It almost reminds them of the growing pains they underwent as a child, but with more intensity.

How peculiar. They let the cuff of their shorts drop.

They entertain the notion of staying home as they stir cream and sugar into their cup, but decide against it. There's been enough chaos as it is, and they would rather not arouse suspicion after the situation in Nadia's room. They can muscle through the day well enough—they hope.

They exhale hard and pour the coffee into their teacup.

There's the meeting with Alienor. Their spoon scrapes the porcelain, forming a ripple in their thoughts, but they drag themself back with a grunt. *Defense through Modern Means, Intro to Glyph Design, Ethical Divination...*

They latch onto the final class in the list, thinking of the Serenity they've tucked away in their room. It can remain as a last resort, can't it? They'll have to consult their notes for ideas.

Before long, the pain lessens to a dull throb. Not ideal, but it will have to do.

On their way out of the apartment, a subtle doubt nibbles at them. Before they can stop themself, they march for their bookshelf and grab their box of trinkets. The button on the spine gives a soft click. They shove a hand into the cavity without looking and close in on the vial. It clinks against their thumb ring as they shove it into their bag.

***

Alienor is waiting for them when they enter the cafe, balancing her cane over one knee. Staring out the window, she pulls her powder blue capelet tighter around her and doesn't look up until Simone pulls their chair out with a loud screech.

"Oh," she says, gaze vacant. "You've arrived."

Simone sits down and sets their satchel aside. "I am. I apologize for my lateness."

"It's fine."

On normal mornings, they launch into lively conversation at once, jabbering until the first bells ring. Magic, philosophy, their classes for the day... nothing escapes the wide net both of their minds cast. This morning, however, there is a storm of nerves brewing between them. Simone shifts in their seat, fighting to meet Alienor's eyes.

"Rough morning?" they ask when the silence grows too deep.

Alienor scrapes her teacup around in its saucer. Under the table, her knee begins to bounce.

"Alienor?"

"I..." The sigh she expels whips her hair into a frenzy, "Have many thoughts lingering is all."

They take her hand in theirs, examining the splints on her fingers. "I see." At once, guilt forms a weight in their chest. How could they have thought to stay home, when other people endure worse?

"I've had plenty put into perspective, I'll say that much." Then, adjusting the splints on her fingers, "But I suppose it doesn't matter. How have you been?"

"Better in comparisons, it could be said."

Alienor turns away once again, knuckles white where she clutches her capelet. She drums an uneven beat on the side of her cane.

"Mx. Allard, if I may be so forward...?"

They lean forward, pulse fluttering. "Yes?"

"What is it that made you decide to pursue Abjuration?"

Simone's brow furrows. "Well, plenty, I suppose. My enbei is a prominent Abjuror in the A.C.A.S., so it feels... almost expected. But aside from that, it's the field of Casting which calls to me the most."

"And you've never had a change of heart? Not once?"

Perhaps, when Simone had first began pursuing their Abjuration degree a year prior, there had been the faintest inklings of doubt. To pinpoint your studies to such a finite degree is indeed a daunting task. And sure, towards the end of their first year they had made themself sick with worry over their career prospects, or if they had made the right decision.

They can't say when exactly the cold chill of certainty had settled within them. Perhaps it had been a culmination of numerous smaller moments—moments which, upon reflection after their passing, had helped cement the notion that, yes, Simone was making the right decision.

"Never a change of heart," they respond at last. "An examination of my values, perhaps. Overall, I've been quite satisfied with the trajectory of my life."

Outside, the courtyard is a rainbow of capelets. Alienor watches each one pass, statue-still for a good while. When she turns back, tears make a gleaming patchwork of her cheeks.

"My sister was killed last week. Monster attack, they said."

Simone winces. Another one in Mertaln? How peculiar. "I'm... terribly sorry to hear that," they say, unsure how best to respond.

Alienor nods as if that's the reaction she's expecting. "I just found out," she continues. "A whole week went by. We were making plans not too long ago to see each other after my graduation, you know. She's always wanted to go to see the Festival of Lanterns in Latuka and—"

Simone takes her hand again, unsure of what else to do.

"It just. It makes me angry, you know?" Her fingers curl tight around Simone's. "Why wasn't I called? I graduate in a few weeks. What difference would it make? We have phones, for shards' sake. Why wasn't I called?"

All at once, her composure crumples. With quiet, whole-body shudders, the tears on Alienor's face flow anew. She looks back out the window.

"I just..." She hiccups before continuing. "I wish I had been there to protect her. That's what our realm of Casting is all about, isn't it?"

Simone nods. Then, realizing she isn't watching, they say, "I suppose so."

The first bells ring, snapping them both to attention. Sharing a look, they rise in unison.

"Mx. Allard." Alienor props the door open with her cane, letting Simone out first. Then, as she steps out after them, she says, "Do you know what the word 'abjuration' originally meant?"

They play with the strap of their satchel, pulse quickening when they realize they don't have an answer. Though their knowledge spans many a topic, language was never one of their strong suits. After an uncomfortable pause, they say, "I don't."

"A renunciation of one's oath." Voice cracking, Alienor rubs her thumb over the head of her cane. "How far we have taken that, hmm?"

***

Upon receiving the summons to visit the faculty office, Simone almost convinces themself it is a cruel joke, a dollop of sour icing on top of an already-shit day. Regardless, prank or not, they know refusing to respond will not be advantageous.

Reality settles over them like fog as the door clicks shut behind them. Professor Darzi's is the first face they see. Beside him, Professor Favreau shifts her shoulders an imperceptible degree, worrying at her lip with too-white teeth. A third professor sits on the other side of her, unfamiliar to Simone. They're an older figure, a map of wrinkles across their face and a long, snow-white beard pooling into their lap. At Simone's approach, they gesture to the empty seat before them all.

"Please have a seat, Mx. Allard."

Simone's heart hammers in their throat as they oblige. They can't help the nervous glance they cast around the room. In their time at Voterique, they've never been in a situation like this. The lack of familiarity feels like treading water. The possibilities are an ocean, bottomless and nauseating.

Adding to the uncanny feeling in their gut is the room's decor. Floor-to-ceiling shelves make the cramped room even smaller, books from a variety of authors and ages collecting dust in the dim light. The chairs are the sole other decoration in the room. The slim windows bear a thin coating of dust. This room sees minimal usage, it seems.

"Thank you for responding to our summons," Professor Darzi says, a soft but unconvincing smile tugging at his mouth.

On their march up to the office, Simone had gone over potential routes of handling this conversation. Though they couldn't be certain, they suspected this summons was related to their recent break in to Nadia's apartment. Again comes the bone-chilling anxiety. Did they really think they could get away with it? Then again, had they not taken precaution?

They cannot help but play innocent all the same. "Am... Am I in trouble?"

"Trouble?" Professor Darzi's eyes widen. "No, no—"

"Professor." The aged professor's eyes on Simone makes them shrivel up. They rest pruned hands over one knee. "Mx. Allard, we have called you in regarding a recent breaking and entering incident in the Diviner's tower. Perhaps you may be aware?"

Simone grimaces as they swallow down the thorned lump in their throat. How awful it is, knowing they were right. "A break-in?"

The professor's shrewdish gaze narrows. They run gnarled fingers through their beard, a stylus gripped tight in their free hand. As they allow the silence to stretch around them, they begin to scribble something on the notepad balanced on their thigh.

"Mx. Allard." Professor Darzi speaks again, pleading to them with the curve of his brows. "We understand you were engaged in a relationship with a fellow student. One Miss DuPont?"

He doesn't need to continue. They know what it is he wants them to say.

I cannot, Professor. Guilt turns their stomach to lead. *Even if it risks everything, I cannot give up this desperate search.*

As soon as the thought crosses their mind, Simone scans each professor's tattooed hand for an activated sigil. Though none of them appear to be Diviners, there's no telling if any of them have taken on the realm as a minor. At any moment, a careless thought can spell their expulsion.

And yet, with no glowing sigils and a lack of the tell-tale scent of magic being cast, they allow themself to slump in relief at last.

"I am familiar with Miss DuPont, yes." The words drag from the back of their mouth. "We were..." *Paramours. Lovers. Something wholly knotted together and impossible to untangle.* "We were intimate."

The aged professor again takes hold of the conversation. "And is it correct of us to assume you would often visit this student's apartment?"

"It is."

"So then, would you happen to be familiar with the break-in?"

Simone's jaw sets. "I would not."

"Do you have an idea who might be responsible?"

Simone turns the question over in their mind. "Could it have been her best friend?"

The moment the words leave their mouth, they long more than anything to snatch them from the vacant air and cram them back down their throat. What are they thinking? If Etienne is imprisoned, they can kiss their search for answers goodbye.

And yet, it's a better alternative than them being caught.

"Etienne LaChance? The man in the hospital?" The professor stills, strands of beard hair tangling in their fingers. "Surely, you do not think us fools?"

Simone bristles. Of course. No one else is aware he's awake yet. "He's the only person aside from me who was quite close to her is all. Forgive me. It is still... difficult for me to consider their circumstances."

"And since you both were so close to Miss DuPont, and one of you is indisposed, well. You can understand our suspicion, right?"

The lump in their throat returns, so thick they cannot swallow it down.

"Professor Chapeau, that is enough."

Three pairs of eyes flick in Professor Favreau's direction. She doesn't flinch under the attention, instead sitting up straighter and tipping her chin in defiance. A woman with her kind of tenacity, it's a wonder why she and Nadia didn't get along.

"This line of questioning is getting us nowhere," she says. "It is clear this student was not involved in these recent events. Perhaps we should release them and extend inquiries elsewhere?"

A beat, then Professor Darzi dips his head. "I can attest to Mx. Allard's reputation. A crime like this would be beyond them."

Professor Chapeau's glower remains. "Very well," they say. They flip to a new page in their notepad and the scratch of their stylus fills the silence for several seconds. Then, with a resigned sigh, they brandish the back of their tattooed hand. As their Caster's mark glows green and purple, tendrils of ice fill Simone's mind, shocking them in place. They don't have the time or sigils to prepare a defense as the magic invades their every waking thought.

No, no, no, no—

"Chapeau."

At once, the tendrils recede. Simone doubles over in their seat, panting as they struggle to comprehend what just happened. The beginnings of a headache bloom to life. Their entire body rattles like they've been doused with ice water.

"What are you *doing*." Professor Favreau's chair screeches against the ground. "We have a process."

Static overtakes whatever comes next. Simone loses themself to the swirling vortex inside their mind.

When they snap back to, they're standing in the hallway, Professor Darzi's arm around their shoulder. Raised voices emanate from the closed door. They don't remember leaving the room.

"I am incredibly sorry, Mx. Allard," he says, for likely not the first time. "What happened was uncalled for. I don't... it will be addressed."

Simone struggles to parse the sequence of events for themself, but they know Professor Chapeau is the cause. When they think of them, of the way their hand had flashed, how Simone's mind had been seized like a child's plaything, the headache between their ears grows in intensity.

Simone shrugs off Professor Darzi's arm, guilt creeping through them at the way he flinches in response.

"May I go home?" they ask. They don't dare utter how his colleague is responsible for the discomfort lingering beneath their skin, how all they can think about now is taking steel wool to their mind and scrubbing until nothing remains.

"O-Of course. Of course."

It shouldn't end this way. And yet it does. Students who turn their magic on their peers and are caught for it risk expulsion, if not worse, but a faculty member doing the same to a student is met with half-hearted hand-wringing. Simone supposes Professor Chapeau possesses their Caster's mark as it is. Nothing they do can undo the magic stamped into their skin. Still, is there not a punishment befitting of such a slight?

The discomfort continues to nag at Simone as they begin the trek out of the administrative hall. By the time they step foot into the brisk spring air outside, they know there will be no recourse for them. Not this time.

TEN

Nadia DuPont || Before

Light stabs through Nadia's eyelids, dragging her to conscious-ness. The steady throb in her temples accompanies it, so sharp she grits her teeth against the pain. The crash is the worst part of the high—though, thank the Gods, she was lucky enough to sleep through it this time.

She sits up, the movement broken down into minute fractions to keep the swelling in her temples at bay, and takes stock of her surroundings. The pile of clothes at the foot of her bed has shrunk. Or, at least, it had *looked* larger last night. And gone, too, is the clutter on her bedside table. The cup included, she notes with a soft frown.

She's done plenty under Serenity's influence. Dance on tables like a drunkard. Make out with Chantal in front of everyone. Other, equally mortifying acts she can half-remember. Clean her room, however? That is something entirely out of the ordinary.

Her brows furrow, the epicenter of an impending migraine lurking between them. A white gap consumes her memory like missing frames in a motion film. What the fuck did she do last night?

Nadia's attention flicks to the blankets encasing her in bed. On a normal night, they're a trap for her to escape from, one she does so with much vigor. On the rare nights that Etienne has snuck into her room, he'd tease her for kicking in her sleep.

Today, however, she's been perfectly wrapped. Had someone tucked her in? Then, heart lurching, a worse thought presents itself. Was someone in her apartment? It wouldn't be the most unusual circumstance, she supposes. More than once, she's come back to herself in the embrace of a stranger, hands in places they don't belong. More often still, she will wake up in an apartment she doesn't recognize. In comparison, waking up alone and untouched is an oddity for her.

Dio sits in the corner of her bed, one eye half-open to regard her. With a soft chirrup, he returns to his gentle snoring.

Her brain continues its slow churn. The afterimage of a memory burns itself into her thoughts.

Simone.

Her palm is halfway to her face when she forces herself to soften the blow. Even the brief touch sends a black wave of pain through her, strong enough to eclipse her vision. Nadia grits her teeth.

She has to apologize somehow. Given that it's the end of the week, though, there are no classes to attend. They could be anywhere on the campus—or off it.

The simplest solution would be to call. But how to explain what happened? Especially with the operators listening in. One wrong word and she can surrender any hope of graduating. Anything worse and she risks Simone's place in Voterique, too.

Still, it would be a start.

Nadia clings to the bed post as she rises, pain barreling through her. Each step makes her gut twist and her knees shake.

I have to fix this.

It takes her another ten minutes to make it into the hall. By the time she enters the kitchen, she's sweating like she's back in Perov in the dead of summer. The bottoms of her feet feel like they've been stuck with pins. Still, she has enough energy left to pick up the phone and hold it to her mouth.

"Simone Allard, please."

A faint crackle. Then, silence. She counts out the seconds under her breath until she hears the fizz of their lines connecting.

"Hello?"

Nadia's heart leaps. "Simone. Hi."

"Hello." A soft breath, then, "May I ask who's calling?"

"It's... um... Nadia."

Before she can say anything else, there's a harsh smack from the other end. The line clicks as it disconnects. Dumbfounded, she brings the receiver down to regard it. Did they just hang up on her?

She expected that response, if she's being honest with herself. Any sensible person would have done the same. Still, her heart tears as she gently recradles the mouthpiece. It would have been better for them to scream at her, to call her every name imaginable. Instead, they'd decided she wasn't worth a single word.

With a soft sigh, she lumbers in the direction of her bedroom. She had to make things right between them somehow... but it will have to wait until she's physically able to.

***

The next day, she looks for Simone everywhere. Despite the gelatin feel of her bones and the unspeakable agony coursing through her, determination lights the way.

She's never let anyone get this close with her. Etienne is the one exception, forgiving the fact their relationship is not romantic, and even he gets kept at arms' length at times.

So what makes Simone so different? Perhaps it's the way they carry themself. She knows they're intelligent from the few conversations they've had. They've a good head on their shoulders, as her mother used to say. She'd be proud.

With that heart-sinking realization, Nadia comes to a final conclusion. She has to make things right between them. She has to.

Winter is making its slow descent on Voterique. It's the first day of the year she feels the need to wear a scarf with her ensemble—and it certainly won't be the last. A wealth of trees and bushes from all around the world frame the perimeter, most of them shifting from soft greens to brown-speckled oranges.

She takes a deep breath, inhaling the sickly sweet aroma of decay. Perhaps today her luck will be good enough she will run into Simone.

And yet, they aren't in any of the halls, nor in the administrative buildings she limps into and gives a cursory glance. They aren't on any of the eight floors of the library—or, at least, she hopes not after the hour she spent scouring it. With every location she comes up empty, her heart sinks a little more.

Finally, as she thinks to give up, she sees them.

They're escorting a third-year Abjuror off the tram, arm linked through theirs. From this far away, the person with them is hard to identify, but there's something familiar about the shock of pale blond hair and the mahogany cane in their grasp. *A mentor, perhaps.* Then, with a twinge of jealousy, *A fellow lover?*

It's not even that Nadia has an issue with having multiple partners—at least, not in theory—but it's definitely not something she has the time or the energy for right now. And, if they were being intimate with other people, the least they could do is tell her about it.

Her knees shake. It's not too late. She can turn around and return to her dorm and pretend she never saw them. Besides, she's sure Simone has better things to do than to handle the disaster that is Nadia DuPont. But if she doesn't seize this chance now, she knows she never will.

With a final deep breath and a prayer for courage, she strides forward. The moment they lock eyes, Simone's grip on their companion tightens and they turn to leave.

"Simone, wait!"

Their gate slows, but they don't stop. Despite the growing ache in her knees, Nadia pushes forward until they're close enough to grasp.

Over their shoulder, Simone's companion gives Nadia a once-over. Their grey eyes flash in the thin sunlight. Recognition flickers in their gaze at the same time as it does within Nadia. This is Alienor, head of the third-year Abjurors.

Nadia can't help the wave of relief she feels. This isn't a date. How could she have been so foolish?

Her hope curdles at the dagger-sharp edge in Alienor's eyes.

"Keep thinking on what we said, Simone," she says, patting their hand before stepping away. "And let me know how it goes."

With this, she walks away, leaning a little heavier on her cane than before.

Good. Nadia is unsure where the rage within her is coming from, but it hardly matters. She watches Alienor walk away until she's a spec across the plaza.

Simone's expression remains neutral. Taking a glance at their watch, they say, "You have one minute before I walk away."

"I... I'm sorry I forgot about our date. I didn't mean you to see me like that." As she speaks, she ducks her head down, cheeks bright with shame. She should say more, she knows, make some kind of case for herself, but...

"Is that all you wanted to tell me?"

Each word is a dart in her side. "I don't expect you to forgive me," she says without looking up. Her throat swells hard enough to make her next words an effort. "Gods know I have wasted enough of your time, but nevertheless... I am sorry."

She should have brought them a gift of some kind. At the end of the day, it's giveaway enough about her state of being that she hasn't. All she can offer by way of apology is herself, and she doubts it's enough to truly sway them.

Simone's face is unreadable. Looking over the brick railing, they stare out into the nauseating depths of the world below. Nadia's heart teeters on the precipice of the silence between them.

Then, softly, they say, "What was wrong with you?"

Nadia rubs her sleeves. "I was..." *High. Inebriated.* And then, a strike of mercy, a gentle lie conjures itself on her tongue. "I've been prescribed some new medicine that had an adverse effect on me. I wasn't expecting it to be so bad."

Not too far from the truth, if one didn't squint too hard at the details. But when Simone turns back, the kernel of hope she's clung to shrivels in her gut. Though their face is still mask-like, the faintest quirk in their brow betrays the frustration underneath.

"I told you during our last conversation that I do not tolerate my time being wasted. If you want to lie about it now, you should at least be more convincing."

Her throat dries to an uncomfortable degree. Before she can respond, they turn on their heel.

No. I'm not letting it end like this.

"Y-You're right. It was a shitty lie," she says, scrambling to follow their hurried march away from her.

"I'm done with this conversation."

"Wait!"

She looks down. Their wrist is so small in her grasp, each slim finger stiffening and then flexing as the shock wears off. Simone wrenches their hand free. Now, their mouth curls in disgust.

She's too threadbare to keep the tears hidden. They stream down her cheeks in thick rivulets. Simone's figure blurs beyond recognition, but she catches their movement all the same.

And then, as they resume their march away from her, she chokes out, "I'm dying, Simone."

They stop, so suddenly their shoes scuff against the bricks.

Nadia swallows. *Now or never, I suppose.* "I... I got the news the day we were supposed to meet again. And—and so I was miserable, alright? And perhaps I might have been..."

Silence. Nadia closes her eyes, feeling the way the individual muscles of her face crumple as she tries to reign in the tears. The attempt is futile. Within seconds, she's a breath away from sobbing again.

A cold hand presses against her cheek. Thin fingers flick the metal hoop dangling from her ear. Still she doesn't move, doesn't breathe. In this moment, anything can happen. She doesn't dare open her eyes.

"How am I supposed to believe that, Nadia?"

Gently, she takes their hand in hers. Her tears dampen their skin. "Sanguina Malefica. Are you familiar with it?"

"I am."

A soft, sad chuckle slips free before she can stop it. "When I was younger, my mother came home crying one day, so hard she shook until she collapsed. I never understood why. Stubborn woman she was, I didn't know she was dying until months later. Doctors came for her without warning one day and I never saw her again."

When she opens her eyes, Simone's brows are knitted together. They chew on their lip, gaze drifting across the courtyard. Their hand remains, the heat of their skin seeping into her bones.

"I've been sick for a while," she continues, desperate to fill the silence. "I'll be lucky to see graduation."

Their mouth opens. Closes. Opens again. Scrunching their nose, they sigh. "Why are you still here, then?"

"Pardon?"

They gesture towards the cluster of buildings behind them. "At Voterique. If you have the rest of this year to live, why spend it here?"

A second goes by, then another. In the distance, the campus clock tower announces the turning of the hour.

If Nadia is being honest with herself, she hasn't had the time to consider her options yet. She could stop attending class entirely, go home for the time she has left. Gods knows her mom would appreciate the company. But then, having lost her wife the same way... would she be strong enough to handle the loss of her daughter? Could Nadia's brother? How old was he now, anyway?

Alternatively, she could disappear from society in its entirety. Find a cottage in the woods and live her remaining months in solitude, or scrounge up the rest of her meager savings and explore the world. She'd always wanted to go to the Isles, despite their weird customs. Or she could explore her home country of Perov in a more thorough fashion. She did miss the astronomy tower in her hometown, after all.

Her chest tightens at the maelstrom of possibility. It's all too much.

"I don't... I don't know," she says at last. "In theory, I could leave and do anything."

"So why don't you?"

Nadia gazes over the side of the mesa for a long while. Trams rattle on their cords, drawing students up from the city below and bringing them back down again. The sheer drop is enough to make her stomach curdle. "As much as I could plan out my final days, I don't think I have it in me to fulfill any of it. I can't... I can't see myself being anywhere but here. I've been on this campus for seven long years now." Her hair catches on one of her rings as she takes a hand through it. "I think I'm just too used to this, now. And if I'll die before I can see graduation, what's the point of changing?"

"I think I understand."

When she looks back to them, they're shuffling from foot to foot and making faces at their pointed shoes. It's been more than a minute now, she realizes.

"I understand why you're angry," she says.

"What even *was* that?"

They've changed back to speaking of their last encounter, she thinks. For a heart-wrenching second, she recalls the feel of their memories cradled within her own. Then, stomach clenching, she says, "Serenity. Medically, it's supposed to be good for pain management and is a good balm for psychological problems."

"From my perspective, you were near-vegetative."

Nadia's lips curl in a sheepish grin. "The effects of Serenity are more severe at higher doses."

"And you take that... how often?"

"Often enough," she says, wiping a hand over her eyes. Then, "I meant what I said that night, by the way... I didn't want you to see me like that, Simone, and I'm sorry."

They suck in their cheeks and say nothing. The silence makes her want to scream. It doesn't matter if they tell her to leave them alone forever. At least the truth would be out there, no matter how messy.

"Nine months is a long time," they say at last.

Nadia flinches. "Not long enough," she says after a pause. *Where are they going with this?*

"And there's no sort of treatment aside from what I saw?"

It's barely a treatment at all. It's putting gauze on a festering, necrotic wound. If anything, I'm sure it limits the time I have left. Not that I care much about that. "There's not a cure, no. The most the doctors can do is prescribe me medicine for the pain and wait for me to die."

They look again over the brick wall. The afternoon sun paints their skin in shades of gold. "My enbei said recently they've never seen a disease crop up so suddenly, or so fast. There's no common cause yet to be determined. Strange, wouldn't you say?"

"I—I guess."

She's seen the gleam in their eyes before, the white-hot flames of a person determined. Etienne wears it when he's elbows-deep in another art project. Something always tells her not even the Gods could tell him no if he sets his mind to something.

She sees it again now. Something about it makes her knees weak.

"Nine months is a long time," she echoes. And, in this moment, it feels like a lifetime. For the first time in a long while, an ember of hope forms in her chest, one bright enough she doesn't stamp it out.

ELEVEN

Simone Allard || After

E tienne is asleep when Simone enters his room. For real this time, they think as they examine the steady rise and fall of his chest. The sigils over him are different—or, at least, they *look* different. It's difficult to tell when Simone is unfamiliar with the language of those realms.

In case he isn't asleep, though, Simone guides the door closed and creeps deeper into the room. They want to have the upper hand if he wakes up. As gentle as possible, they edge a chair closer to his bedside and sit down. Their hands shake at their sides.

A lot of his color has returned, thank the Gods. Right after the attack, he'd been so grey he'd rivaled Nadia on her better days. Now, however, he's almost... normal.

Simone almost has enough pity in their breast to regret their next course of action.

Reaching into their satchel with their free hand, they produce the vial of Serenity. A last resort, they remind themself. Setting it between their knees, they snap their Casting glove against their skin and finally look up.

"Etienne."

He doesn't stir beyond the scrunching of his face. It will be easier to see inside his mind if he's asleep, they think, but they owe him the pretense of inviting themself in. There's two ways this conversation will go. Perhaps he will choose the easier route.

"Etienne," they say again.

Still nothing. They take his hand in theirs and lean in closer.

"Etienne. Wake up."

He gasps as his eyes snap open. Flinching, he yanks his hand away, as if he expects their skin to poison him.

"What are you doing here?"

His voice is still thick with sleep. Perhaps they can convince him to take the more humane approach before he's realized...

"Have you found a way to get me out of here?"

Or perhaps not.

"Not entirely," they reply, face filling with heat. "But that doesn't matter right now."

His brows furrow. Without looking, he reaches for the bedside table—and for his glasses.

"You need to tell me what happened to Nadia."

He stills inches from his glasses. The muscles in his neck twitch, worms straining for the surface. "I already told you," he says in a low tone. "If you want to know anything, you need to get me out of here."

"Not so." Simone takes a deep breath and attempts to channel some deeper, colder part of them. They think of their younger years, how they'd presented speeches in an unflinching, unchanging tone as their enbei lobbed question after question at them. Any hesitation had been met with immediate ridicule. Though callous, their enbei's nitpicking had hardened them.

But now, it's too soft an experience to draw on. They need something firmer to anchor to.

Nadia. Think of Nadia.

They like to try to think well of her, even now, but they can't help the memories swarming them in this moment. The way her jaw sets when she's angry. The way her voice turns gravelly when she's on a tirade, like the force of her fury is grating her vocal chords. How, in her worst moments, she is an incarnation of wrath itself, hair standing on end. A Goddess of brutality all her own.

Professor Chapeau's sneering face swims to the front of their mind before they can cast it aside. The edges of their vision turn crimson.

Simone focuses on the discolored spots on Etienne's face, on the angry pink scars running across one side. They warp their features in as close an approximation of Nadia's that they can. "There are two ways this can go," they say in a voice like tempered steel. "Firstly, you can volunteer the information willingly. I get what I need from you and I leave and we pretend this never happened."

He snorts. "I don't have the patience for this."

"Which leaves option two."

"Get out before I call the nurses myself."

They retrieve the vial of Serenity and hold it in his line of sight. At once, his white skin is even paler.

"Wh...Where did you get that?"

"Doesn't matter, so long as you know what it is. I don't want to do this, Etienne, but I'll make the both of us drink it, right here and now, and I'll force the information out of you in a different way entirely. And who knows. The way you are, perhaps I will stumble upon some of your other secrets as well. There's no telling what I find when I force my way into your head."

His throat bobs. "You wouldn't dare." Though his gaze is cutting, it doesn't keep the tremble out of his words.

"I've had enough of being kept in the dark, Now that you're awake, I want answers."

He chews on his cheek for a long while, his glare icy. Still he says nothing.

"We don't both have to drink it. I'll make the sacrifice for both of us." As they speak, they ease the cork loose. "Either way, I'm leaving this room with what I want."

"Enough!"

The single word bounces off the walls and back into both of their ears. In the silence that follows, Etienne shoots a panicked glance to the door, then to Simone. Shock slackens every inch of his face, replaced in a flash by ice-cold fear.

"Fine." He spits it like a globule of acid in their direction. "Fine. Just... put that away."

Their brow quirks. "I thought you and Nadia consume it a lot."

"We *did*." A single tear rolls down his face. "But..." Then, with an inhale and the cracking of several of his vertebrae falling into place, he meets their stare with reddening eyes. Still, he doesn't speak. His shoulders shudder, his expression sullen as he takes a breath, then another.

"Etienne," they say in warning, flashing the vial nestled in their palm.

His lips press into a thin line. After several seconds, when Simone is becoming certain they'll need to take drastic measures after all, he lets out a long breath. "Nadia... she—"

"Oh!"

So caught in the moment, Simone hadn't heard the footsteps in the hall. Neither had Etienne, they realize when his eyes grow wide. In unison, they turn at the creaking at the other end of the room.

Doctor Aiza regards them both from the doorway, face beaming.

"I was beginning to think you wouldn't wake up," she continues. "But this changes everything." Then her focus shifts to Simone. "I'm sorry, but I'm going to have to ask you to leave."

"Pardon?"

"Well, we have some tests to run. I don't want our friend here to get more overwhelmed than he is, do you?" Doctor Aiza adjusts her clipboard, grey eyes flashing. "If you would please come along?"

Etienne is ashen when they look back, a pleading gleam in his eyes. Whatever his silent request is, however, they aren't sure they fully comprehend it.

Doctor Aiza props open the door and steps closer. "Mx. Allard?"

They stuff the vial of Serenity in their pocket, glad they'd been positioned in such a way as to hide it from her view. Then, with a stiff lip, they replace the chair and step away. They've waited this long, after all. As maddening as the thought makes them, Simone knows they can wait a little longer.

And yet, they can't help the foreboding knot forming in their gut as they step out into the hall. Their biggest chance has been snatched from them all too swiftly. It's enough to make them spit.

***

A week passes in the blink of an eye and still there's no word from Etienne.

Not for Simone's lack of trying, of course. Every day, they return to the medical ward, hoping beyond hope the news will be different. Each time, Doctor Aiza's response is the same.

"We have to continue monitoring Etienne now that he's awake. I'm sure you understand."

The first time, and perhaps even the second, Simone allows themself to believe it's the truth. On the third day, they take careful note of the way the doctor guards herself in their presence, the way she stays out of arm's reach and pins her clipboard to her chest like a trapped animal.

They tell themself they're being paranoid. Voterique wants what is best for its students, foul administration aside. And, if nothing else, Etienne is more a danger to himself than the doctors are.

Still, they can't ignore the kernel of doubt buried deep in their stomach.

The week ends the way most do, without fanfare or hurry, spring is giving way to a gentle, balmy summer. It's still chilly enough they hesitate to stay outside for too long.

Then, at the end of the week, something different.

By now, they've learned not to expect much from the nurses roaming the off-white halls of the medical ward. While they hope for good news—an update, even—they know they're likely to be sent away. So when they see Doctor Aiza behind the front desk, they take a deep breath and brace themself for disappointment.

"Oh, Simone," she says at their approach, smile warm but her gaze distant. She's preoccupied with shuffling through loose pages and envelopes. "How nice to see you again."

Simone doesn't miss a beat. "Am I able to see Etienne today?"

"He was discharged this morning, I believe." Doctor Aiza pauses her half-hearted digging to flick through the clipboard at her side. Then, after a pause, "Yes. Yes he was."

A frown twists their lip. The news would be good were it anyone else, but having Etienne back on campus proper makes it all the easier for him to avoid them.

"Are you sure?" they press.

Her brow quirks. "Etienne LaChance, right?"

"Yes."

She examines her clipboard again with a frown. "He was discharged to his apartment as of dawn. Perhaps check for him there?"

As if he would open the door to them. Still...

"Okay," Simone replies with a stiff nod. "Thank you for your time."

They should be elated, they think, no matter how unlikely they are to pin Etienne down now. Finally, after weeks of worry and sleepless nights, they can try to *really* get their answers if it means they have to corner him in his home. But something about it all feels... strange. It nags at them as they march back across campus, eager to think it over in the comfort of their own home. A soft pain lingers in the crux of their elbows.

If they were a lesser person, they would let Etienne have the full force of their fury now. Best to strike while you have the upper hand, as their enbei is wont to say. But it's early. They're certain he's tired, and they've already waited this long. Surely, a little longer won't hurt them.

Before long, the temptation is too great to ignore. They grasp the phone mouthpiece in shaking hands. "Etienne LaChance, please," they say to the crackling static beyond. The phone rings and rings and rings.

Finally, in a gentle tone, the operator says, "I don't think he's quite awake yet, dear."

With a grunt, they replace the receiver and go back to bed.

An hour before first bell, they come back to the phone to try again. The yogurt curdles in their stomach as they wait for the lines to connect. To their disappointment—though not their surprise—he doesn't answer.

On the verge of tears, they do the one thing they've been dreading doing since Nadia disappeared. They call their enbei.

The line rings for a long while before they pick up. "Candide speaking."

Their gut sinks like a stone. Eyes watering, Simone holds the phone away to softly sniffle before saying, "Good morning, bei-bei."

"Simone?" At once, their voice is a touch softer, but still retains the hardness of a profoundly busy researcher. "Won't your classes begin soon?"

"T-They will." Now their stomach is a sea in the throes of a violent storm. "I just…"

Silence. Then, "Has something upset you?"

Plenty, they want to scream. Their paramour has disappeared and no one can tell them why. Her best friend loathes them with a passion they cannot understand. Everywhere they turn, doors are closing in their face, one after another.

To confirm anything would be admitting defeat. They want to stiffen their lip, to spit in the face of the turmoil they struggle to hold back. Still, the realization they're being read so thoroughly crumbles the last of their resolve.

"Bei-bei, what am I doing here?"

Their enbei sighs, the sound soft and distorted by miles of telephone wire. "Studying," they reply, terse but not unsympathetic.

"You've spent your life following in my footsteps. Don't claim to have doubts now, so close to the end."

Simone's gaze wanders around their living room. Placards from primary school gleam on the walls, catching their attention. The years of academic achievements are splayed out like an autopsied animal. On good days, Simone finds solace in those placards, reminders of how far they've come. Now, they feel like a threat when coupled with their enbei's words. *All of this will be for nothing if you turn away now.*

"I don't have doubts," they say at last. "I am fine with what I'm doing and how I'm performing." They almost believe themself, they think, given how difficult it is to place where it is their hesitance lies.

"And yet you sound displeased."

There's an edge to the words, a hard warning beneath the surface. *Do you want to waste your life on something else? Would you rather suffer starting all over? Has all of my teaching of you been for nothing?*

There is no good answer. A tear rolls down their cheek. "I'm sorry, bei-bei."

A soft exhale, punctuated by the static. "Simone, what spurned on these doubts?"

"I just..." Simone pauses again to drag one sleeve across their face. "It's been a difficult month is all."

So quiet they almost miss it, they hear their enbei mutter, "Aurelia has always been better at this than I." Their heart squeezes at the mention of their mother. Then, before Simone can comment, "Press forward, Simone. Whatever plagues you will wash away soon enough."

While their enbei's words are meant to be encouraging, they know, Simone finds the platitude hollow. How easy it is to tell someone from across the world that they have nothing to worry about. How can one understand a crisis of thought when they themself are already secure?

Simone could scream themself hoarse and it wouldn't make much of a difference. So, forehead pressed to the wall, Simone relents at last. "Of course," they say, praying the disappointed undercurrent of their voice is lost to the miles of static. "Thank you."

"My greatest hope is you continue to do well. For now, however, I must get going."

"Thank you, bei-bei."

Before they can say more, the line disconnects. They re-cradle the phone with a soft sigh.

This illuminates nothing.

And yet, it shines a paralyzing light on everything.

***

Between classes, Simone scours the courtyard, desperate for a glimpse of Etienne's green capelet and curdling sneer. And yet, by the time the final bell tolls, there is nothing.

He is surely being bombarded, some rational sliver of them argues, and they shove the thought away. He should know better than anyone they're looking for him—especially now. Anyone else seeking answers regarding him can wait.

Still, hunting him down will solve nothing. The more they persist, the more he's sure to slink away. Instead, their enbei's words echo in their mind: *Press forward, Simone. Whatever plagues you will wash away.*

"Struggling with a problem?" Chantal asks from across the table. The two of them have met early for their study session, books sprawled out along a library table. When they look up, she has her head cocked, black hair tied back with a silk scarf. She's bent the corner of the page she's reading, book half-closed in preparation. Despite her curiosity, there's a sullenness in her cheeks that everyone at Voterique seems to wear nowadays.

"Pardon?"

She gestures to their clenched fist. The stylus in their grip groans at the force they're exerting on it.

"A lot on my mind, I guess," they say as they drop the stylus with a clatter. A spiderweb of cracks run along the wooden surface.

"I think it's that way for all of us."

Simone stares at their notes. Over and over again, they've scrawled out, *What is Etienne hiding?* Some of the iterations have carved deep grooves into the paper, on the verge of tearing. They frown. Gone are the notes they were supposed to be taking regarding their course, *Ethical Miasmic Disposal and Containment.* How could they have blundered this badly?

Chantal's jaws part in a sudden, loud yawn, snapping them back to. They regard her out the corner of their eye. "I see your sleep is as disturbed as mine," they say.

She leans closer, her orchid perfume drifting from her in waves. "I've been to see Etienne today."

They still. So, he isn't avoiding everyone after all. It confirms their hypothesis, at least. "Oh?" they ask after a moment to recollect themself. They slide an arm over the page to hide their scribblings.

"He looks... better. I've been worried about him, of course, but after the first couple of nights..."

Simone's jaw sets. "I understand." Then, flipping the page, "The good news is he was sent home this morning."

Chantal's smile is watery, but it's present all the same. "So you've been to see him as well?"

They shake their head. "I tried to at the clinic, but he had already left."

"Perhaps for the better." Then, halting, Chantal continues, "He seemed... strange."

"Of course he did. He's been asleep for days."

"No, not just that."

They arch a brow in silent encouragement.

"He... I hate saying this about a friend."

"What do you mean?" they ask, more terse than they intend. Irritation gnaws at their nerves.

"Do you remember Celio?"

Simone swallows hard. A former member of the study group, Celio had disappeared after classes one afternoon. Simone's knees ache at the memory of the vigils they'd attended, the candles they'd lit and bowed over despite not having faith in the Gods they were supposed to pray to.

And then, a miracle. Perhaps the Gods had been listening, after all.

Except, he had returned changed. It wasn't a simple matter of whatever horrors he had experienced. No, when Celio had returned, it was with no memories of his time away. No one could get him to speak of where he'd gone, let alone why. Any time he *did* try to speak on events, his eyes glazed over and he would stutter endlessly until the topic was changed.

Simone gulps. "Yes," they say. "I do."

"Etienne behaved in a similar way when I tried to talk to him."

Under the table, Simone's fist clenches. *So close to answers and they're being stripped from me.* They chew on the inside of their cheek. *I should just go visit him.*

They don't know why the thought hadn't crossed their mind before, but the moment it crops up, they grip it tight and don't let go.

Their skin prickles. Chantal is watching them, head tilted as she regards them and a question in her eyes.

"How strange," they say, if only to get Chantal's attention off of them.

She nods, apparently satisfied they acknowledged the information she's shared. "Trauma is one thing." She shivers. "Shards, if I had been in his place… I don't think I would have ever woken up. Still, it doesn't feel right."

"Perhaps I should go see him for myself, then." With this, they rise from their seat. "Could I come by your apartment for today's notes sometime later?"

"Of course."

Shrugging off their sudden apprehension, Simone marches towards the exit. Their heart beats strong in their chest, as loud and all-consuming as war drums.

TWELVE

Nadia Dupont || Before

"You will read this," Simone says, expression soft but otherwise unreadable as they leer at her from her bed, "until you can recite it from memory."

Nadia had expected giggling library dates and study sessions ending in a different sort of studying, lingering glances across cafe tables and endless flirting. Much to her dismay, however, she soon learns Simone's true meaning.

She regards the book they've offered her as she sways back and forth in the center of the room, brow quirked and bare skin buzzing. The cover is all worn brown leather, the title once gold-plated and now rubbed nearly beyond recognition.

"I know you're a serious student." Nadia pauses to finish reading the title, *To Be Loved By Gods*, with a snort. "But I never took you for the religious sort."

Simone's mouth quirks. "I'm not. This is part of your Divination and Mysticism assignment."

"I wasn't aware I had one."

"I know."

Nadia takes the book from them after a moment of hesitation, wincing at the sudden weight. Still, she doesn't let go. "How *did* you find out what I was assigned, again?"

Simone had been on the verge of combusting when they learned of Nadia's awful grades. "We cannot continue this relationship," they had said, much to Nadia's dismay. Then, as tears pricked her eyes, they had continued, "Not unless you start performing better. Especially if you are intent on staying on this campus."

And so an arrangement was made.

Simone's cocky, dominating aura recedes as a soft blush consumes them now. "I may have filed an academic inquiry on you." Then, as she sputters in offense, they continue, "I saw your truancy notices when I was over. Wanted to know what I was getting myself into."

Creepy, she supposes, but not the worst thing someone has done for her. "And I'm supposed to read this whole book?"

A playful twinkle lights up Simone's eyes. "Of course not." Then, more serious, "You would know this if you'd been paying attention in your classes."

Simone's gaze is a persistent prickling between her shoulders for a long while. Between sly glances, she stares at the pages until the letters—and she—refuse to sit still. Whenever she looks up, Simone brandishes their thin switch rod and arches a brow.

With a couple of lashes, she learns to keep her eyes on the pages.

Before long, she's lost in the rhythm of the words. The cadence rolls over her like water. The longer the session goes on, the less she feels the lick of Simone's switch at her back... and the more she aches for its sting.

The end of the hour is punctuated by Simone's sharp, "Stop."

The word comes to her from some faraway place, like a misted-over dream. It isn't until Simone is perched over her, delicate fingers caressing the rounded nub of her chin, that she registers their command at all. She wants them to keep touching her like that. Or, perhaps they could swat her until she cries instead.

What is she thinking? She's been to the occasional session with people who direct her with a stern word, or stretch her emotionally and sexually, but nothing she's experienced has been able to dig into her psyche like this.

And yet, she likes it. She *craves* it.

Do it again, she wants to tell Simone. *Hit me again.* Would they think her odd if she begged? Perhaps they would punish her for speaking out of turn.

"Stand."

Shrugging the post-meditative numbness and the ache in her hips, Nadia is quick to obey.

"Stay."

Her breath hitches. The bed frame creaks as they settle into a comfortable position. Then, eyes shadowed, they flip to the beginning of the book. "Tell me what you read. Summarize for me."

Nadia's gaze swims. The words on the paper jumble together in her mind's eye and, for a moment, is lost behind a thick fog.

Their voice sinks sharp claws into her conscious and drags her back. "I gave you a command, Nadia."

She shivers, and not just because she's stripped bare in her room on a chilly autumn day. From her canopy bed, Simone is reading through the book, quirking their brow every time they look up.

"It goes over the, um…"

The lash of wood on her thigh stops her. "Without the use of filler words. Again."

She struggles to conjure the pages in her mind's eye. How can she not remember the last hour she's spent, the words she'd carefully packed into her memory?

To Be Loved By Gods. She chews her lip. It was a study on the differing deities who had Ascended a couple of centuries prior, as well as the consorts They kept. Who amongst Them had she just read about?

Simone sighs, tucking the book under their arm. "Would it help if you read it again?"

Though their tone is light, she notes the undercurrent of disappointment. Her stomach drops. Above all else, the last thing she wants is to waste more of their time.

"No," she replies. "Give me a moment longer."

The switch smacks her forearm and she hisses. "'Give me a moment longer,' what?"

Her gaze lowers on instinct. "Professor. Give me a moment longer, Professor."

"Very good. Again."

***

The next few weeks pass in this fashion. After the final bell for class, Nadia claws her way through the throngs of people and into Simone's arms, though more often she ends up on her knees, or balancing objects while trying to recite passages. To her amazement, though, and that of her professors, she's improving.

As she's getting ready to meet Simone one morning, there's a knock on her front door. Her brows knit together. Was she expecting company today?

Etienne stands on the other side, hands buried in his pockets. His hair, normally soft as bird down, is ruffled with sleep. Something must be bothering him. Etienne is renowned in their gaggle of friends for his preening. He would rather leap from the rooftop of the library than be seen in less-than-perfect condition.

She smooths out the front of her dress to avoid staring at him. "Etienne. I was wondering when I would see you again." In truth, since beginning her sessions with Simone, it had been some time since she'd been to see Etienne. Had she really let their friendship lapse this much?

He steps into her apartment and shuts the door. "Yeah," he replies, smoothing back his hair. "Me too."

"What's that supposed to mean?"

His lips press into a thin line. "You haven't spent as much time with me is all."

Nadia frowns. Of course she hasn't, given how often she works on homework now. Or, Gods forbid, engage in Simone's study group—personal or otherwise. Their quick wit and rapport with faculty is what allowed her to turn in her plethora of late assignments to begin with.

"I guess I haven't. I'm sorry, Etienne." She fingers the myriad of bracelets she wears and says, "We'll have to do something."

"Right now?"

His eyes gleam with hope. Her stomach clenches at the thought of quashing that emotion. Sighing, she says, "I can't. I promised Simone I would meet them for tea before class."

A shadow crosses his face at once. His gaze drops to the floor. "Do you fancy them?" he asks softly.

"Yes," she replies. Warmth pools in the pit of her stomach. "A lot."

"I was worried you would say that."

Her stomach boils with indignation. "Why?"

He still refuses to look up, but his cheeks turn the color of an autumn moth. "I don't know."

"You're lying," she replies without missing a beat. *Lest I forget we've had this fight before.*

Lest. She represses a snort and shakes her head. Simone is getting to her. Not that she minds. If they can keep making her toes curl and bring a halt to the tedium her life has become, then she welcomes their influence.

"Need I repeat myself?"

Nadia's brows pull together. Incredulous, she takes his face in one hand and forces him to look up. "Are you serious? You're *jealous*?"

He tries to jerk away, but her nails keep him pinned. Then, "Yes."

"What is there to be jealous of, Etienne?"

He rolls his eyes and breaks their contact. "You know what, I shouldn't have come here. You're too busy for me, right?"

Her fingers twitch. She has half a mind to slap him, to grab his shoulders and shake him until the foolish thoughts flow out of his brain. Doing either would make all this worse, though. "That's not it at all!"

"Then what, Nadia? You are replacing me. That's clear enough to fucking see."

Another flex of her fingers. Shards, he makes it *incredibly* difficult to remain civil. "Is that what you think this is?"

This time, when he pulls away, she doesn't stop him. His fists curl and uncurl at his sides. "I don't know," he says. "Maybe."

The way his voice cracks sends shivers down her spine. A twinge of pity plucks at her heartstrings and all at once, her frustration leaves her. How could she have become so self-absorbed so as to neglect him? How could she let him think he was being replaced?

No, a different section of her conscious argues. *The time I've spent away has been to my betterment. Who is he to think he can stand in the way of it?*

Sighing, Nadia reaches across the chasm yawning between them. It will do her no good to go torching relationships. Though Etienne stiffens, he lets her take his hand. "I'm sorry," she says. "Please don't stay mad at me."

Etienne's pout deepens. "Kind of hard not to be."

"I'll—I'll redeem myself, okay? I'll tell Simone that I can't make it to their study group tonight. Time for me and you, right?"

He flinches at the mention of Simone, then slouches once more. "Fine."

"I mean it, Etienne. Just the two of us." Nadia lets his hand drop, scanning her living room for her satchel. How strange, she thinks as she catches sight of it, the way I'm changing.

In the distance, a bell tolls, a warning to Casters all across the campus. Etienne stuffs his hands back into his pockets.

"Tonight," he says. "Be there in my apartment."

His mouth opens, like he wants to say more, but then he shuts it with the shake of his head. Before she can confirm, he stalks out, leaving her to tremble like a mouse from her newfound spot on the couch. Her body refuses to still for a long while afterwards.

***

Her final class can not end fast enough. As soon as the bell chimes, she's stuffing her books in her satchel and walking as fast as her aching joints will allow her.

Simone was surprisingly civil about her last-minute cancellation when she told them this morning. She had expected them to scoff at her, or to make a statement about her wasting their time again. Instead, they had smiled.

"Okay," they had said, crossing one leg over the other. "You have made good progress, after all. You've earned some time away."

The way they had said "earned" had made her blush, but it was permission enough and she wasn't about to argue.

Still, despite her quickness, Etienne isn't waiting for her. On a good day, he would somehow be outside the building of her final class in time for her to meet him. Perhaps he's more upset than she thought.

Tugging her capelet tighter around her, Nadia strides for the towers with a frown. We'll make up, she tells herself. We always do. Still, the first kernels of doubt sow themselves in her breast.

She takes her time going up the stairs of the Enchanter's tower, but she still ends up panting at the top. Faculty has met recently regarding installing a lift to go between the floors, given the rise in disabled students in recent years. As she catches her breath, Nadia wishes they would hurry up and install the damn things. What are people going to do, fornicate in the lift? In front of everyone?

Her cheeks flare at the thought. Best not mention such a thing to Simone, or they'll be sure to take advantage of it.

Mood soured, she marches up to Etienne's door and knocks harder than intended. It takes a long while for him to answer. The kernels of doubt take root.

The instant she sees his face, she throws herself into his chest.

Etienne gasps, arms closing around her on instinct. Together, they take uneasy steps backwards into the room. The door swings closed.

"Welcome back, Etienne," says a voice at her back, muffled by her capelet. Her heart clenches. Though the mural is inspired by his mother, she knows as much as he does it's not as good as the real person. Still, he can't seem to get rid of it.

Etienne eases her back after several moments. A soft frown tugs at his lips as he regards her.

"Say you don't hate me," she blurts. Even as she speaks, the first of what she is sure is many tears comes to her eye and threatens to fall.

"W-What?"

"Say you don't hate me. Say I haven't fucked up too badly. Please."

Etienne scoffs, shoving his glasses further up his nose. "What are you talking about? Of course I don't hate you."

Had she imagined their discussion this morning? Had it all been some strange, sour dream?

As she's still ruminating, he continues, "I mean, I *was* upset... I still kind of am."

It's a shock of cold water down her spine. "But I haven't done anything wrong."

"No," Etienne says after an uncomfortable pause. "I suppose not."

He's let her into his apartment. It's a start. Still, his expression remains guarded as they face each other. He crosses his arms tight across his chest. The soft clicking of his tapping heel fills the room.

This is stupid. Her jaw sets. *How is it my fault he's jealous of my...*

She stops. Are Simone and her partners? Kinky classmates? Would they consider the two of them a romantic relationship? They fuck her every so often, but does that mean they're dating?

Nadia makes a note to have that conversation with Simone. For the moment, though she can't understand why he's so disgruntled, she needs to make things right.

Disgruntled. Ha. Simone really *has* changed her.

"I'm sorry," she says at last. "I guess entering a relationship *did* make me distant from you."

With a sigh, Etienne unfolds his arms. "Thank you."

The gloom wreathing the two of them eases, but doesn't disappear entirely. Nadia sweeps closer once more, the force of her hug more gentle this time. A soft sigh escapes as Etienne holds her to him. His fingers, like spokes on a spindle and all too cold, thread through her hair and tangle it. Despite their proximity, Nadia's skin prickles.

"Promise you'll make more time for me, Nadia."

She buries her face into his chest, positioned just so to keep the buttons of his coat from injuring her. "I promise."

After a second longer, Etienne shrugs out of her hold. "Enough of this stoic shit," he says with a half-hearted laugh.

When she meets his gaze, he's practically bouncing on his heels. An excited Etienne is a dangerous Etienne. "What is on your mind?"

He digs a hand into his breast pocket and produces a small vial, the contents black as pitch. Nadia's pulse quickens at the sight. Her throat dries.

"Serenity."

His grin turns wolfish. "I've kept this on hand for weeks." Then, after a pause, he says, "...For you."

Nadia hesitates, then hates herself for hesitating. Though Simone had not outright requested she stop consuming Serenity, given her deteriorating health, they never looked pleased when she brought it up. And with their variety of *study* sessions, she didn't have as much time for it.

He must notice the way she falters. He's always known her so well. "When was the last time you dropped?" he asks.

It's all the invitation she needs.

Minutes later, Etienne has his arms thrown across the back of his couch, eyes the size of tea saucers and impossibly dark. She smiles at the sight of him, at how at ease he seems to be in her presence. A pang of guilt lances her, not the first she's felt all day.

Then her eyes close again and she is drifting within a strange, warm void. Sparks dance on her tongue. Her mouth fills with the scent of the earth. A hand closes around her own. It's not until Etienne's thoughts bleed into hers she recognizes him, but then it's as though a part of herself has been re-fused to her. It's the way the two of them should be, always and forever.

That is, until a headache forms at her temples.

The pain is a foreign enemy in her blissed-out state, an errant fly buzzing around her mental feast. She carves craters into the couch with her nails, clinging to the peace she's fought so hard for.

In these moments of twisted desperation, the pain intensifies. It blooms into a storm of sensation behind her eyelids. The blackness she's previously been suspended in comes alive in a wash of oranges and reds and greys. A dull roaring like the approach of a storm fills the silence. After several seconds, she recognizes what she thinks are words.

Meat. Consume. Food. Bite. Meat. Meat. Meat.

Her stomach drops with the swarm of thoughts. She's so *terribly* hungry. How had she not noticed it before?

She takes a deep breath, hoping it will calm her down. Instead, she breathes deep the scent of salt and pine and blood and meat...

Nadia snaps back to with a gasp.

Etienne raises his head from the opposite couch with a giggle, his body wreathed in darkness. "Are you okay?"

"I-I think so." As she speaks, she runs a hand through her hair, hissing when her nails drag too-sharp across her scalp. She untangles her fingers and examines them for blood.

An ear-piercing shriek escapes instead.

The skin on her hands and arms is ink-black and gnarled like the bark of an old tree. Each finger ends in claws the size of daggers. The veins in her arms pulse in time to her racing heartbeats.

Etienne bolts upright. "What's wrong?"

She holds her hands out for him to touch. When he brushes against her, a maelstrom of memories and thoughts surges through her brain. Etienne sitting at his ailing mother's bedside. Nadia throwing crumpled flowers into an open grave. A cold breeze rolls over her skin. Blood, sharp and metallic, coats her tongue.

"Am I supposed to be seeing something?" he asks.

"Yeah." It's an effort to keep her voice level. "My hand is—"

And yet, as Etienne rolls his thumb over her knuckles, she realizes her skin has returned to normal. Only the darker hue to her veins gives her a hint that anything has happened at all.

"It's what?" His thumb stills. "A bit wrinkled, sure. You're growing up." *For now.*

The thought floats to her through the bond, a sharp, sudden reminder of her ever-dwindling lifespan. Nadia pulls her hand back with a harsh swallow, eager to sever the connection. Massaging the skin some more, she says, "No. It... I can't describe it."

"You're getting too into your psyche," Etienne says with a half-hearted chuckle. Though he means to be encouraging, doubt clings to his words and flickers through the remnants of their link. Shocks of green light up the turmoil boiling behind her eyes.

"Yeah," Nadia replies, as equally unconvinced. "That's all it was."

Reality waltzes away from her once again. When she closes her eyes, her visions are thick with disembodied shadows and the howling of dogs. Something dark and undefinable lingers in the fringes of her mind, disappearing when she focuses too hard on it. And then, when her mind drifts away, it looms over her once again.

Whatever it is, it's enough to make Nadia shiver.

THIRTEEN

Simone Allard || After

It occurs to them as they reach the third-floor landing they've never stepped foot inside the Enchanter's tower before. They've passed by it every day for the last two years, and had seen it in the distance for years before then, but never once had they had a reason to enter it.

It's the same as the Diviner and Abjuration towers, complete with portraits of famous Enchanters lining the walls. All of them brandish the back of one hand, Caster's mark tattooed upon it.

Simone stops to catch their breath before examining the hallway. This late in the day, there aren't any students milling about outside of their apartments, so they're free to venture forth unencumbered.

Etienne's door is decorated with soft gold filigree, his name embossed in the center. Splatters of paint in a rainbow of colors pepper the surface. It's as flashy and unnecessary as he is.

A storm of possibilities swells to life. He could not answer. He could slam the door in their face. He could call the faculty on them—the worst outcome of all. All of these and more form a hurricane in their mind.

With a deep breath, they knock. Their pulse beats strong in their throat, hard enough to make them dizzy. After several seconds and no response, they try again. Nothing.

Well, that answers that. They shove a hand into their pocket. *I was hoping to not have to use this...*

Getting into his apartment is easy enough. Slapping a square of paper against the doorknob, they focus on the current of magic running within them and channel it through their glove. The Caster's mark and the sigil on the page glow in unison, an unearthly yellow, before dimming.

With a click of the lock, the door swings inward.

A while ago, they had commissioned the spell from a Transmuter in their study group. They hadn't meant it for nefarious purposes—mostly, it was to get into the library late at night, or into the restricted section within. Now, pocketing the slip of paper, they feel a twinge of guilt, but they're quick to squash it back down again.

They've never been inside Etienne's apartment before. They've never had a reason to, given the terse relationship between the two of them. Still, they aren't prepared for what lies beyond.

Three of the walls are a snowy white, streaked with a rainbow of paint. Thin wire criss-crosses the room. From it, pictures of all sizes hang from metal clips. A mural of a river spans the wall opposite them, so detailed that from this distance, it looks real.

Did he paint this himself? From the scant information they've gleaned from him, Simone knows Etienne has a proclivity for art. Nadia often fell back to talking about it and how excited it made her. On bad days, Simone allowed themself to feel bitter about it; there wasn't much the two of them talked about that made her as animated as Etienne did.

Still, if *this* is his handiwork, it's no wonder why Nadia enjoys it so much.

"Welcome back, Etienne," says a voice behind them. Simone jumps with a squeak. When they turn, they expect a fellow Caster to have followed them in. Instead, they stare at a life-like portrait of a taller woman, her short black hair streaked with gray and fashioned into waves. To their shock, her eyes flutter closed as they regard her. A soft, golden beam of light shines through the trees overhead.

Did he paint this, too? How could he even get it to move?

They have a vague awareness of art thanks to Nadia, but none of the knowledge they can conjure explains what they're witnessing. With an impressed hum, they turn back for the room beyond.

A section of the floor has been lowered, forming a sort of platform. Orange couch cushions form a ring around the edges. In the center, an oak table stretches out. Save the small stack of books on top, it is devoid of decoration.

With another glance around the room, Simone realizes they won't find their answers here. The space is too sparse. They head for the hallway stretching towards his bedroom. Then, at the threshold, they hesitate.

Am I willing to cross so personal a line?

The thought stills them, just for a moment. Though they're no friend of Etienne's, is it right for them to go through his room? His most private of spaces?

Their lip curls. At this point, if they can find any lead, they'll take it.

What was once Etienne's bedroom has been torn asunder. Though it's evident some attempt at cleaning has been done in the aftermath, the space is otherwise decimated. Shredded pillows bleed their feathered stuffing. Liquid, black as pitch, has formed permanent stains in the carpet. It's difficult to pinpoint one area in the room to focus on, until they catch sight of his desk. A long, smeared handprint runs across the surface, rusted red in color.

The pieces connect in their mind. This was the sight of the monster attack.

With shallow breaths, Simone steps deeper into the room. The floor moans under their weight. Perhaps the second-year unlucky enough to have an apartment below Etienne's won't notice.

They examine the desk. Aside from the garish handprint—too smeared to determine who it belongs to—the surface is bare of decoration.

And then they see it. A single page with a small collection of scrawled lines. The first couple of sentences recap Nadia's litany of symptoms. The next words steal the breath from their lungs.

"Could Sanguina Malefica and the monster epidemic be related?"

A vital clue, perhaps. Would Etienne notice if they took this to study?

"Welcome back, Etienne."

Simone stiffens, ice-water filling their veins. Stuffing the paper in their pocket, they take a cursory glance around the room. Two methods of escape await them: the window over the desk will alert him to their presence right away—and looks too small for them to slip through, regardless. The doorway into the living room is their only other option.

Simone grabs the first writing utensil they see and a loose scrap of paper. Fighting the panicked jitter of their fingers, they try to recall the sigils Shae had used in casting the invisibility spell on them. When they think they have it, they crumple the page up and will the magic through their glove.

Nothing happens.

With a desperate hiss, they try again and find they're still as corporeal as before.

Shit, shit, shit.

A soft sucking sound comes from just behind them. Simone spins on their heel, expecting Etienne to have ambushed them, but he isn't there. Their gaze sweeps over the room—the tattered pillows, the strange stains in the carpet, the scraps of cloth and paper all around the room—and struggle to find what has changed.

Then, with a soft exhale, it comes to them. The stains in the carpet have shifted.

The soft pad of Etienne's feet come from the next room, drawing closer. They don't have time to ponder the state of his bedroom anymore. Paralyzed, they can only watch as Etienne's shadow falls across the floor. He taps a lantern at his side. Blue light from the magicite within fills the room.

Their eyes lock.

Etienne limps deeper into the room with a frown, easing the door shut behind him. He looks at them with the same feral hatred they remember, but it is clouded by a strange vacantness all the same. Disbelief flickers across his face. Then, "What are you doing in my apartment?"

They clench their concealed fist. "You should know the answer to that."

Without breaking eye contact, he shrugs his coat off and lets it drop. The multitude of buttons clack against the door. After a beat, he sucks in his cheeks and says, "I don't know what you're talking about."

Despite his words, his brows are scrunched together. He gives them a vague, pleading look, as if he's suggesting something but can't outright say it. Chantal's words float to the forefront of their mind. *He seemed... strange.*

They break eye contact, shaking their head. "Etienne, what happened to you?"

"I was almost killed." Despite his recent brush with death, his words drip sarcasm all the same.

"By what?"

A soft sigh. "I don't remember."

"And what happened to Nadia?"

"She was…" The hesitation is multi-layered. Simone closes their eyes, waiting with growing impatience for the answer.

Then, finally, "I don't remember that, either."

They don't remember crossing the room, don't remember picking Etienne up by the scruff of his shirt and slamming him against the door so hard it groans, but then they're there, panting with exertion and the suddenness of their movement. Teeth grit against the pain lapping at their bones, they keep him pinned.

"Bull. Fucking. Shit."

Simone has never thought themself an imposing figure. Bookish, perhaps, depending on the person they speak to. But intimidating? Never. They can posture all they want, they can fake it, but never has someone's voice quaked when speaking to them. Never has someone's eyes widened in fear at their presence.

Until now.

Etienne whimpers, trembling like a soaked cat. Something about the stench of fear wafting off him makes their chest swell. It's a high they know they'll never be able to replicate.

"I will not ask you again."

"S-Simone, please put me down."

Their head tilts. A strange, cold calm settles over them. "Tell me why you're lying first."

"I'm *not*!" As he speaks, he tries to wrench their hands free. "Put me down and let me explain."

After a breath, they lower him, caging him in with their hands in case he attempts to flee.

"Can we sit down, at least?"

Simone flexes their glove and gives him a pointed look.

"Fine." He rakes a hand through his hair. "I don't... I don't know how to make you believe me, but my memory of the day has been shrouded."

They have half a mind to pluck the vial of Serenity from where they left it in their apartment and force it down their throat. Then there will be no secrets. Despite their rage, though, they won't resort to that. Not yet.

Their muscles flex with the force of their fury. "So unshroud it."

"It's not that simple!" He crosses his arms, shrinking away from them and against the door. Then, quieter, "I shouldn't even be aware of it."

"What the fuck are you talking about?"

The moment his mouth opens, his gaze loses some of its focus. He slumps against the door. Clasping his head in his hands, his whole body heaves and he lets out a low, pained moan.

Chantal's warning. Celio. The erratic oscillation between clarity and confusion. All of it snaps into place. Of course. How could they have been so foolish?

"Someone altered your memory, didn't they?"

He stills. Stares at them from between his fingers. Slowly peels his hands away. Exhaling, he says, "I always knew, despite my own misgivings, there was a reason I had a grudging respect for you."

And then, without further ceremony, Etienne's eyes roll back in his skull and he drops to the floor.

They are at Etienne's side at once, scanning him for a pulse. "Shards," they hiss, skin clammy as they touch him. His heartbeat is weak, but by some small mercy, it's steady. He's alive.

They give his face a testing pat with their palm, hard enough to make a sound but not enough to cause damage. He doesn't stir, so they strike him again. Harder. A pink splotch blossoms across his pale skin. Aside from a harsh inhale, Etienne still doesn't wake up.

"Shards, Etienne..."

Digging their fingers under his arms, they drag him back towards the living room with a grunt. They make it a few steps before they have to drop him and pant. He's heavier than he looks. Or they're weaker than they believed.

Okay. Think, Simone. They lean into his doorframe and survey their surroundings. Etienne remains sprawled out at an awkward angle beneath them. They can't drag him into the living room, clearly. They can't call the medic ward. What *can* they do?

As the panic bubbles up within them, Etienne snorts as if waking from sleep. His eyes open, lashes fluttering like butterfly wings.

A stifled gasp escapes as they survey him. "Etienne."

He brushes the back of his head, the movement done in sluggish slivers. After an eternity, he sits up. "That fuckin' hurt," he says, staring up at Simone with narrowed eyes. His hands come away tinged with blood.

"Easy," Simone says. He flinches when they get too close, but they don't let his fear dissuade them. "You just... collapsed."

He frowns. "I did?"

They nod. "You were trying to tell me about Nadia when—"

"I'm sorry, who?"

Dread sinks into their stomach like a stone, heavy and cold. "You know who."

And yet, when they search his face for any sign of recognition, there is nothing. Etienne's brow furrows as he continues to rub the back of his head.

"You know who," they say again, more desperate this time. Their nails press harsh crescents into their palm. "Nadia DuPont. Your best friend."

Etienne's nose scrunches. "I'm sorry, but I'm unsure who you're talking about."

Silence. Simone scans his face for any trace that he's joking, but it's scrunched in confusion. Real, genuine puzzlement.

Etienne cocks his head, brows drawing together as he studies them. "And... who are you?"

A soft chuckle escapes, then another. How absolutely absurd, the situation Simone finds themself in. And yet, somehow, hilariously pitiful.

Before they can stop themself, they are heaving with delirious laughter, clawing at their collar to get more air into their lungs. Tears stream down their cheeks unhindered. And then, with a painful scream, they throw themself to the floor and let out a low howl, keening until the sorrow threatens to swallow them whole.

All the while, Etienne says nothing.

Etienne. How can he sit here and toil with them like this? What gives him the right to play at idiocy? He's lying. He has to be. He's lied this whole time. They want to claw their way into the depths of his brain and hollow out the recesses of his memory. Who could forget something so painfully important?

Simone forces themself off the floor. When they look up, Etienne's expression has shifted from confused to terrified.

"I-I don't know who you are," he says, lip trembling, "but you need to leave before I call the faculty."

They should care, but they don't, even when the memory of Professor Chapeau's magic within their skull assaults them. If they leave this apartment empty-handed, then all their weeks of torment will have been for nothing.

They launch themself at him, fists curling tight around his capelet, and slam him against the floor.

"I know the answer is in there, Etienne." Their voice is a deathly growl. "It's hidden, but I know it's there."

Etienne's breath catches. He stills beneath them, eyes unbelievably wide. Then, whimpering, "Please let me go."

Their fingers curl tighter. "Your name is Etienne LaChance. You are a third year Enchanter. Your best friend is Nadia DuPont and up until a few weeks ago, the two of you were *fucking* inseparable. And then she vanished. A monster tried to kill you both."

His pulse quickens against their fingers. "I don't remember any of this."

They bring his face in close and slam him down again. "Think very, *very* hard. Your name is Etienne LaChance. You are a third year Enchanter. Your best friend is Nadia DuPont and you two are insep- arable. A monster tried to kill you both. Say you remember!"

He licks his lips, breaths shallow. They scan his face for any flicker of recognition, some kind of sign to tell them he's playing a sick joke on them, but there's nothing. No awareness, no memory. Only fear. Pure, unadulterated fear, the kind they know he couldn't possibly fake.

All at once, they crumple. They collapse on his chest with a choked sob.

After a long pause, a hand comes to the small of their back. "I... I am sorry for your loss, and I am sorry for whatever part you think I would have had in that. But... I don't know anything. I'm sorry."

Then he nudges them off him and settles their grief-limp body against the door. Simone tries to watch as he picks his way across the apartment, but their tears sting too greatly, reducing Etienne to a watered outline.

Before long, he returns to their side. "Here."

Hugging themself, Simone rises. They look from Etienne to the book in his hands. As they wipe their face, hiccuping, they say, "What is that?"

"It's all I can really offer you." When they don't take it, he sets the notebook in their lap and steps back again. He doesn't stop until he's on the other side of the couches, keeping the sunken platform between them. Not that the extra space would protect him, if Simone truly desired to cause him harm. But they don't. Not now. Now, they're exhausted of it all.

"I won't ask you again," he says as he edges for the phone hooked on the wall, snapping them back to. "Please leave."

Simone holds the book to their chest. Whatever it is, they can read it at a better time than right now.

"I... I'm sorry," they say, standing. Their anger abandons them in waves, replaced with stark embarrassment. "I'm sorry."

With this, they feel for the doorknob and wrench the door open. They stare Etienne down as they step into the hall, and they keep staring as the view they have gets slimmer and slimmer. A woman's voice follows them down the hall.

"Goodbye, Etienne. Have a good day."

***

They spend the rest of the day locked within their apartment. All they can think about is how painfully blank their walls are compared to Etienne's. Any time they drag their gaze to something else, it inevitably flicks back.

Not that there is much to see, given they can't stop crying. For weeks, they've remained steadfast in their faith that, even if they wouldn't find Nadia *alive*, they would at least know what happened to her.

Now that faith is gone, along with the rest of Etienne's memories.

More than ever, they ache for the warmth of their enbei holding them close like they did when Simone was a child. All they offer now are short phone calls and empty praises.

They stay curled in a ball in the corner of their apartment until shadows paint their room in shades of grey. Even then, wincing at how sore their muscles have become, it's an effort to rise. They manage, though, stumbling towards their bed and falling face-first into it, desperate for the lights within their mind to darken.

The next morning, they have half a mind to stay home. Bright light pierces them through their eyelids. As they come to, their mouth is a desert.

The book Etienne gave them catches their eye from their desk. A glance at the clock tells them they have some extra time this morning. Surely, a quick flip-through won't hurt them.

The book, as it turns out, is a copy of Etienne's notes from his Enchantment classes. The errant scan they promise themself quickly turns to determined scrutiny. They find themself making faces at the array of sigils scribbled haphazardly on every page. When were they last able to read something without comprehending it?

The first bells for classes ring from the clocktower across campus, shattering their astonished trance.

Simone closes the book and regards themself. They're half-dressed as it is. Their morning tea has long since gone cold. As underprepared—and exhausted, they realize as a sudden yawn wrenches their jaws apart—as they are, attending classes today would not be to their benefit.

Besides, they have Etienne's book to read. It's a clue. It has to be. They got through to him, somehow, and this was all he could offer in return.

It's a stretch of a thought, they know, but they cling to it all the same. Etienne—the old him, the Etienne that hates them so intensely—is trying to help them. They have to believe that.

They spend a long while looking over his sigils, tracing their finger over the deep-set lines and smudging the charcoal. The back of their Casting glove glows as they try to decode the spells he's written. At times, they get a spark or two off the tips of their fingers, but nothing further.

Then they flip to a section in the book titled "Influences on the Mind" and their heart stops beating.

Etienne's notes on this section are sparse, which makes Simone disheartened the moment they register it. Worse still, he writes in a cryptic shorthand. Each page takes Simone several minutes to parse. Would it have wounded him to give them an Etienne-to-normal text translator?

Still, at the end, he's left a list of citations.

Snapping the book shut, Simone dashes for the hallway.

FOURTEEN

Nadia Dupont || Before

That night, when sobriety has settled back over her like a wet blanket, Nadia tosses and turns in bed. Her bones groan with every movement. Her body is a maelstrom of agony.

Still, the pain is nothing compared to the whirlwind in her mind.

Every time she closes her eyes, she sees her hands, blackened and monstrous. No matter how hard she tries to convince herself it was a trick of the light or an errant hallucination, the image remains.

She's seen plenty on Serenity before, all of it difficult to describe with a sober mind. Lifelines, memories born from the minds of others, slivers of a reality so like hers and yet so different. All of these, but never anything so... dark. Is it a sign she's been corrupted? Some fragile, irreparable thing? Is this part of the deterioration Doctor Aiza had warned her about?

Nadia stretches one arm to the ceiling, then the other. Her teeth grit when her elbows pop. If she doesn't think about it, she can pretend what she saw never happened. Really, couldn't she say it was a manifestation of how she feels about herself.

That's just wishful thinking.

Her arms fall to her sides once again.

She spends the rest of her night this way, staring at the ceiling and lying as still as she dares. More than ever, she wants a drug-less reprieve, but she can't make herself get up. Not when the pain wracking her is so immense, no matter how tempting the cure to it.

The shadows on her walls move in slivers. Before long, the first lights of dawn stream into her bedroom. From his spot between her feet, Dio blinks one eye and then the other before rising. The rumble of his purrs thrum through her.

"Good morning, sweet boy." She reaches to scratch him behind the ears, but can't quite stretch far enough.

She slumps against the mattress and closes her eyes. In the silence that follows, a thought prickles her from the edges of her consciousness. Hadn't this last batch come from Chantal?

Her eyes snap open once again. Chantal. Perhaps she had received a bad shipment this time. It could happen to anyone, couldn't it?

She'll need to check with Chantal, though. Just to be sure.

Nadia flexes her body one muscle at a time to prepare herself for the venture. As she works to adjust to the waves of pain, her alarm blares at her from the living room. During one of Simone's last visits, they moved it. "To help entice you out of bed," they had said with a teasing wink. So far, it's working.

She drags a hand over her face. "Fuck."

Every subtle sound—the creaking of the cabinets, Dio's soft steps, the click of the alarm as she disarms it—is another spike into her skull. Thank the Gods she doesn't have classes today. She doesn't think she could stand to go, nor could she stand the disappointment Simone would flash her afterwards.

She stills as she reaches for the phone. Could they... be in danger because of her?

No. She shakes her head. *Of course not.* She will get this sorted out before it becomes any bigger an issue.

"Chantal Bellarose," she says into the mouthpiece the moment it connects. Then, hugging herself tight, she waits for Chantal's tired sigh.

"Hello?"

"Hey, it's Nadia."

"Nadia!" Is she imagining the brightness in her voice? "How nice of you to call."

Guilt grabs at her stomach and wrings it like a towel. "I've been meaning to. Could I come over?"

"Right now?" Shuffling. Chantal's voice is deafened for several seconds. Static crackles across the line. Then, "I think that would be okay."

Nadia thinks she hears Chantal go to say more, but she doesn't care. She slams the mouthpiece back onto its holster and spins. Teeth clenched, she pops the joints in her body one by one and prays for the pain to stop.

***

She can't remember the last time she stepped foot into Chantal's apartment. They've passed each other between classes, certainly, and Nadia has seen her a time or two in the study groups Simone likes to drag her to. But when was the last time she spent any time with Chantal, just the two of them? Weeks? A couple of months?

The thought nags at her like the unsightly mole on her chin as she sits on Chantal's beige couch, cradling a teacup in one hand. The heat emanating from the porcelain is near-blistering, just enough of a distraction to ground her from the otherworldly groaning in her bones.

Across the room, Chantal is pruning the variety of plants lining the shelf on the wall, errant vines from the ceiling catching in her hair. Her apartment is a gardener's paradise, arrays of plants meticulously placed throughout the mostly-white space. Her living room window has been fashioned into a stained glass portrait of orchids, a further testament to her passions.

When Chantal turns to face her at last, a sliver of purple light falls across her face and dyes her brown skin lavender.

"So," she says, setting down her plant mister, "what brought you to me today?"

Nadia bites her lip. She has dragged herself this far, but now a precipice yawns before her. Does she dare venture into a situation she doesn't know the outcome of?

As she ponders, she traces the rim of her teacup. Finally, "That last batch of Serenity..."

Chantal frowns. "Are you out of it? Nadia, perhaps you need to slow down."

"No, no." She waves a hand for emphasis. "I still have a few doses left. Anyway, that's not what I wanted to talk about."

"Oh?"

Nadia's swirling finger stops. When she looks over, Chantal is regarding her with narrowed eyes. The purple light from the window shifts across her face. For a moment, Nadia allows herself to get lost in the beauty of it.

When she doesn't speak, Chantal waves her on in encouragement. "And...?"

She sighs and sets her teacup down. Already, her hands are shaking.. "Chantal, have you ever had... nightmares when using Serenity?"

Chantal's lips purse. "I suppose."

The weight in Nadia's chest loosens.

"However, I wouldn't classify them as nightmares in the traditional sense."

She feels her lungs constrict once more. "What do you mean by that?"

"Well…" Chantal steps closer, sandy-colored skirt swirling around her ankles like waves on the shore. "Do you ever stay awake at night, thinking about past experiences you had that went wrong?"

All the time. "Yeah, I suppose."

"It's similar, but magnified if I start thinking too negatively." With this, Chantal throws herself into the cushion opposite Nadia, tight curls swaying as she settles. "It's none too difficult to get me back to a more neutral state, though. That's the beauty of Serenity: it's quite easy to reign my thoughts back in."

Nadia keeps her gaze locked on the table before them as she digests this information. After a long pause, she says, "And you've never… hallucinated? Like what you saw was right there in front of you?"

"Can't say I have. Why?"

She slides her hands beneath her, desperate to keep them still. The image of them from last night, all blackened and gnarled, flashes in her mind. "No real reason," she replies with a harsh swallow.

Chantal sits up once more, tucking stray curls behind her ear. "You aren't as grand a liar as you think you are." The twitching in her cheeks is enough to betray her concern. "What happened?"

Where to begin? Rocking in her seat, Nadia debates the best place to begin explaining. "Last night, I dropped with Etienne. Except—and I don't know what prompted this—at some point… It's as though I was having a daydream. I didn't feel like myself. And then I looked at my hands and—"

At once, the monstrous image assaults her. Nadia squeezes her eyes shut and shakes herself hard enough to make her brain rattle, but the image doesn't clear.

"What did you see, Nadia?"

She pauses to take a sip of tea, eager to ease the sudden dryness from her throat. "I was... something else. Something dark."

When she looks up, Chantal's face is scrunched in a thoughtful way, gaze far-off. She's seen that look before, the deep-in-thought, lost-to-the-world expression. Simone wears it sometimes when they read a challenging book or try to solve a Ximuchian number puzzle. "You're making the face again," she will often point out to them.

"What's on your mind?" The words spill out before she can stop them.

Chantal doesn't respond right away, instead marching for her bedroom and slamming the door. Nadia jumps in place at the sound. Heavy thudding sounds from the other room, accompanied by the groan of wood. She has half a mind to offer to help, but the itching under her skin makes her reconsider.

Minutes later, Chantal emerges, hair untucking itself from her carefully-constructed puff. Wiping beads of sweat from her forehead, she comes to Nadia's side and sets down a small stack of books.

"You're so like Simone," Nadia says before she can stop herself. And it's true. Who else, when faced with a problem, would turn first to books? Still, though her compliment is meant to be genuine, Chantal's reproachful look tells her the meaning was lost along the way.

Cheeks warm, she shifts her attention to the stack of books in Chantal's lap. The cover on top depicts an embossed image of a brain, the words *On Matters of the Mind* circling it. She flips through without a word, the silence punctuated by the whisper of the pages running together. Then, when she approaches the end of the book, she slows down. With a grunt, she produces her find for Nadia to read.

While Serenity is oft-regarded as a cure-all for even the most traumatized of patients, it should be known numerous side effects can occur while under its influence, including disorientation and hallucinations.

Nadia's brow furrows. "It wasn't a hallucination." And yet, even as she says it, doubt settles in the back of her mind, an unwanted guest. Perhaps she had imagined the horror, after all.

And yet...

The sting of the claws in her hair pricks her again, a phantom memory. "No," she says, voice steadier than before.

"Okay." Chantal's reluctance is evident enough, but she sets the book aside with a nod regardless. "How about this one?"

And so it goes, Chantal flipping through each book with growing impatience as Nadia refutes her suggestions. Before long, Chantal's impressive stack has been combed through, whittled to a single thin book at the bottom: *Modern Folklore.*

Chantal chews on her lip as she flicks through, twirling an errant strand of hair with a well-manicured finger. For a moment, Nadia is transfixed at the sight of her.

"Perhaps it was one of these," Chantal says, breaking the spell.

Nadia looks down at the page she's presented. Most of the paper is wreathed in black, making the figure in the center stand out all the more. Though it's human-shaped, the flash of its eyes and the dagger-sharp claws jutting from its hand makes her heart lurch.

"Y-Yeah," she says, voice strained as she tries to swallow down her brewing nausea.

Chantal pauses, examining the image. She flips the page so only she can read the back, which she does with a worsening frown.

"What?" Nadia urges when she doesn't speak.

"You... you're certain this is what you saw?"

She jabs a finger at the ghastly image. "This is what I *was*, Chantal."

Chantal closes the book without a word and sets it in the space between them. For several seconds, she chews on her thumbnail, face an ill-fitting mask over the turmoil brewing beneath. Then, as Nadia thinks she will end the conversation all together, she says in a voice so terribly quiet, "Do you remember Professor Duval?"

Of course she does. Some stubborn part of her keeps the memory of the woman close to its chest. "Yes."

"Did you ever listen to her audio logs?"

Nadia's nose wrinkles. "What are you going on about?"

"The vocite, Nadia. Countless copies were made of the Professor's research. Perhaps it was not required listening for you, but weren't you ever curious?"

"N-No," she says, something not unlike shame welling up within her. "It never occurred to me to."

Chantal sighs, hand halfway through her hair before it gets tangled in her tresses. After a moment to unravel the mess she's made, she picks the book back up and finds the page again.

"Professor Duval was investigating miasma. Specifically at Idune."

"I know that part."

"Of course you do. But did you know there's missing parts to all of those recordings?"

Nadia's mouth opens. *How absurd,* she almost says, but then stops herself. She's never listened, after all. What would she know?

At last, Chantal has found the page again. She holds it up for Nadia to examine once more, tapping emphatically at the figure in the center. Now Nadia has a chance to regard it better, she notes the way the figure seems to emerge from the shadows themselves, skin so slick it drips. Not any kind of dew or blood, if the image is to be believed, but the same pitch clinging to its claws.

"In it," Chantal continues, earning her attention once again, "she speaks of these creatures in more detail. Living but not. *Human* but not. A-And it's with this last recording the A.C.A.S. came to understand the phenomenon we know of as monsters. So I've heard, anyhow. I've only seen the recordings for myself once when I snuck into the restricted section."

Nadia's chest tightens seconds before the words register. Then, blinking, she tears her gaze from the image. Heart in her throat, she says, "You mean...?"

"What we know is not precise." Chantal closes the book again with a snap. "But... yes, Nadia. If this book is correct, this is a monster."

FIFTEEN

Simone Allard || After

Voterique's library is a wonder of architecture and knowledge. Modeled after the old cathedrals in Hadorae, the building is topped with a spire tall and sharp enough to pierce the clouds. Stained glass images of historic events separate each of the eight floors, one for each realm of Casting.

Simone strides towards it, book tucked under their arm, and shoves the front door open before marching up to the front desk and slamming their book down. An archivist with heavy circles around their eyes looks up at Simone's approach.

They purse their lips. "How may I assist you?" they ask in a voice suggesting they would rather impale themself than offer assistance.

Simone flips to the list of books Etienne had written and presents it to the archivist. As they look through the selection, Simone studies them more. A mop of curly brown hair hangs over their face, a good brush away from detangled. Their name is pinned to the collar of their third-year Evocator's cape: Cyril. Someone from Perov, Simone would guess, given the slight tawny hue of their skin and their lilting accent.

After several minutes reading and cross-referencing different books around them, Cyril hands Etienne's notebook back. "A lot of this will be on the eighth floor with the rest of the Enchanting texts... and a couple of these are on the Diviner's floor." They point to the last two books in the list. "I'm afraid you won't have access to these two, however."

Simone frowns. "Why?"

"They're restricted," Cyril says, sucking on their cheek.

Not a problem for me. The sigil they've used one too many times flashes in the back of their mind. No problem, indeed. They tuck the book back under their arm, hoping the disappointment they flash comes across as genuine. "Thank you for the direction."

"Sure." A beat, then, in the same disinterested tone, "Anything else?"

"Not that I can think of, thank you."

For once, they take the elevator up to the floor they need. The thought of walking too much sets their knee to aching. They need to reserve as much energy as possible for their search.

The gates of the elevator creak open on the fifth floor. The Diviner's floor. With a stiff nod to the students planning to board the lift next, they scan the first shelves for the books they seek.

***

The restricted section of Voterique's library is a wonder unto itself. Not a floor so much as it is a separate pocket of space, a small section of the Enchanter's floor has been cordoned off to accommodate it. Makes sense, considering how many of the books in that realm of Casting have been kept under strict supervision here.

Getting inside this section is a wonder, too. Simone knows the general rotation of the library staff, thanks to comments they've squeezed out of the faculty and Didier, who helps run the building part-time. Still, each time they enter the rift, it's with a racing heart and sweating palms and the knowledge that, at any moment, they can be caught for this transgression.

This time is no different.

Like the rest of the library, the books here are sorted by realm, then title. Rows of shelves tower over Simone as they pick their way through. They scan the spines with a lump of blue magicite in their fist, heartbeat pulsing in the tips of their fingers and goosepimples raising along their flesh.

Before long, the watery blue light catches on the first title they seek. *Memory: A Hidden Power of the Brain.* A slimmer book, Simone frowns when they pick it up. They skim the first few pages, almost missing the section titled "Memory and the Means to Alter It", but it seizes their attention on a second look. A short read-through reveals to Simone why this book has been transferred to the Restricted section.

People alter memories every day in minor ways. If you've had to convince yourself of a truth, that is an alteration. If you tell someone a small lie, just enough to nudge them towards your truth, that is an alteration. The realm of Enchantment treats memory no differently—though often, its approaches and results are more severe.

Simone's hypothesis is all but proven in this single paragraph. Of course Enchantment would have a role. Lip between their teeth, they stuff the book into their bag without a second thought.

The next tome they seek proves a more difficult search. The title alone is enough to tell Simone their quest will be harried—*Enchantment: The Art of Memory Magic.* They hadn't paid as much attention when asking the archivist for assistance, but now as they check their notes again, they let out a soft groan.

It had to be Enchanting. They shove their list back into their pocket. *Eight realms of magic and Etienne was swayed by the most dangerous of all. Why couldn't he have chosen Evocation? Transmutation, perhaps.*

Their footfalls reverberate throughout the space. The magicite flickers. The scent of books old and new drifts to them from every corner of the rift, crumpled paper and glue and aged leather. Scents that Simone normally finds comfort in, now enough to make the back of their neck prickle.

They've scanned every book in the Enchantment section twice before they find the second tome. It's much thicker than the first, more a textbook than a novel, and bears a respectable heft when Simone picks it off the shelf. The spine creaks as they lift the hard front cover and flick through.

This will take some time to read. The table of contents alone is several pages long, though thorough enough they think they'll be able to find the sections they need without much effort.

Finished with their quick skim, they settle the book in their bag and scan the dim recesses of the Restricted section once more. Their feet carry them of their own accord as they take slow steps through the liminal space. They should leave, they know. The library staff will be changing shifts soon and they can't afford to be caught here. Still, their curiosity nags at them as they catch sight of a glowing cabinet in the distance.

Before they can stop, they're walking in the direction of the cabinet. Inside, boxes fitted with small gems gleam in the dim light of their magicite, each bearing their own label. Collections of vocite, they recognize after a beat. The gems are small compared to magicite, but bear the same off-blue tinge and have a similar crystalline structure.

Most of the boxes are unfamiliar to Simone, despite their labels. From their best guess, perhaps recordings of lectures or academic logs. But then their gaze catches on a larger box in the corner of the cabinet and the label stops them cold.

THE FINAL RECORDINGS OF DOCTOR CHLOE DUVAL

How strange to find them in the restricted section, given almost everyone on campus was given a copy of the vocite to study last year after...

Simone counts the gems in the box, then again with a deepening frown. The logs they listened to last year were a series of eight, but there's twelve in this box, each winking at them in turn.

More logs? Their lips press into a firm line. *How curious.*

They've just finished settling the box of vocite within their bag, grunting at the added weight, when they hear a faint fizzle. The pressure in their ears builds before releasing with a pop. From far away, someone hums, their footfalls echoing.

Fuck.

Simone dims their magicite and shoves it into their pocket with a sharp inhale. Darkness presses in on them with the absence, as heavy as lead. Their mind flicks to the time they'd hidden in their enbei's closet during a meeting, how their own breaths had covered their skin in an uncomfortable dew, how terrified they had been to move lest they make a sound. Though they had been heavily admonished by their enbei after, it had been one of their first forays into geopolitics.

Focus, Simone. They press their palm to the shelf closest to them, breath fluttering.

They've reached the end of the row when they catch the cold glow of a magicite stone in the distance. It's a small pinprick of light, hidden as the bearer disappears behind another row of books. Simone sucks in their cheeks.

The entrance is somewhere in the dark beyond, they know. Some place past whoever is within this rift with them. If they can safely extricate themself...

The stranger rounds another corner. The light bobs with their steps, painting the shelves in shades of blue. Simone stiffens as it draws nearer.

I have to get out of here.

All they have is their fingers against wood to guide them as they take their first steps into the dark. The temperature around them gets warmer, then cooler. The smell of ozone tickles their nostrils, guiding them the rest of the way. Their pulse continues to beat in the pads of their fingers.

Then, when they're so close to the entrance their entire body prickles, their hip slams against a shelf. The books at their side rattle, the sound enhanced by the distorted space. They choke on a strained hiss of pain.

The blue light in the distance flashes. "Hello?"

They're so close, they can reach out and touch the flickering shadows forming the exit if they try. The hairs on their arms raise to attention.

Without pause, they take the final step. The world spins violent enough to make Simone's stomach twist. The pressure builds in their ears before again releasing with a pop.

When they open their eyes, they are back on the eighth floor of the Voterique library, facing a door simply labeled RESTRICTED. Clutching their bag tighter, they spin on their heel and race for the exit.

***

Even before coming to Voterique, before taking their entrance exams and facing the panel of professors eager to interview them, Simone had known about the basics of magic. It was hard *not* to know them, given the lessons their enbei had instilled in them. From childhood, they had often been subject to their parent's lectures, engaged in test after vigorous test.

Casting, at this point, is as easy as breathing.

And yet, somehow, they find themself on their apartment floor, brow furrowed as they study the array of sigils before them. The books they've collected form a ring around them, and they flick from book to book, page to page, Caster's glove hovered over the parchment and waiting for something to happen.

It would be easier with a subject to test on, they know, but the only choice in the apartment is Dio and the ethics of performing spells on an animal are nebulous at best. Still, the option is becoming all the more attractive to them the longer they read and don't get results.

As the prospect of testing the spells on Dio grows too tempting to ignore, a knock on the door disturbs them.

Simone rises to their feet, grunting with the effort, and nudges the books under the couch with a foot. For good measure, they take the blanket Dio had been resting on, earning a chirrup of complaint for their efforts, and lay it over the books. A good enough hiding spot—for now, at least.

Another series of knocks urges them to abandon doing anything further. Alienor stands on the other side when they peer through the peephole, hugging herself tight. She leans hard on her cane, looking the door up and down with a sour expression.

They ease the door open to face her. "Good afternoon," they say with a respectful dip of their head.

She barges her way into their apartment and shuts the door with the flick of her cane. Her eyes, a cold and piercing grey, rake over Simone before shifting to the rest of their apartment. She's never been inside their space before. She's never *had* to be, they think.

"You didn't come to meet with me." She takes a step closer, straightening to her full height, as she speaks. "And you weren't in any of your classes. And yet, you don't appear to have taken ill."

Simone swallows, shame gurgling in their gut. It isn't like them to abandon their courses. "I apologize if my absence caused you concern."

Her cane thumps against the floor. She gives the room another appraisal, gaze settling before long on the lump of books by their couch.

"When did you get a cat?"

Their blood runs cold. *Dio.* A lie forms itself on the tip of their tongue. "I was... watching him for a friend for a couple of days." Even as they speak, they pray Alienor won't feel the need to follow up on it. Their willpower is stretched impossibly thin as it is; they don't think they can craft a lie convincing enough to placate her.

Alienor's gaze remains glued to the couch as she passes Simone by and takes a seat. She spins her cane between her palms, gaze finally going vacant in an expression Simone recognizes. She's thinking.

Then, "Simone, you do understand you're being watched quite closely, do you not?"

The hairs on their arms raise. They stuff their hands into their pockets, mind whirling as they struggle to think of an excuse.

"Every step you take out of line is being recorded, you know," Alienor continues, as if Simone hadn't reacted at all.

Their throat dries. Does she know about how the faculty cornered them? How Professor Chapeau had forced their way inside their mind?

"Why would faculty want to watch me?" they say at last. Perhaps, if they feign ignorance, she'll let slip some information they can use.

"You are directly involved with someone who recently disappeared, Simone. Our professors are not fools."

Simone swallows hard. "But I didn't..."

"But you could have knowledge of where she went." Now, her stare pins them where they stand. "Not to mention your own personal exploits. You did not think you could get away with sneaking into the Restricted section, did you? You checked out books with the front desk. Your presence there is recorded."

Their nails dig craters into their palms. Jaw set, they check the lock on the door before striding to Alienor's side. She doesn't flinch from their hard stare, but they wish she would, if only to give them an iota of power over the situation. Instead, she arches a brow, chin tipped in defiance. Then, with a sigh, she sets her cane aside.

"You are very lucky, Simone, that it was I who found you in the Restricted section earlier. You are luckier still I don't have the will to report this transgression."

They can't help it: they flinch. "Why?"

"You've always been one of my favorite prefects, Simone. Your kindness has earned you kindness in return."

Simone mulls this over as Alienor wrenches her gaze away. No one can possibly be this altruistic. "What do you want from me?"

Her lip twitches in something not unlike a smile. "Let go of this hollow pursuit. Lower your head and strive for the end of your second year with no further issue. Voterique has lost one student recently, after all, and I…" She shakes her head, gaze forlorn. "No need for it to lose another."

Despite the gentleness of her words, the meaning behind it is enough to knock the wind from Simone's lungs. *Is she… threatening me?*

As they ponder her words, Alienor rises again with a groan. "Maintain caution. That is all I ask." Then, she limps back to the door, a gentle hiss escaping with every step.

At the door, she turns back. "A final piece of advice, should you deign to take it."

Simone gives a stiff nod in encouragement.

"Reading books on a realm of magic is not the same as the practice of it itself. With that in mind, I might suggest you visit the campus Enchanter's council to get their insight. They will get farther with their spells than you will, after all."

Simone's brain swirls. Before they can think of a response, Alienor is gone, the door shutting with a click behind her.

***

Later that night, head aching from the amount of sigils they've forced themself to look at, Simone at last sits back and unleashes a deep sigh. Truth be told, they haven't been able to focus since Alienor's visit, but they've made an attempt at it regardless. The sooner they can figure out how to decode Etienne's mind, the better.

And yet, it appears they will make no more progress tonight.

Throwing their papers down, Simone pops their back against the couch. The clicking of their vertebrae is a familiar—if mildly uncomfortable—sensation, one they relish in as tingles spread from their crown to their toes. Time to begin their nightly routine.

It's not until they're returning the pages to their bag they remember their other unorthodox find. The box bangs against their knee with considerable force, enough to inform them of its existence. For a moment, they consider leaving it hidden away, but their curiosity wins out in the end when they pull the oak box free. Inside, the gems are as lustrous as ever.

They put the box aside and seek out their Caster's glove.

Vocite, like magicite and its ability to project light, are specialized crystals attuned to sigils for capturing sound. They're used sparingly, given how difficult it can be to cultivate them, as well as recent technological advancements, but as Simone snaps their glove against their skin, they remember childhood days spent bent over stones much like these, listening to one lecture or another at their enbei's behest.

They adjust their Caster's glove with a grim set to their mouth. The box of vocite perches with a precarious toddle on their knee when they set it down. The first piece they pick up is the smallest, casting soft rainbows across the carpet as Simone holds it up to the light.

What are you hiding?

With the slightest nudge of power through their glove, they activate the sigils engraved on the stone's surface. It pulses with light. After several seconds of crackling, a thin voice permeates the apartment.

Simone closes their eyes and listens.

INTERLUDE

Recording #1

Today marks the first day of the newest A.C.A.S.-funded expedition into Idune to reclaim it for archaeological use. Gods willing, we will be up-river and studying the ruins by the end of the fortnight. There's a wealth of miasma there, ripe for the sampling.

[A long stretch of static broken by the snapping of twigs, the stamping of boots, and unintelligible murmurs.]

I'm hoping these new preservatives prove useful.

As am I, Laurent. The samples we collected during our last expedition proved too volatile to give more than a cursory scan. Without them, it's difficult to determine the success of the preservatives... but I maintain faith, regardless.

Professor Duval, do you think we'll find success out here?

Time will tell. At the very least, our new group of Abjurors should make our current trek leagues safer than the last one.

So you allege.

[Several seconds of static. Then, barely audible, a sigh.]

I have to believe that Idune will be different now, Laurent.

Of course. Forgive me. I haven't been feeling well as of late is all.

Do I need to tell our entourage to take a break? Let us rest? To tell you the truth, I've been needing to—

No... no, that will not be necessary, Chloe. I'll be just fine.

Recording #2

The forests in Elrick are trickier than I gave them credit for.

The first day, I found myself trampling a circular path around the same set of bushes. [A soft chuckle.] How many times did we do that, Professor Blanc?

Four or five, I think.

That sounds right.

[A cough, followed by a sniffle.] *Suffice to say, it has been murderous on my joints. And this weather! Has Elrick always been this cold?*

[Softly.] Hush, Laurent. These logs are being sent back to the college when we're done.

[At regular volume.] We've been walking for a couple of days now with the map Doctor Guérin provided for us. It seems the path has seen some changes since their last expedition. That's nature for you. Still, I have ensured the appropriate updates get made as we go.

[Papers rustle. Twigs snap in the background.]

Professor Duval?

Yes, Dominique?

It... I feel like we're being followed.

Ah, yes. [The rustling of papers continues.] Nature, for all its beauty has a way of making you feel paranoid. This is your first expedition, is it not, Dominique?

Well... yes.

As I thought. The feeling will pass.

[Footfalls trail off in the background. Moments later, heavy crunching.]

I'd be remiss if I did not confess to you I felt similar, Professor Duval.

It gets easier to ignore. The wildlife gets curious, takes to poking around a bit. So long as we ignore them and keep our wards in place, we will be fine.

It feels different this time.

[A sigh.] Go speak to Professor Kontos, then. Perhaps between them and Agnis, some extra preventative measures can be taken.

[Stomping and snapping twigs fade into the distance. A long pause punctuated by static.]

I must confess to feeling the same... but the Gods would not allow us to let their most holy of sites remain in corruption. Though the trek is long and full of brambles, I am not so eager to retire from it.

Besides, the chairwoman would have my head for wasting funds.

[Another sigh.] Laurent's paranoia is getting to me. That's all this is.

Recording #3

[Soft knocking pierces the static.] *Professor Duval? May I discuss something with you?*

For a moment, perhaps. I am finishing my observation logs. What is it, Dominique?

It's regarding Professor Blanc.

Laurent? What of them?

I worry for them, Professor. Earlier, I happened upon them. [A sharp inhale.] *They were dreadfully sick.*

Laurent is fine, Dominique. The—they're struggling to acclimate to this new environment is all. But if it will appease you, I'll check on them once I have finished.

Recording #4

I've updated the map to an incomprehensible degree at this point. Professor Blanc has had to make copies for the sake of legibility. Keeping the interns at bay, though, has proved to be a challenge most unique.

Dominique continues with her insistence on there being something in the woods. Our zoologist, Professor Kontos, assures me they'll remain out of our path. [Harsh metal jangling.] As a precaution, they've distributed clackers to keep us from stumbling upon things we shouldn't.

Still, our fumbles have delayed the timeline considerably. Alas... where the Gods give, they also take away.

[Distant jangling stops.] *Professor?*

What is it now?

Look.

[Clanking continues.]

Ah. It seems you've come across the remains of something's dinner. A deer, I think. Laurent, get a look at this.

[A long pause, filled with crackling static and jangling clackers.]

Seems too neat to be a prey-kill. And it's still intact.

I thought similar. It's unsettling. Dominique?

Yes, Professor?

Take some blood samples and a few photos, if you please. Professor Kontos is still a ways behind and I'm sure they wouldn't want to miss this.

Recording #5

I submitted Dominique's sample to Professor Kontos and found the deer carcass had been covered in miasma, not blood. This struck me as odd, given every miasma sample I've recovered from Idune looks the same: viscous and black and inky. These new samples seemed more like a halfway stage, something in between. Does this mean blood can turn miasmic? Can blood be so easily corrupted?

Enlightening and troublesome in equal measure.

Another interesting discovery is the sample collected appears to have limited activity. It was practically alive when we rested for the night, straining against the glass. I've never seen a sample behave this way.

There's been slime molds that look like this before. *Lindbladia tabulina* comes to mind, known for its dark color and dense clusters. Still, slime mold wouldn't kill a larger organism. Not by itself, anyway.

[Glass clinks together.]

Looking at it now, this sample has lost much of its animated properties, but I'm unsure if that's due to decay or something else. Gods willing, I can keep it preserved enough to compare to samples in Idune once we arrive.

[More glass clinking before, suddenly, silence.]

It also, strangely, reminds me of the samples collected back in Voterique of the unfortunate students who have contracted *Sanguina Malefica*. Especially in the later stages, their blood becomes more muddled. A lesser person may think there's a connection there.

But there couldn't be. Such a thought is ridiculous.

Recording #6

The Gods aim to keep me vexed. The miasma we collected has lost its color and reduced itself to a sort of grime at the bottom of the tube. This decay, at least, is a constant with all other samples I've ever observed. It seems any research I'm capable of doing will need to be immediate and harsh.

I'm still not certain what to classify this fluid as, though it is reminiscent of miasma. A subtype, perhaps? I wish the sample was still viable, so I could better compare.

There's no time to turn back, alas. It's been almost a fortnight since we landed on Elrick's shore and we've barely made it halfway. The chairwoman will not be pleased at our tardy return.

Recording #7

[The recording opens with shuddered breathing and stifled gasps, followed by silence lasting several seconds.]

Dominique was right.

[Shuffling and more gasping.]

We had made camp for the night, as usual. I had Laurent and the group do chores while I continued my (unsuccessful) port-mortem observations of the material we collected. It was while doing so Dominique herself came to visit me.

"I've felt it again," she told me. I told her it was the paranoia of an amateur explorer.

And yet, she was right.

Not long after her visit to my tent, I heard it. A creature reminiscent of a human, wearing what looked like an insect carapace and dripping with pitch. It looked... it looked like Laurent. It couldn't have been. But it did. It was.

It's easy to describe them in retrospect, I suppose. In the moment, I could only focus on how absolutely *wrong* they looked.

The hunt was already on when I emerged from my tent. Dominique's blank expression focused on me across the clearing. A mix of blood and black slime seeped from the wound in her side. Dead before she hit the ground. I pray the Gods were merciful and took her swiftly.

Most of the research team was killed in the attack.

It's just two of us left. Myself and Professor Kontos. I still don't know how to describe the full depths of what happened.

As for Laurent, well.

[A long pause. Low, pained groaning in the background.]

I will stop my recollection here. It appears Professor Kontos is coming back to.

Recording #8

Professor Kontos is dying.

The wounds they sustained during the attack have festered in a way I've never seen before. Each time they're leeched, the fluid is brackish and putrid. The scent that rolls off them is equally as foul.

"Leave me here," they said last night. [Shuddered breathing.] I had half a mind to comply.

But... I can't. If Professor Kontos dies, I'm alone. I can't bear to try to continue this journey on my own.

[More shuddered breathing, accompanied by sniffling.]

In a sick twist of fate, Laurent's monstrous corpse has allowed me another look at the fluid we recovered from the deer last week. It appears this fluid surging through Laurent's system now is like what we sampled and recovered before. It's behaving in similar fashion, animated and reaching. I have no doubts now as to what caused it. There are monsters stalking these woods. Are they related to the miasma we've studied in Idune?

Better yet, how is it Laurent came to be transformed in the first place?

By my new counts, we will be in Idune within a couple of days. I have to keep us moving.

Recording #9

This recording will remain brief. Professor Kontos passed on overnight. I am now, more than I ever have been, utterly alone.

There is nothing to distract me from this truth, and that terrifies me. Worse still, the samples I harvested from Laurent died with them.

Laurent, my beloved. [Heavy sighing and sniffling.] I'm terrified. More than I can possibly say. But I am determined. There is a reason we were sent here. As such, I will finish this expedition. Your death can't have been in vain.

[Several seconds of sobbing, followed by crackling as the recording suddenly stops.]

Recording #10

Idune, once a massive and holy gravesite, has become naught less than an overgrown hovel in the years since its formation. Nature in Elrick, it seems, is aggressive and quick to reclaim any stolen land. The statues here look more like poorly-trimmed hedges.

But, at last, I've found it.

I don't know how I'm getting out, if I'm being honest. The exploration team has been reduced to... me. Can I truly brave the wilderness all by myself?

Ah, well. I am wasting time thinking of my own mortality. For now, it is just me and the wealth of miasma bubbling around me. I should get to studying.

[A long pause punctuated by static.]

Laurent should have been here for this. It was their department that backed the expedition, not mine. I'm just the woman with the vocite clusters and the knowledge of miasma. I've been at this for longer than I've had any right to. And yet, here I am, in the place they should have been.

[Soft sniffles.] I went back, you know. To the campsite. I buried Laurent, like I should have the night I killed them. I... killed them.

[Several seconds of sudden, heaving sobs. They slowly taper off to shuddering hiccups, then silence.]

There isn't much to their grave; I had only our resources at my disposal. But I do hope they find it appropriate in the afterlife. May the Gods bring them comfort.

It's just... it's just not fair.

Recording #11

The pools of miasma here have grown considerably since our last expedition two years ago. I tried to take measurements to compare to the old notes and ran out of tape for most of the sites. The smallest mass of it I've found thus far is an impressive five feet wide. It swallowed the stick I used to try to measure depth, however. For now, the notes just say "very deep". An unscientific approximation as any.

Another feature of note is the activity. Much like the small samples I've obtained from corpses along the way, the pools here gurgle constantly. If I turn my back for too long, I find they've shifted position, like they're reaching for something.

It's difficult to quantify their makeup, but it's reminiscent of slime mold. Only... more sentient. I set traps and fed a couple of the sites what small vermin I managed to catch. They consumed the offerings. Or perhaps, like the stick I lost, the animals drowned in their depths and are fermenting somewhere below.

A final, strange observation I've had, the whole of Idune—miasma and all—becomes incredibly active whenever I cast a spell. It livens. It *notices*.

For example...

[The crackle of magic being cast.]

Here, I have produced a wink of Evocation magic, a simple ball of flame. Despite the weakness of the spell, the puddles around me have reacted in an instant. They reach towards me, forming unfathomable shapes from within their depths.

[Another hiss.]

I've tested this theory with the avenues of magic available to me. The result is the same. Somehow, this is all connected. I just hope I have time to decipher it all.

[Distant groaning.]

I'll have to pick this up la—

[Growling in the background. The sound of a pistol cocking.]

[A single gunshot, followed by an astonished shout. Static slowly builds to a crescendo before the audio suddenly cuts.]

Recording #12

This will be my final recording of my findings for this expedition.

It is no longer possible to purify Idune. The cynical part of me believes it is only a matter of time before the rest of the world is reduced to such a miasmic state. Monsters have overwhelmed the world to an insurmountable degree. When Laurent and I first set out to investigate this site, we sought a solution to the world's plight.

And yet.

[A soft sigh.]

As I record this, a ghastly wound has gone necrotic in my side. Any attempts of conjuring magic, strangely, seems to affect the blackening tissue. Much like the miasma, it reaches. I feel its pull within me.

I do not have long left in this world. An hour or so ago, I broke out in a gruesome fever. I am in a forest, far from home and all alone. For all my knowledge, I see not a means to get out of my predicament.

Ah, I suppose it no longer matters. These chunks of vocite will outlive me now. With my final moments, I shall seal them within their box and activate the spell meant to teleport them home. Then it is up to the good faculty of Voterique to do with my findings as they may.

[Shuffling and pained groaning.]

I do not have much longer. These recordings will stop here and I shall complete my task as I promised I would.

Laurent, my beloved, I will see you soon.

SIXTEEN

Nadia Dupont || Before

"**S**imone, I can't let us continue to have a relationship."

Her haggard reflection stares back at her, brows furrowed in concentration. She tries to see beyond herself, to envision Simone standing in front of her, but can only get the image to settle for seconds at a time before it ripples and fades.

She's practiced this conversation for hours. Ever since she's returned home for the day. Simone has attempted to coax her into coming over, eager to put her through another rigorous study session, but she doesn't have the stomach to see them today. Not after everything she's learned.

"You're too fucked up," she whispers to her reflection. "If not in body, then in spirit."

Her reflection frowns in response. It has the gall to even look hurt by her words. *How can you deface yourself?* it asks her. *How can you go on pretending we are not the same?*

With a final, frustrated growl, Nadia spins on her heel and stalks out of the bathroom.

She has to distance herself from Simone. Hallucination or not—and she's less and less certain what she saw was a figment of her imagination—she poses a danger to the people around her. She wouldn't be able to forgive herself if she caused Simone harm.

If only she could get the words out.

Planning never goes how she wants it to. If she wants to follow through at all, she will need to be spontaneous. And so, before she can think of the consequences, Nadia throws her bag back over her shoulder and stalks out of her apartment.

The walk to the Abjuror's tower is a short one. Before she can blink, she's in front of Simone's door. No turning back, she thinks as she brings a hand up to knock.

Before she can make contact, the door swings open.

"Somehow," Simone says from the other side, "I knew you would change your mind."

Despite herself, a relieved sigh leaves her. It doesn't matter how her hair sticks to her sweat-slicked cheeks, or how she's sure her skin smells the wrong side of pleasant. As soon as Simone's face is in her view, she throws herself into their arms, allowing them to rub circles into her back.

Focus.

At once, the comfort of Simone's attention on her evaporates. She pushes herself back and forces herself to look them in their eyes.

They must sense the change in her. With a frown, their grip shifts to her shoulders. "Is something wrong?"

"May I come in?"

Without a word, they step back and allow her into their apartment.

Simone's space is as organized as they are, all white space and severe angles. Several dark wood shelves line the walls, a contrast to the vastness of everything else. There is not an item out of place—from what she can tell, anyhow.

As she shuts the door, Nadia takes a breath and debates how to begin. *Hey, Simone, I think I'm turning into a monster.* Is that too straightforward? It's a better explanation than, *We shouldn't see each other anymore.* Less likely for them to get upset.

"Nadia?"

Simone's voice cuts through her, sharp and knife-like. She stiffens, back pressed flat against the door, a strange warmth gathering in the pit of her stomach. Perhaps they hadn't meant to, but their voice has a dominating edge to it.

Perhaps she could let them put her through another lesson before she cuts them off. Would that be selfish of her? Would they hate her for it?

Their brows pull together. "Nadia?" they say again, softer this time.

She takes their hands in hers, phrases of all sorts turning over in her mind.

Finally, "We cannot continue to see each other."

Their dark eyes flash. The frown they wear deepens as the full weight of her words sinks in. Their grip on her shoulders tightens. "What are you talking about?"

"Simone, I can't keep dating you. It isn't safe."

"What are you talking about?" they ask again.

Nadia traps her bottom lip between her teeth. How much can she explain?

"I..."

"Tell me you're trying to be humorous. Tell me this is a joke."

"Simone..." Despite herself, Nadia's voice cracks. "Why are you wasting your time on a dead woman?"

Simone shakes their head with great force. "You aren't dead. Not yet." Then, after a pause, "You *won't* die. I will make sure you won't."

Nadia chuckles sadly. "You can't know that, Simone. This could all be for nothing. You warned me from the beginning how much you hate your time being wasted."

Their mouth opens, but nothing comes out. Instead, they press her forehead to theirs, ragged breaths fanning across her face. They haven't brushed their teeth yet, but she finds the soft sourness a strange sort of comfort. Their warmth envelopes her, a sharp contrast to the door at her back. Nadia's resolve slips, just for a second.

You are a weakling. If you were a better person, you wouldn't delay the inevitable.

She wants to shove herself away, wants to yank Simone closer and ride them through the waves of misery threatening to consume her. And yet, if she moves, it will be her total undoing.

They hover on the edge of this precipice for a long while, Simone's tears dampening her cheeks.

"Do not play with my heart like this," they say at last. "I beg of you."

As their lips hover over hers, her resolve hardens. "Simone..."

Before she can speak, they capture her in a kiss, body hiccuping against hers. Their tears mingle together as she closes her eyes and loses herself to the moment.

Then, as they grab a fistful of her hair, she shoves them back.

"Don't. Please."

"Why?"

"You are blinding yourself. The facts here are this, Simone: I am dying and there is nothing either of us can do to stop it. And if I am not dying, I am turning into a monster."

Confusion clouds their gaze. "You are the furthest thing from a monster imaginable, Nadia."

"But it's the truth. Something is wrong with me. Something vile and twisted."

"Don't be absurd."

"*Look at me!*"

The shriek bursts from her before she can stop it, echoing off the walls. Does she appear as desperate and distraught as she feels? Can they see the cracks forming in her human veneer? How close is she to spiraling out of control again?

Simone scans her from head to foot. They're looking, but are they *seeing*? She doesn't know. Which is worse—seeing the reality or buying the lie?

"You want to know where I was yesterday? You want to know why I called off our date? It's for this reason. I went to Etienne's house, we took Serenity, and I... I can't even describe it to you. It was like being someone else. Some*thing* else."

Their brows crinkle. "You were intoxicated," they say. A statement, and yet it feels like an accusation. Their gaze hardens around the edges as they say, "Of course you couldn't process properly."

"For several, heart-wrenching seconds, all I could think about was tearing out Etienne's throat. And I *liked* it."

For the first time this conversation, Simone's response is what she expects: wide-eyes and a half-step away from her. Their outstretched hand begins to shake.

Her resolve wobbles at their expression, but she presses forward. "If I hurt him... *Gods*, if I hurt you, Simone. Either of you. I could never forgive myself for that. You understand, now, why I am stopping our relationship? You understand why this thing between us cannot continue? Even now, you are afraid of me. Deep down, you know the truth as well as I do: you cannot love a monster."

She hates herself for the way their face crumples at her words. It's for the best, she tells herself as they press their face into their hands and shake with the force of their silent sobs.

She can't let this conversation go on.

"I truly am sorry, Simone. I wish it wasn't this way."

Before she can stop herself, before she can watch their heart break further, she throws herself back out the door and towards the exit. Simone's anguished shriek follows her down the hall.

***

Nadia did what was best for everyone. She tells herself this over and over and over again, but she can't quite get herself to believe it. How can breaking Simone's heart be the best answer? Why did she bother with any of it at all?

If she was a better person, she could wipe away the traces of her existence entirely. Jumping off the edge of the mesa would be enough to take care of her, she thinks, if not for the mess her body would leave behind. As an alternative, she could fling open the door of the tram and plummet into the forests below. No one would find her—not right away. They would be spared the agony of cleaning a corpse, left instead with sun-bleached bone.

She could also keep her death more personal. Enough Serenity could numb her to the pain of however she deigns necessary to end herself, if the drug isn't enough to kill her outright. A river of blood from her veins, perhaps, or smothering herself. It would be selfish of her to inflict her final trauma on others.

With a shriek that strains her vocal chords, Nadia shoves her face into her pillows, tears flowing anew.

For a couple of months, she has become an expert in forgetting her own mortality. The pain is ever-present now, true to Doctor Aiza's warnings, but it wasn't until the distorted visions she experienced that she realized she would die. And, if the churning in her gut is any indicator, the line between her life and death is slimming.

The room is grey with the first lights of dawn by the time she emerges from her fugue. The dull slap of her feet echoes through the apartment as she drags herself to the bathroom. Then, as ice-cold water drips from her fingers, she lumbers towards the phone on the wall. One person, perhaps, may know how to guide her.

The click of the line is sharp enough to draw the breath from her lungs. In the silence that follows, she teeters on the edge of collapse. Then, a voice, soft and thick with sleep. "Hello?"

Nadia's throat tightens. She had forgotten the difference in time-zones. "Maman."

A gasp, so faint she almost misses it. "Nadia?"

"Maman," she says again. Years in Mertaln has softened her Perosh accent, but now it settles back into place. Has it been so long since she called home? "I was thinking of you and Ines lately."

"Oh, your brother is getting on as he always has. Catching more frogs, covering himself in more mud, getting into more trouble. His grades are finally picking up, though. Oh! Did I tell you he's decided he wants to…"

And on and on she goes. Nadia listens to her prattling for a while, allowing the stress of this week, this month, this whole *school year* to melt away. At least, she does for the first couple of minutes. Then, as her mother continues to speak, the calm settled over her like snow thaws.

"…Nadia?"

All at once, she's on the floor, heaving sobs tearing from her breast. She cradles the phone's mouthpiece like a child, keening into it until she has to stop to catch her breath and then sobbing anew.

You have no one to turn to, her conscious goads. *You're a danger to everyone you love. Everyone who is foolish enough to love you.*

"Darling? What's wrong?"

You never told her you were dying, did you?

The thought sobers her, somewhat. With a sigh, she recollects herself, storing all of her grief and anger and pain into a jar somewhere deep inside herself and screwing the lid on tight. Wiping her eyes, she regards the mouthpiece in her hand.

"Nadia?"

The voice inside her, no matter how insidious its intentions, is right. "I am sorry," she says in a breathless whisper. Then, before she can think, she slams the mouthpiece back into its cradle.

She doesn't remember the march back to her room—not until her face is pressed into her pillows and fresh sobs claw their way out of her throat. The phone continues its ear-piercing refrain in the hall. The pillows tear under her nails, spilling feathers like animal entrails. Even this wanton destruction isn't enough to satisfy. It's too sanitized. Too neat.

And yet, despite the lilting voice in her ear urging her to move, to find something new to tear apart, she cannot. Instead, she lays there, palms warm against her bare stomach, watching the time pass with the shifting of the shadows on her wall.

SEVENTEEN

Simone Allard || After

The last of Simone's pilfered vocite dims with the completion of its recording. In the aftermath, all they can hear is the staccato of their uneven breaths, the squeak of the leather of their Casting glove as their fist clenches.

Everything Simone has understood regarding Professor Duval's expedition has been a lie.

They shove the chunks of stone into their velvet-lined box and slam the lid down, pulse hammering. Professor Duval's words—her true, unedited words—swim laps in their mind. How could they have been so wrong?

Someone tampered with her findings.

Sensing their distress, Dio comes to Simone's side with a soft chirrup. Though he ensures he keeps his distance, he allows himself close enough for them to rake their fingers through his too-soft fur. The action helps bring the roaring storm of their thoughts to a dull hum, then to a stand-still.

Did Nadia... become a monster?

They want to shake the thought off as a flight of fancy. How preposterous a notion. She couldn't have, could she?

But... why else would she have disappeared?

Their brain fills with tingling static. With a frustrated grunt, Simone scrubs their eyes free of grit. This is too much for them to contend with, they decide as they force themself to their feet.

Etienne. Focus on Etienne. It's the one puzzle I can do anything about now.

As they stride down the hall, the slam of their apartment door is as loud as a gunshot.

***

The Enchanter's Society. Simone's next clue. While the Enchanters have their dormitory tower like everyone else, the Casters therein more often spend their time in this hall instead. Simone has heard whispers of the Society before, a sort of cult where the Enchanters of Voterique gather. Really, Etienne is the only Enchanter they know who doesn't attend the Society at all, save any mandatory meetings.

Simone doesn't know the full details of the goings-on within the Society, either. Between Etienne's dislike of them and the far-off, tight-lipped way he gets whenever they've asked (or rather, had Nadia do so), he's not been one to divulge. The members of the Society could have anything: Extravagant orgies; A grey-walled prison full of mind-warped drones; A chaotic pocket dimension.

In Simone's mind, it's an exaggerated, exclusive study group, one with which other students of Voterique—and perhaps a professor or two—have entered seeking guidance. Although, of the eight realms of

Casting, Enchantment requires the utmost discipline in order to use, so it makes sense to seclude students who elect to specialize in it.

Still, their shadowed reputation and dangerous Casting proclivities does the Enchanter's Society minimal favors.

Much in the same way the medical ward is an unsightly growth amongst the faculty buildings, the Enchanter's Society lurks in the background like an abandoned child. Despite its impressive width, it's the shortest of the faculty buildings—and yet, it's the one that makes Simone's skin prickle now as they approach. But perhaps it's not the building itself, but the way fellow Casters-to-be give them a narrow look and a wide berth as they approach, as if the building is diseased and, by entering, Simone will become the next bearer of its contagion.

With a shiver, they pull their capelet tighter around them.

The entrance doors, filigreed and gaudy, stretch open at their approach. If the rest of the Society is decorated like this, it's no wonder Etienne has such a flair for the dramatic.

From the darkness beyond, several blue pinpricks of light flare under Simone's assessing gaze. And then, as they step inside with a shuddering breath, a soft gust of wind catches their hair and the rest of the lanterns light.

"Welcome to the Enchanter's Society," says a voice. Simone scans the foyer for the source. The bang of the doors startles them, and it's not until they're trembling, hand to their fluttering heart, that they locate the person who had spoken. An attendant at the front desk stares at them with lake-still eyes. Brown curls frame their face like brambles on a bush. Their light green capelet gives their pale skin a nauseating hue. When Simone doesn't respond, they blink their too-wide eyes and tilt their head. "How may we provide assistance?"

Simone's knees lock. Though the attendant's lips move, the voice emerging from them has multiple sources. On impulse, they look around the foyer for other figures.

"I..." They pause, swiping their tongue over their lips. What *had* they come here for, again?

The attendant blinks, some semblance of sentience settling over them at last. Adjusting the clasp of their capelet, they say, "Either ask for what you seek or leave. We do not tolerate loitering."

Simone falters, just for a second, before standing up straight once again. They've contended with far worse, *been* far worse. A multi-voiced attendant is manageable in comparison. "I must consult the Society regarding magics of the mind."

The attendant's eyebrow twitches. "This is what we are here for, after all."

Of course. Simone dares themself to step closer. "Rather, it is about a friend of mine—"

"How vague."

"—who has been behaving... in an odd manner for a while."

They've practiced their lie for hours in front of the mirror, and yet this iteration feels the most ridiculous. Warmth floods their face and they shuffle on their feet, unable to say more.

The attendant's face remains unchanged. "Seems it may be a matter for the medical ward, no?"

Simone's jaw clenches, but they relax it with another breath. *Patience.* "It would be, under normal circumstances. Except..." As they think of how best to phrase it, they pull one of the textbooks free from their satchel. "He's in some kind of strange daze. He went on a trip a week or so ago, but the next thing I know, he's returned and he cannot tell me a single thing from his time away."

At last, the attendant's eyes widen, just enough to tell Simone they have their attention.

"It's as though... Well, here."

Simone slides the book across the desk, pointing to the title on the top of the page. The attendant leans forward to read through it.

As they wait, Simone takes another look around the foyer. A high balcony overlooks the space, accessed by a wide marble staircase. Suspended from the ceiling is a massive skeletal structure. It's a beast of some sort, Simone thinks, catching sight of the large horns sprouting from the skull. A drake—one from before the current era, judging by the size. A set of wings sprout from its midsection, too small to be of real use. Over the ages, drakes had shrunk further and further in on themselves. Due to their utilization in various militias, and then being trained otherwise afterwards, they had evolved to not utilize their wings or bulk. The handful of living specimens Simone has seen are barely bigger than a housecat now.

They're so enraptured by the skeleton they miss the attendant's next words until, in their stupor, Simone's gaze lands on them once again.

"I'm sorry," Simone says. "Did you say something?"

The attendant slides the book back in Simone's direction. "I do not know what sort of situation your friend was in for certain. But, if it's anything like this, it is possible they are suffering from arcane amnesia."

Simone represses a shiver. Now, at last, their hunch has been confirmed. "I... was afraid you would say that." And, despite themself, they mean it. Taking the book back and replacing it in their satchel, they say, "What can be done about it?"

The attendant fiddles with one of their earrings, a thoughtful gleam in their eye. "I am afraid I am more of a... spokesperson for the Society and as such, my knowledge is limited. Allow me a moment."

Before Simone can respond, they pick up the receiver at their side. Their voice drops to a whisper, so low Simone cannot make out what they are saying. Then, after several seconds, they hang up again.

"If you will wait here a few minutes, I will have someone down to assist you."

***

A few minutes, indeed.

Simone glowers as they leaf through one of the many books in the foyer. Though they are sure their growing impatience is evident to the attendant—and to the person who takes their place before too long—they do not have it within them to care.

They are halfway through reading about the ravings of an esteemed writer of Prophet Prose—some phenomenon Simone never understood but would have Nadia rambling for *hours*—when a shadow falls over them. When they look up, a figure with skin like a sun-warmed beach and eyes as dark as an inkwell stares down at them. Their down-turned nose crinkles as they lock eyes.

"You aren't an Enchanter, so I suppose it is safe to assume you are the one who requested assistance?"

Simone replaces the book on the table at their side with a nod.

"As I assumed. A pleasure to make your acquaintance. I am Pro-fessor Erestia Altonis."

Their skin prickles. Of all of Voterique's faculty, Professor Altonis is one of the higher-ranking members. Even Simone, who doesn't care much for Enchanting or the intricacies surrounding it, knows this much. And, if her penetrating stare and the scars across her hands and chest are anything to go off of, she is not a woman to be trifled with, let alone disturb.

All at once, Simone's prospects of getting an answer sour. With someone as esteemed as her attending to them, it's only a matter of time before the rest of the faculty knows of their goals. Still, they swallow their trepidation. They've come this far, right?

"Pleased to meet you," they say before standing.

Professor Altonis takes them in again with a sniff before spinning on her heel. Without a word, she stalks for the staircase, footfalls echoing with every step. Simone lingers for a heartbeat, uncertain if she's expecting them to follow. A sharp glance in their direction and the jerk of her chin is enough to convince them to fall in step at her side.

They don't speak further as she leads them up the stairs and down a series of hallways, each turn as disorienting as the last. Portraits line the walls. They remind Simone of the dormitories, how prominent Casters frame each hallway in an attempt to inspire. A lot of the faces Simone recognizes from their brief trip to Etienne's tower, though the portraits in the Society are more severe. They scan the hall for a portrait of Professor Altonis, but they're moving too quickly to see for certain.

Before long, they stop before a plain wooden door, an equally-plain nameplate hanging from the top. Professor Altonis produces a key and the door opens with a soft click. With a touch of a magicite lamp, the office beyond flairs to life and the small wooden desk inside gains a purplish hue. A tank sits atop the windowsill. Inside, a snake wriggles back and forth, stomach pressed to the glass. Posters of several enlarged sigils in various states of construction line the wall, all of them

Enchantment in nature based on the swirled lines and arrows. Of the realms of Casting, the language of Enchantment is the most fluid in construction.

The door shuts with the flick of her finger. "Please have a seat," she says as she rounds her desk and drops into a plain chair.

Simone complies with a final, wary glance around the room. The chair they settle into groans at the added weight.

"Now, I have been told you suspect a friend of yours has been suffering from arcane amnesia?"

"Correct."

Professor Altonis reaches for a pen and uncaps it. As she lowers it into an inkwell to fill, she says, "And why would you suspect such a thing?"

"He's been acting strangely lately."

She waits, pen at the ready, eyebrows quirked like she's expecting something more.

"A-And, the other day, when I tried to speak to him, it took him a while to remember who I was."

She writes this down on a spare scrap of paper and pauses once more. When Simone doesn't continue, she says, "And is there anything else?"

They swallow down their rising irritation. Her voice carries a Vahnic lilt to it—and likely, her matter of overspeaking is related to her origins. Worse, her accent reminds them of Nadia. *Don't think about her.* Their fists clench tight.

"He went on a trip recently, and before he left, he was fine." As they speak, they scrape the recesses of their memory for the lie they had told the attendant. It would be all the stranger if they couldn't keep their story in order. "And then, when he came back..."

Professor Altonis recaps her pen with a flourish. "Your capelet suggests to me you are a second-year Abjuror. Is that correct?"

They nod.

"Furthermore, you are unfamiliar with the general philosophy behind Enchantment?"

Jaw set, they nod again. Their knowledge of most of the realms is relegated to a Casting 101 course they had taken in undergrad.

"And did you not take a class regarding Casting theory in your preliminary schooling?"

She speaks slowly now, accent thickening. *Patience,* Simone urges themself yet again as a near-blinding wave of rage crests within them. *It would do little good to lose your calm here.*

They bite the inside of their cheek hard enough to taste blood. "Yes," they say at last. "I did."

Professor Altonis's frown deepens. "So then, you are familiar with a certain adage, I should think. How do you Mertish say it? Mundane over magical?"

Their nails bury deep into their palms. Still, the only trace of anger they allow to show is the flair of their nostrils. "That is correct, Professor."

"With this in mind, *have* you made every attempt to disqualify the mundanities?"

If I had assumed the cause was mundane, he would've gone back to the medical ward. "I believe so."

Professor Altonis purses her lips, taking them in with the slow drag of her gaze. "And yet, you still suspect arcane amnesia."

Simone's grasp on their calm is fraying. Each word they think of to say is more foul than the last. At last, in defeated silence, they nod a third time.

"I see." Professor Altonis rises from her desk, turning to the tank on the windowsill. Rubbing a nail against the glass, right over where the writhing snake's stomach is, she says, "As much as I would love to lend Society resources towards your cause, I remain unconvinced."

The world drops out from beneath them. *No...*

"What I would advise you do is speak to the medical ward. Or, perhaps speak to one of the Divination professors. It is certain your friend has experienced a traumatic event, either in the physical or psychological sense. Asking the Society to go digging through his brain could cause more harm, however, and I do not have the patience to sit through a malpractice hearing if it can be avoided."

All of this. All of this was for nothing.

"But perhaps I am wrong. If you can have your friend provide some documentation which would suggest the presence of arcane amnesia, we would be willing to assist you. Until then, I would like to have all possibilities examined."

A scream bubbles in the back of their throat, but they force it down. *Wait until you are alone. Throwing a fit will not behoove you now.*

Professor Altonis's head tilts as she regards them. "Do you have nothing to say?"

"Thank you for your time." They stand quick enough the chair rattles in place, but they stop it before it can fall over.

They don't cry. Not yet. Not as the first tendrils of rage wrap themselves tight within Simone's ribcage. Not as they march themself back towards the exit, though it takes them several false turns. Not as they pass by a portrait of Professor Erestia Altonis's portrait at last. Their fingers twitch at their sides. How they long to jam the pointed tip of a pen into the canvas, to see the professor's visage torn from end to end.

But they don't. They can't. And so they continue walking.

The maze of hallways constricts tighter around them, as suffocating as the ball of words and frustration lodged in the back of their throat. Simone's skin itches with the fury of an anthill disturbed. As they round another dead-end corner, they let out a gargled growl and slip into the first door that isn't locked.

Beyond, the room is so quiet the silence pulses, womb-like. Several shuddering breaths hiss between their clenched teeth. Thick carpet cradles them as they slump to the floor.

It takes a long while for their skin to cease crawling.

When they're able to get their scattered thoughts back into order, they creep back into the hallway and scan it for a hint of familiarity. They don't know what they're seeking, if they're being honest with themself. Enchantment has never been their forte, let alone something in their realm of interest, so they've never seen the need to pay it more attention than necessary. Regardless, if the Professor won't give them any answers...

As they read each door plate, they strain to check for people on the other side before they gently test each knob. Most of the doors are locked, they find, but a couple open into blank rooms with naught but a single chair and some sort of medical apparatus. These rooms Simone exits with a shiver and their lip between their teeth.

At last, they find a door labeled Sigil Study. Their first attempt to open the door is thwarted by it being locked, but the sigil they've commissioned is more than capable of granting them entry. With a faint puff of ozone and a flash of light, the door clicks and parts under Simone's guiding hand.

The room beyond is so dark they can't see further than the tip of their nose, even with light from the hallway bleeding through. They slip into the dizzying void, fumbling through their pockets for a chunk of magicite to light their path as the door clicks shut behind them, but the light it provides makes a minimal dent.

A cloaking of some sort, then.

The scent of ozone is strong enough now it makes Simone's stomach clench. Each step further into the room is like wading through sand. Their head aches with the exertion, but they press on until they catch the sharp corner of a filing cabinet with their shin. A curse hisses through their teeth as they stoop down.

The top drawer opens with a muted rattle. Inside, a modest stack of slim books gleam in the subdued light. Clutching their magicite, Simone flicks through the pages of the topmost book. It's a collection of sigils, a pristine copy of a former Enchantment student's graduation spelltome. Each page has been painstakingly annotated with the intent behind the design. Amicability spells, spells for sleep aids, sigils capable of creating bravery charms...

Nose wrinkling with disappointment, Simone closes this book and moves to the next. This one, too, offers nothing of use. Same with the next book.

As at last they think to give up this endeavor, the book at the bottom of the stack catches their eye. Plainer than all the rest, Simone almost skips over it entirely, but it calls to them as they make to close the drawer. After a beat to listen for activity in the hallway, they unearth the tome from the bottom of the stack and riffle through. There's fewer annotations in this tome, and Simone's limited understanding of Enchanting makes finding sigils of import a difficulty. What sigils are titled serve little use to them.

The last page evades them until they're ready to snap the book shut. Then it unsticks itself from the page before it and flops against the back cover. Simone catches one word: Memory.

With a start, they yank the page free and shove it into their satchel, trying and failing not to let the first inklings of hope take purchase in their breast. Even if they can't make sense of it, perhaps Etienne can.

EIGHTEEN

Nadia DuPont || Before

Simone doesn't visit. They don't even call. Nadia finds herself by the phone more often than not, praying for the telltale ring. And yet, day after day, it never comes.

She wishes she had it in her to be angry at their dismissiveness. Anything would be better than the soul-crushing despair gripping tightly to her throat. A dozen excuses float through her subconscious, and on especially foul days she allows herself to entertain them. Simone decided she wasn't worth chasing. They weren't strong enough to handle this final antic of hers.

On and on the excuses go, nipping at Nadia's thoughts, but they each ring hollow. Of course they would be done with her foolishness. Of course Nadia is not worth pursuing. Especially not now, bundled up tight in her bedsheets.

In the days since the breakup, she's formed a cocoon of sorts. If not for the truancy notices piled up on her nightstand, she wouldn't bother leaving her apartment at all. And so she wallows in the nest she's made, emerging only to attend classes and come right back home.

How pathetic, she tells herself when she puts herself to bed for the weekend. *As if you could have deserved anything better.*

It's the last thing she thinks before she closes her eyes.

***

"You're moping."

Nadia unpeels one crusted eye and peeks out from within the bundle of blankets. Watery blue light streams in through the hole she's formed for breathing. The warmth of Dio on her ankles comes to her next, light enough pain doesn't register yet.

A throat clears from across the room. The clicking of heels draws closer.

"How did I know I would find you here?" Etienne asks. His weight settles next to her, forming a dip in the mattress.

Her other eye opens to join the first. Through the gap in the bedding, she sees the ends of Etienne's brown hair. It's gotten longer since she last saw him. When *did* she last see him?

"I know you're awake, Nadia. We've shared a bed long enough; I know what your snores sound like."

With a grunt, Nadia nudges Dio off of her. Otherwise, she doesn't speak.

"I won't leave just because you ignore me."

Threads of pain weave themselves across her now-upright hip when she rolls over. Jaw clenched, she tries to find a more comfortable position. "Go away."

Etienne scooches closer despite her groaning. The desire to kick him crosses her mind, but the spare energy she's mustered flees the instant she thinks to use it. Instead, she remains stiff against him.

"You know, I never thought you'd be one to be knocked down by a breakup."

She sniffles. "What are you talking about?"

"Oh, come on," he says with a scoff. "Both you and... Well, you were both tight-lipped all week, by the sounds of it. And Chantal told me she heard it from the source. And since you haven't even seen *me* all week, well."

Sighing, Nadia throws the blanket off of her. A cold gust runs over her in an instant. She wants to sink back into the void the nest she's built has brought her, but she knows Etienne won't allow such pathetic measures.

"I don't think I even took breaking up with Aleksi this harshly."

Though her hip continues to ache, she curls in tighter to herself. "Do you think telling me that is helping?"

His hand settles on her thigh. "If you wanted someone to coddle you, I know you could send me away and call someone else."

Nadia's jaw sets. "You think you know what I need?"

"I did, once."

"And now?"

She knows she's being callous, but she can't help herself. Since she's awoken, irritation has scratched at her like stray grains of sand. Each word from Etienne worsens the sensation. Her skin tingles. What does he know about how she feels? Why should he even care?

"You're angry," Etienne says. "You're wounded. I understand. Driving the world away won't solve anything, though. Relationships end. Life continues. Just because Simone broke things off—"

At once, Nadia is upright. So, Simone chose to save face instead of tell the truth. Fighting the waves of nausea threatening to drag her back down, she spits out, "I was the one to leave them."

Etienne's eyes widen, just enough to notice. "What?"

She doesn't meet his gaze.

"You…Why did you do that?" Etienne's brows pull tightly together, like he's examining a particularly intricate puzzle. He reminds her so much in this moment of Simone, and the thought is enough to steal the breath from her lungs. Her throat constricts tighter.

Another flash of her monstrous self comes to mind. She squeezes her eyes shut against the image, but another, more sobering thought crops up from the back of her mind. *If Simone was in danger, Etienne surely is as well.*

"You should go," she croaks before she can stop herself.

"Don't be ridiculous."

She shoves him as hard as she dares, the ghastly vision granting her strength. "Get out."

One of his pencil-thin brows arches. "Not when you're in such a state." Then, softer, "…Don't close yourself off from me."

Her jaw clenches so tight it ticks. Anger, viscous and black, bubbles within her. "As if you haven't done the same?" He opens his mouth to speak, but she surges forward. "For weeks, you've scorned me and pouted and thrown your childish fits because you can't stand not being the center of attention for *once* in your fucking life!"

He reels back as if she's slapped him. She almost wishes she had.

"I—I'm sorry," he says at last.

"Don't give me that. You're just saying it because you know, deep down, I'm all you have."

Red fills his face in one fell wave. "Th-That's not—"

"Isn't it?" *Stop this,* some small part of her urges. *Don't shove him away, too.* But she ignores it for the burning indignation consuming her. "You follow me around like a lost dog all the damn time. Don't you know how annoying it can be, trying to placate you?"

He opens his mouth again and Nadia tenses. They've fought before, at times hurling insults like knives. Now, she stiffens in preparation for his retort. All the while, the smaller part of her screams at her to stop.

Instead of speaking, Etienne shakes his head and rises. Before she can challenge him—or apologize, some small part of her argues—he leaves the room.

The only thing you know how to do is to destroy. A sentence she has told herself every waking moment she's had since her conversation with Simone. True or not, it's been a useful enough tool in her self-pitying arsenal. Now, as she watches Etienne's retreating shadow, the thought echoes in her ears, overtaking everything else.

***

And yet, when she wakes up, Etienne is perched on her mattress, flipping through the pages of an Enchanting textbook. Relief is the first tangible emotion unfurling within her, followed by confusion. Why would he have stayed?

As if sensing her stirring, he bends the corner of the page he's reading and sets the book in his lap. "You know, you can be a real bitch sometimes."

The blanket encases her. He's tucked her back into bed? Flashes of their last conversation drift to the forefront of her mind and, all at once, the meaning of Etienne's words dawn on her.

The goal was to get him to leave, not to tell the truth.

She winces at this voice within her thoughts, her and yet not her at the same time.

Etienne shakes his head with a heavy sigh, one weighted with a tangle of unspoken thoughts. She's heard this sound from him before, simultaneously frustration and resignation. And to think, she was the one to do this to him...

She takes his hand, praying he doesn't snatch it back. "Etienne."

He doesn't look up. The unspoken declination takes the breath from her. Still, she must persist.

"Etienne, I'm sorry."

Nothing. No twitch of his eye, no move to shrug away from her. His gaze remains locked on the book in his lap, like it's the most interesting thing to him in this moment.

"You—You're angry," Nadia continues, faltering. This, at least, earns her the faintest shrug. "I said some... awful things to you before."

"Do you really think that of me?"

She flinches. "What?"

"That I am some lost dog following you around. An inconvenience. Is this what you think of me, truly? Of our friendship?"

"Of course not." She grips his hand until both their knuckles pale. "I—"

Now, finally, he looks up. His gaze is all fractured glass, a kaleidoscope of pain. Her own heart is fit to shatter.

"Oh, Etienne..."

With this, he snatches his hand back, rips off his glasses, and buries his face. Thick, choked sobs tremble through him. Nadia represses the urge to wrap herself around him, to shove him away, to have him scream all the terrible things she said back at her. And yet, none of them are enough punishment.

You deserve this. All of it, and worse.

She picks up his glasses first and sets them aside. Black frames hug two circular lenses, each relatively unmarred save the smudges of his fingers. *Since when has he worn these?* The frames she remembers were a tortoiseshell pattern, weren't they?

All at once, the truth in its terrible entirety sinks into her. A schism has formed between them, vast and irreparable.

As Etienne continues to shudder, she envelopes him. The way he stiffens against her is enough to set her jaw, but she doesn't let go. Not when he falls into her lap, still sobbing. Not when he stretches the front of her shirt with the force of his despair. His pain carves its way into the deepest recesses within her.

Before long, she's crying, too, clutching him to her like the moment she lets go, he will disappear.

***

Etienne doesn't stay for long after he finally calms down. Slinging his bag over his shoulder, he mutters something non-committal and wipes the last of the tears from his eyes. Then, louder, he says, "See you around."

Nadia doesn't stop him in his hasty retreat, no matter how badly she yearns to. Instead, as the door slams shut behind him, she sprints for the bathroom. Her knees crack against the tiles as she vomits—dry heaves, really—into the yawning depths beyond.

When she comes up for air, the absurdity of it all is enough to make laughter bubble up in the back of her throat. Her body rattles with manic energy, like she's channeled an electric Evocation through her.

Keep it together. Even as the thought crosses her mind, a sardonic chuckle slips through her teeth, followed by a wave of bile. As sweat breaks out across her brow, she rests against the porcelain. An uneasy quiet settles over Nadia's apartment.

She doesn't know how long she sits there, legs akimbo as she tries to recollect herself. Only how badly her body aches when she drags herself to her feet once again.

The image in the mirror is a woman crazed, all unruly hair and flushed cheeks. "How close we came to ruining everything," it tells her with a wide-eyed stare.

"It's over with," Nadia snarls under her breath.

She's halfway to calm again when a flash of black catches her eye. She's imagining it, she tells herself, even as she gives her reflection another look-over.

There, against her collarbone. The faintest touch whites her vision with pain, but she finally gets the collar of her shirt pulled away enough to inspect it better. A tangle of black veins surge across her chest, starting from the throbbing artery in her neck and spreading to the peaks of both breasts.

Nadia skitters away from the mirror, colliding with the back wall hard enough to knock the breath from her lungs.

You're a monster. She takes a shallow inhale and finds her face in the mirror, looking just as frantic as she feels. For a second, her jaw hangs lopsided, skin sagging, but when she blinks, the image is gone again.

When she again tugs at her collar, the black veins have disappeared. She trails a finger over where she knew them to be, but the pain has subsided as well. All of it, gone, as if it had never happened.

NINETEEN

Simone Allard || After

The sigils on the page before them are a dizzying mess of curve and angle. Small, near-illegible annotations frame each one. *Memory recollection?* suggests one. *A means of breaking locks on the mind*, says another. They spend the rest of the evening pouring over the notes they've been handed, brain aching with the strain required to make sense of it all.

Dozens of sigils, each more complex than the last. It's enough to make their head spin. And, they realize with an ever-deepening frown, who is to say what they've created from the notes they have is even correct?

By the time they retire for the night, they're certain they're no closer to solving the matter of Etienne's mind than they were when the day began. The moment they close their eyes, half-formed sigils swarm their thoughts, plaguing them even in the realm of sleep. And yet, when they stretch an astral arm out to grasp them, the images slip through their fingers like smoke.

Still, the sigils remain when they wake the next morning, stuck to their eyelids like tattoos. They rub the images away with the crust on their eyes. A strange-shaped lump fills the back of their throat, accompanied by a heavy-set lurching of their stomach.

And then, the instant they sit up, bile. They rush for the bathroom, knees cracking on the tiles as their stomach boils over. Brackish liquid and the remains of last night's dinner spill from them in waves. Over and over again, they cling to the rim as they retch.

Finally, sweat-soaked and shivering, they still. They hug the porcelain, limbs stiff. It takes the remaining shreds of their energy to peel themself away. Even now, certain as they are of their stomach being empty, it continues to spasm.

Did I eat something foul? They scrape through their memories of the day before, all of it obscured by a dense fog. What they can gather doesn't match the maelstrom swirling in their gut. Thinking on it too hard sets their temples throbbing, though. Before long, they give up any hope of investigation.

Simone's legs threaten to buckle underneath them when they stand. Leaning hard against the toilet, they flounder for the lever, pausing when they finally catch it. Though the contents of their stomach was mostly water and acid, indistinguishable chunks of last night's dinner bob about. And yet, streams of gray thread through it all.

Funny. I can't remember eating anything that color.

With a final shiver of disgust, Simone gathers enough strength to push the lever and flush the evidence of their sickness away.

A distinct discomfort makes a home of their bones. Each step they take is accompanied by creaking. The sound is enough to set their teeth clenching. They're only in their second decade. Surely, they should have had more time before their body buckled on them?

Still, as sore and as pale as they are today, they do not dare stay home. Not with Alienor's threat looming over them.

They mull over her words as they work their capelet around their shoulders. *Every step you take out of line is being recorded.* She couldn't have been serious, could she? And yet, it would make sense if she was. Between the faculty cornering them shortly after Etienne's disappearance, to the strange way he was treated when he woke up...

Etienne. The moment their mind shifts to him, sigils flash behind their eyes. Their fingers tangle in their capelet clasps. Teeth clenched, they clear their thoughts with a deep breath and re-secure their capelet. The moment the clasps click, their brain resumes its harried sprint.

Of course, there's the matter of them being sick, too. Yet another puzzle they cannot hope to untangle. *A fluke*, they try to tell themself as they search their apartment for appropriate shoes. *And nothing more. The stress and the lack of sleep is catching up with me is all.* No matter how many times they repeat this mantra, however, an undercurrent of doubt remains.

The last thing to gather before they leave are the fresh Enchantment notes they've happened upon. They upturn most of the apartment in their search, chest growing uncomfortably tight the longer their search takes. Despite themself, a dark cloud of a thought brews to life in their mind. Could someone have come in and taken them?

The first bells are ringing by the time they've located the notes. Dio has made a makeshift nest of the pages, white fur spotted with gray from the uncured ink. Simone clucks their tongue at the discovery, mind swirling too viciously to be truly upset. After a cursory glance to ensure the runes aren't smeared—they are, but not enough to be illegible—Simone shoves them into their satchel and rushes out the door.

***

Simone's harried arrival to their Intro to Glyph Design class earns them a raised eyebrow from fellow Casters and Professor Darzi alike. They slump into the first available seat they spot, each eye on them like a knife in their side. From his podium, Professor Darzi jots their presence down on his ledger with the wry twist of his mouth. The silent admonishment is enough to make them want to wither and die on the spot.

As their gaze glues itself to Professor Darzi's veined knuckles, a sickly thought rears its poxed head: How could they be so careless? In all of their years of schooling, Simone has never been late. Sure, on more than one occasion they've cut it close—and an ailment or two has meant missing a day of classes all together—but they've still maintained a reputation for being in the room before the bell rang.

And now, a true dark mark on their record. What will their enbei think?

The thought looms over their shoulder for the rest of the class. Every time Professor Darzi meets their gaze, they wrench it away again. Before long, the shame is all-encompassing, tearing at their lungs with iron claws.

It's all they can do to flee the room when the final bell rings.

And then, at the threshold, "Mx. Allard?"

They freeze in place, breath fluttering. Professor Darzi doesn't say anything further as the other Casters of their class shove past them on their way towards whatever lesson is next, but Simone knows what he wants all the same. They watch their peers pass with something like envy. How lucky they are to be free of a lecture.

When the last student has left, Professor Darzi approaches. This close, the overwhelming wave of his cologne washes over them, cedar and musk and bergamot. It's enough to make their throat ache with nausea. A thousand questions flare to life and die on the tip of their tongue.

"Mx. Allard, something is bothering you."

They stiffen at the suggestion. Perhaps they've been more rash as of late—something Alienor's last conversation with them cemented. Still, they thought they'd been more reserved about their feelings than this.

Or, more likely, perhaps recent circumstances have frayed their mind enough that their inhibitions have shattered. The possibility makes their jaw set.

"Mx. Allard?"

How to toe the line? Alienor's warning again rears its head. What can they say that will allow them a way out of this conversation?

So close. Their jaw clenches harder. *So painfully fucking close.*

They spin on their heel to face him, anger sparking at the concerned crease of his forehead. It must be a facade, a way to get more information from them. Still, a part of them—one which refuses to go silent no matter how badly they will it—longs to divulge him *something.* They owe him this much, no matter how tangled their circumstances have become.

The instant the words form on their tongue, Simone dissolves into heaving sobs instead.

Professor Darzi's eyes widen. With a hand outstretched, he takes a half-step closer to them. "H-Hey, now."

Even this short revelation eases some of the weight threatening to crush them. Hiccuping, Simone wipes their face and rushes to recollect themself. "I'm sorry," they say after a beat. "Sorry. I've just..."

A warm hand claps their shoulder, the touch restrained despite the comforting intent behind it. Professor Darzi looks at them like they're a problem he's been required to solve but doesn't want to touch. All the better, they think. So long as he allows them to slink away at the end of this discussion, he can feel however he wishes.

"I've just been having a rough time is all," they say. "With…"

They cannot make themself say Etienne's name. Their tongue warps around the letters and tangles. *Etienne.* Three syllables, and yet an impossible spell to conjure. And then, beyond him, thoughts of Professor Chapeau. "With everything," they settle for at last. "It's all so terrifying and awful."

Professor Darzi withdraws his hand. "I see." Still, he doesn't step away. "Have you allowed yourself any time to decompress?"

They give their head a hard shake. *I can't stop now, though. There's no telling how long I have left to solve this ephemeral puzzle.*

He sighs. The back of his hand glows yellow. Behind them, two chairs screech against the floor and slide towards them. Simone sinks into one of them.

The moment Professor Darzi sits down, he folds his arms across his thick chest. "Mx. Allard, are you familiar with the Candle Theory?"

Of course they are. Every professor in their preliminary education had drilled Candle Theory into their head. People—and Casters especially—are not unlike candles, so the theory goes. Burning them from both ends reduces them faster. And, much like candles, people only have so much of themselves to offer before they are depleted.

Still, it makes Simone scoff. Candles cannot be rebuilt time and time again. People can. It's illustrative, perhaps, but devoid of real use all the same.

Professor Darzi sighs again. "The Candle Theory suggests—"

"I understand the theory, and its implications." Chewing on their lip, Simone crosses their legs.

"Well, has it occurred to you that you're running low on wax?"

Blood soaks their tongue. They've bitten their lip too hard. "There's only weeks left before the end of the semester. I can prioritize relaxing then."

At this, Professor Darzi's frown deepens. "And you believe you will still be able to sustain yourself?"

"I have to, don't I?"

His brows furrow. Deep, canyon-like wrinkles break out along his forehead. Professor Darzi takes a breath, mouth open to speak, but must reconsider his words. Still wearing that same worried frown, he eventually says, "Such a mindset is not conducive to a healthy learning environment, Mx. Allard."

"Perhaps not." The confession surprises them. Hoping the professor doesn't notice the surprise evident in their face, they quickly add, "But it is what will get me through these remaining weeks, for better or for worse."

"And after?"

Simone's gaze drops to their wiggling foot. For months, they've allowed themself the escape Voterique provided them. It's easy, they think, to forget about the outside world when in such an environment. Professor Darzi's words shatter the fragile illusion. What *were* they planning to do in the interim between their second and third years? An abundance of research for their thesis, no doubt. Was there truly nothing else?

"Ahh..." Professor Darzi's palm settles on their knee this time, lingering long enough for the gesture to be felt before pulling back again. "But, of course, you have another year to ponder it, hmm?"

It takes every shred of energy they have to sculpt their face into a neutral mask. Beneath it, all-consuming terror begins to set in.

"Regardless, Mx. Allard, there are resources available to you, should you have the mind to look. Meanwhile, I would advise you to maintain diligence in your academic affairs."

For the first time in a long while, Simone cannot disguise their confusion.

Professor Darzi offers a thin smile. "A few weeks left before the end of the semester. You reminded me of such yourself. Don't allow yourself to get too lax now, when you're so close to the end."

With this, he gives their knee another soft pat before standing. They remain weighted in their seat as he moves around the room. Chairs shuffle around under his careful guidance. The scrape of an eraser against the blackboard fills the silence. Then, when they think he's finished, he clears his throat.

"I... I will not track your tardiness on your record. Not this time."

Their breath catches. "Thank—"

"*This* time," he says again, the words like the strike of a rod. How odd for them to be on the verbal receiving end, for once.

"O-Of course." They rush to their feet, jolts of pain coursing through their knees. "It will not happen again."

"See that it does not." Then, after a leaden pause, "You are dismissed."

***

Their conversation with Professor Darzi lingers in the back of their mind for a while. They turn it over, examining it from one angle and then another, repeating the motion until the incomprehensible shape brands itself. And then, when the last bell of the day rings out across the campus, they tuck the discussion away and abandon thoughts of it for good. It's nothing compared to the shadow looming over them.

There must be some trick to the sigils, some sort of pattern they aren't seeing. Even studying Etienne's notes has been of little use. True, Enchantment has never been a subject which interested them, but they can't help the frustration itching them as they study their notes for the umpteenth time.

But they're unable to stop themself. With their current trajectory, some sort of reckoning awaits them at the end of their path. The curdling in their gut tells them so. And yet, their need for an answer drags them forward all the same.

Whatever awaits them at the end of this road, they will see it through to the end.

The snap of the banners on the towers catches their attention, taking them back to their first days on the Voterique campus. Oh, how excited they had been to enter a college as prestigious as this, how delighted they had been after the first four years to acquire their Casting license. How the rainbow of banners and capelets had caught their eye as they chose a specialization after. Blue for Abjuration, purple for Divination, black for Necromancy, yellow for Transmutation, orange for Conjuration, grey for Illusion, red for Evocation, and...

Green. The banners of the Enchantment tower strike at the wind like an agitated snake. Returned to the present, Simone eyes the fabric with their lip between their teeth. They can't make sense of the sigils they have, but perhaps—

On a whim, they turn on their heel and strive for the front doors.

Alienor's warning prickles their ears. *Let go of this hollow pursuit. Lower your head and strive for the end of your second year with no further issue.* And now, feet away from Etienne's apartment, they've almost a mind to heed her. Before Nadia, they had resigned themself to this exactly, to keeping their head down and mastering their thesis, regardless of the cost to their social status or health.

At this rate, they've risked everything as it is. Even if they turn away now, they're being watched. It is a matter of time before the faculty catches onto their litany of transgressions—if they haven't already. May as well add one more to the list.

Once, twice, three times they bang their fist against the door, hard enough they're surprised they don't leave an imprint. Their legs wobble beneath them, fawn-like. The hall around them tilts on its axis, one soft breath away from falling apart. In the stillness, they again debate if it would be better to flee, to pretend they were never here.

But then Etienne's door opens and the wobbling world comes to a halt.

He cocks his head at the sight of them, knuckles white around the doorframe. "You again," he says. "I thought I told you not to come back here."

Though his tone is cutting, Simone notes the way he pales under their scrutiny. So their last interaction had some impact, after all. Still, as they open their mouth to speak, nothing emerges. Their hands lock at their sides.

"Didn't you hear me last time?" His eyes narrow to slits. "Do I need to call for the faculty?"

They shove the papers towards him with a grunt. "We have unfinished business."

He stumbles back half a step, just enough to get him back over his threshold. At once, Simone follows them into the space beyond.

TWENTY

Nadia DuPont || Before

"I'm so glad you could join us today, Nadia."

A wane smile tugs at the corners of her mouth. She shifts in her seat, grimacing at the way the wood makes the backs of her thighs numb. No amount of bunching her skirt beneath her eases the ache, but it's enough of a task to consume her. That is, until Doctor Aiza clears her throat.

"Nadia?"

She stills, planting her hands under her rear. This will have to do. Settled, Nadia's gaze flicks from Doctor Aiza to the man sitting next to her. Fresh leather patches cover the points of his elbows. His jawline is sharp enough to chip glass. He adjusts his glasses, stopping at once when he notices her appraising him.

"Who is this?" Nadia asks, swinging her legs. She's not quite tall enough for her feet to touch the floor. She can't remember the last time her circumstances have made her feel so childish.

Doctor Aiza's rapid blinks betray her surprise. Then, clipboard held close to her chest, "This is Professor Darzi."

Nadia adjusts her position once again. Simone has mentioned him before, she thinks. "I thought your specialty was Glyph design," she says. For once, the scorn dripping from her voice is unintentional.

Professor Darzi's head tilts. "I-It is," he replies, tugging at his lavender scarf. It contrasts well with his skin, as warm and wrinkled as oak bark. And his *voice*. Etienne's type of man, for certain.

Still, his presence is an unwanted one, made more unwanted by his lack of justification. Baring her teeth, Nadia says, "Then why are you here?"

"Miss DuPont..."

Professor Darzi holds up a hand, stopping them both. "It is," he says again. "However, my expertise lies also in diplomatic affairs. Negotiations. Counseling. Various items of that nature."

Doctor Aiza clears her throat again. "He is here as a formality and nothing more. The true focus is on *you*, Nadia." With this, she lowers her clipboard, pen at the ready. "It has been five months since your official diagnosis. How have you been feeling? Any new developments?"

Nadia weighs the question with a long pause. Without prompting, the vicious image of herself days before comes to mind, but she squashes it back down. The coils of unease in her gut tell her such information is best left unsaid.

But then, what *can* she say? *Why yes, doctor. Every day gets harder than the last. I can no longer focus on my studies because I am too busy debating which method of ending my life would be the quickest. Tell me, would it be better to drain myself of blood, or should I pitch myself off the roof of the library?*

"Nadia?"

She comes back to with a shiver, the dark thoughts sloughing from her like slime. "Sorry," she says after a pause. "I was thinking."

Doctor Aiza notes this with a frown.

Fuck this. Nadia hugs herself tight, breath quickening. Panic swarms the edges of her mind, poised to strike. *I've chased Simone away. Now I'm here. What is keeping me here anymore?*

And yet, as the truth steels itself to emerge, a lie jumps out instead.

"Aches and pains, mostly," she says, and at once the joints in her fingers swell to attention. She flexes each finger until it pops, pretending she doesn't notice the way both faculty members straighten in response.

"Any worsening symptoms? Mobility issues? Trouble concentrating?"

The nameless voice from her brief hallucination whispers to her from the back of her mind. This, too, she shoves away. "Some, I suppose."

"How about changes in behavior?" Doctor Aiza pauses, gaze flicking from Nadia to Professor Darzi and back again. She holds her pen aloft, ready to record anything, and it's enough to make Nadia's stomach churn. "Increased aggression?" she continues. "Suicidal tendencies? Impending senses of doom?"

Nadia represses a snort. *Every waking moment of my day.* "No."

This too, she writes down. Then, assessing her collection of notes with knitted brows, Doctor Aiza balances her chin in her propped-up hands, swaying a bit with the effort. "I must admit confusion."

Nadia sits up straighter, willing herself to remain stone-faced. "About?"

"It has been five months, and yet you're saying you've experienced no major changes since we last spoke. Sanguina Malefica is not normally such a... kind disease. A lesser physician might find your progression confusing."

As she shrugs, thoughts of her mother flare to life. She'd been healthy one day, dead and gone four months later. "What you've prescribed me has been useful."

"Perhaps." Even as she speaks, Doctor Aiza chews on her thumbnail. Then, blushing, she stops herself again. "Still," she continues, but whatever thought she has, she does not complete it.

Professor Darzi regards the doctor for a long moment before leaning forward, hands balanced on his knees. Nadia steels herself the instant his greying beard twitches.

"The road one must take when confronting difficult circumstances can be... arduous."

At once, Nadia represses the urge to roll her eyes. Barely.

"That road comes with its own set of steps, too. Denial being the first—"

"I'm not in denial."

"—which gives way to anger."

"Nor am I angry."

Professor Darzi holds up both hands, as if by virtue of the display, he can avert her temper. The gesture makes her blood boil all the greater.

"The point that I wish to get at, Ms. DuPont, is that the first option one takes in a situation like yours, statistically, is avoidance."

She clenches her jaw until it aches, saying nothing. All the while, Doctor Aiza continues to write.

"Not that I aim to accuse you of anything, of course," Professor Darzi says. "However, is it at all possible you are underplaying your developments? A mistruth here or there in the hopes of prolonging the inevitable?"

The world fades to a dull static. Nadia's pulse ticks, fast enough to make her dizzy. The ringing in her ears grows, grows, grows, until it is an all-consuming haze...

...And then, with a shuddering breath, it clears once more.

"Perhaps I should be blunt," she says, teeth warping around the words. Her nails dig into the meat of her palms, but she uses the pain to stabilize herself. With a glance to Doctor Aiza's clipboard and Professor Darzi's irritating brow-furrow, she continues, "I am well aware of the nature of my disease. I know how this will end, the same way I know how it consumed my mother. It saps, and it saps, and it *saps*, until all you are is a husk. My mother was a prisoner inside her own skin by the time she was taken from me. Do not think for the slimmest of seconds that I am playing at denial, or that I do not have a right to be angry, Professor. The truth of it all is more real to me than it will *ever* be to either of you."

With this, the static in her ears grows to a crescendo. The last of her resolve turns to grains of sand in her chest. Unable to meet either faculty member's gaze, she looks to the floor instead.

There isn't much to say afterwards. Professor Darzi and Doctor Aiza share uncomfortable glances as they prep her for a final test. "Just a sample," Doctor Aiza says as she stabs a needle into Nadia's forearm. "So we have a better timeline to gauge from."

And as her blood floods through the intravenous tube and into a vial, Nadia tries not to think about how it looks like mud. She doesn't need to look Doctor Aiza's way to know the results will not be promising.

She doesn't have much time left. But how much?

***

Despite her insistence to the contrary, an oddness within nags at her for the next couple of days. It starts as a feverish sweat on her brow, a strong uneasiness she can't quite shake. Each day she awakes, desperate to return to some semblance of normal—or, as normal as she can be with her state of being—and is instead sorely disappointed.

By the end of the week, it has blossomed into an outright sickness. Pain wracks her from every angle. After clawing her way through her classes, it takes everything within her to limp back up the Diviner tower steps and into the waiting arms of her bed once again. A fever hangs heavy on her brow, in sharp contrast to the chill running bones-deep within her. Before her head hits the pillow, her eyes are fluttering closed. Perhaps, some dwindling part of her hopes, she will fall asleep and never wake up. Wouldn't that be lovely?

To her partial dismay, she awakes again some time later, gaze swimming around the room. Orange beams of light penetrate the holes in her curtains, painting her in copper streaks.

"Nadia?"

The voice comes from someplace far off, so disorienting she could almost believe she hallucinated it. And she must have, because...

Simone's head appears around the doorway, long black-and-tan braids swaying around them. Nadia can't make out their expression in the low light, but her arm trembles when she reaches to activate the magicite lamp next to her. Slumping back down, she can only watch as they tiptoe themself into her bedroom proper.

"W-What..." Her voice comes out a croak, so she coughs and tries again. "What are you doing here?"

A thin beam of light falls across their face, illuminating the concerned crease of their brows. "I had to see you," they say. "The way we ended things... It didn't feel right."

With the last dredges of her strength, Nadia turns her head for the wall, suddenly aware of the warm sweat patch she's left against the pillow. A shudder of revulsion rolls through her.

"I don't know why you're wasting your time, Simone."

"Don't try to dismiss me. Not without giving me a chance first."

"I told you how this would end." Even this short a conversation sends the back of her throat to itching. She coughs again, the motion enough to make her whole body tense.

"You look like shit," Simone says, a heartbeat before their footsteps draw closer.

She doesn't have it in her to give them a cutting response. More conscious now, she's aware of the way her entire body shudders with chills, the way pain oscillates between each of her joints, highlighting spaces of her body she didn't realize existed. And, beneath it all, an undercurrent of longing, powerful enough to snatch the breath from her. Longing for Simone. Longing for the black ichor she's stashed in vials under her bed.

A cool hand brushes her brow, highlighting the sheen of sweat sticking to her like a second skin. "Is there some way I can help you?" Simone asks.

Leave me alone. She can't get the words past her lips, nor is she sure she wants to. A vigorous itching blooms to life under her skin. A soft, pathetic mewl escapes.

"I'll make you some tea," they say when she doesn't speak.

"Wait."

Her head flops the other way again. Simone has stopped in the doorway, brows still pulled together. Under her sickly gaze, they sway back and forth and tuck strands of braided hair over their shoulder.

"In... In the kitchen, in a cabinet over the sink..."

Pathetic. Unable to shove them away, unable to curb your habits. What good are you?

Nadia closes her eyes and hisses through her teeth. "I have medicine in the cabinet."

Simone cocks their head. After a pause to process her words, they bound for the kitchen. The gurgle of the faucet fills the quaint apartment space. Cups clink together, followed before too long by the scream of a kettle. Nadia listens to it all with half-closed eyes.

"Hey."

She reawakens to a fragrant cup of tea under her nose. Mint-flavored steam floods her senses, cold and refreshing. It revitalizes her enough to attempt to sit up—though after her attempt leaves her sprawled out, Simone rushes to her side.

"How long have you been like this?" they ask, face buried in the crook of her neck as they help her up. She tries not to think about how she likely reeks of sweat and illness, or how they in comparison smell as fresh as a summer's day.

"Some time," she grunts out before taking her cup. "Thank you."

The lack of instant bliss tells her it's not Serenity in her cup. Nadia takes a hesitant sip, then another. Despite herself, a subtle warmth unfurls itself within her.

"This is nice." Nadia settles her cup in her palms, relishing the warmth.

"I found the Serenity."

She doesn't speak, mouth suddenly dry. Her heartbeat skitters as she waits for their next words.

"That was what you were hoping for, wasn't it?"

She wants to dash their cups to the floor, wants to scream at them until her voice gives out, wants to shove her face into the pillows and sob until her eyes crust over with salt.

And yet, she does none of these things. Instead, she watches Simone's face, scanning for any twitch or crease which would betray how they feel.

They heave a sigh. "Is this how you want to live out the rest of your life, Nadia? However long you have left?"

She bites the inside of her cheek until she tastes blood. "I'm dying." With a bitter laugh, she takes another slow swallow of tea. "The faculty has given up on me. *I've* given up on me. Makes me wonder why you haven't."

Perhaps that is the true tragedy. Nadia is not worth the time Simone has devoted to her, and yet they keep trying. Why?

"I'm sure the faculty hasn't—"

"Oh, they've asked how I have been. After months of ignoring me, of course. They have the luxury of ruining my life and then continuing on with theirs. Does it matter to them if I waste my days in a stupor?"

"That's... That's not..."

Perhaps it is only the fact she has someone to talk to now, or perhaps it is having some semblance of sustenance in her. With the scraps of renewed vigor she has, she gives Simone a pointed look. "You cannot possibly be this naive."

Their cup settles in their lap with a clatter. Their knuckles pale around the ceramic. Too late, Nadia longs to cram the words back down her throat. Of the two of them, she's the naive one, isn't she?

Then, to her surprise, they laugh. A soft, sad noise, more exhale than sound.

"What is it like?" they ask in a broken whisper.

"What?"

Simone sets the saucer down on the bedside table, face scrubbed blank of emotion. Instead of responding, they chew on their lip until the skin is a raw, angry red. Then, when the silence is so thick Nadia thinks she'll choke on it, they say, "Serenity."

Now it's her turn to be taken aback. "You want to know?"

The blue beads on the ends of their braids clink together.

Her cup joins Simone's on the table. Sighing, she grips her blanket with both fists. Where to begin? "When I wake up, my body is on fire. It's like... It's like I go to war, every single day. A war against myself. And then I come home, I go to sleep, and I wake up the next morning right back on the battlefield.

"Some days, it's as though Serenity and its influence are the only reason I can function anymore."

Simone processes her words, face frustratingly blank. "There is more to it, though."

"Of course there is." Even as she speaks, the first tendrils of shame cling to her vocal chords. "It doesn't just *help*, Simone. It... It is the best feeling in the world."

"Mmm." Another pause. They're debating something. She can tell by the slightest pull of their eyebrows, the way a hesitant crinkle forms on their forehead. Perhaps they are realizing, finally, that they are better off abandoning her to her own devices.

"Show me."

The words echo through the apartment, louder and more powerful than the chiming of the campus clock tower. Nadia's grip on the blanket tightens. "You can't mean—"

"I do." Their confession seems to shock them, too, judging by the way their eyes widen. They take her hand in theirs, fingertips calloused and ink-smudged.

You really are a toxic influence, aren't you? If not for your entrance in their life, they would be much better off by now.

Nadia exhales, low and slow. Something about the determined edge in Simone's expression carves the nagging voice from her mind. "You're certain?" she asks.

Simone nods. "I am."

"Then there's only one thing left to do." She pulls her hand back. "You know where the vials are. Go grab one."

***

For all of Simone's bravado, it takes a long while before Nadia can convince them to leave her alone long enough to collect the vial. Longer still before they return, slim tube in their fist. By the time it's uncorked and they're pouring drops—"Just a couple," Nadia says before they get too overzealous—into their cups of tea, Nadia is salivating at the sight. An unconscious reaction, she tells herself as they pass her one of the cups. *Giving in to your urges*, her conscious goads.

At last, Simone corks the vial again and sets it aside. They stare into the depths of their cup for an eternity, vein in their neck throbbing.

"You don't have to do this," Nadia says, if only to fill the silence.

They don't raise from their bowed position. "I know."

"You're scared."

"I know."

And then, before she can say anything else, they throw the cup back and swallow the contents whole.

The change is instantaneous. Simone's pupils swell to the size of saucers. The coral flush in their cheeks turns to wintery grey. Blinking several times, they set the cup down. Nadia rushes to take it from them, lest they drop it in their newfound stupor.

"Woah." In the skirmish, the back of their hand brushes hers. Even sober, the sensation is enough to make her shiver. An unseen force envelopes her mind in the split second of contact. Then, when she pulls away, it's gone.

"What is this?" Simone's lips don't move, but their voice fills the space between them. With widened eyes, they take her in. All of her.

She should follow them down the ink-black rabbit hole. In the other forays she's had, she's often been the first person to drop, and the dive is the loneliest when there aren't other auras to bounce off of. And yet, she's entranced by the way Simone examines themself like a science experiment, twisting their hand back and forth, studying the gaps in their fingers.

"How does it feel?" she asks.

"Strange. Foreign. Kind of... good."

"And that isn't the best part yet."

The Serenity washes over her in rapid but gentle waves. One moment, the room is quiet and ordinary. The next, it buzzes with lights of indescribable color. Nadia's brain swells attempting to comprehend it. Brightest of all is the figure before her, so luminescent it hurts.

Simone.

"*Fuck*." The letters take shape as they leave Simone's mouth.

Without a second to consider, she takes their hand. "That isn't all."

Wind rushes through her ears. Their clasped hands form the epicenter of a vortex. Within seconds, she isn't fully sure where Simone ends and she begins. And with each passing second, the line between them grows thinner and thinner, until...

...Like two pieces of glass overlapping, they meld together and are one.

They blink. The sun shines down, bright enough to blind them. As they raise a hand to shield themself from the rays, they take stock of their surroundings. A wheatgrass field surrounds them, tendrils providing a far-off itch they can't seem to scratch. Then, as they settle, a young boy rushes by. They watch him as his too-loose sandals kick up clods of dirt, which sprays near enough they have to dodge out of the way.

"Nads," he says with a chuckle, running a hand through his swoop of dark brown hair. For a moment, their entire being ripples with confusion—Nadia? I'm not—but they settle when the boy holds out a small, wet frog. Its skin inflates between his fingers, the soft croak filling the silence.

"About time you caught it," they hear themself say, voice familiar and yet not. A fog drifts through their mind, softening the edges of the scene. When they look at the boy again, a thin mist obscures the details of his face. Then, with a breath, they force the scene back into focus.

"Nadia! Ines! Come inside for dinner!"

Ines releases the frog with a scowl. When his mouth opens, his words come as if from the end of a long tunnel, too faded to decipher.

In the blink of an eye, the scene is gone, leaving behind a blank world of grey. It wrinkles and warps, a puddle disturbed. When the image is clear once more, they stand over a clay jar, dusting their fingers over its smooth surface. A warm hand claps their shoulder.

"What age is this artifact from, Simone?"

Before they can answer, the scene changes again. They pull their hair back in a long, too-tight plait, brows furrowed. Grasping the ends in one shaking hand, they pick up a pair of scissors with the other. The metal slides together with a soft whisper that crawls up their spine. They catch their mom's solemn gaze from the mirror, noting her own freshly-shorn bob. Once, her hair had dusted the floor in soft curls, but mourning rites require a sacrifice.

"It's okay," she says as she steps closer. One ring-laden hand wraps around their own, supporting their grip on the scissors. "Do you want me to help?"

They pause, lump thick in their throat, before nodding. As one, they guide the scissors to the clump in their fist. As the first strands drift down around them, their mother leans in close. "The first cut is always the hardest." Then, as their hair mingles together on the floor, "It's a reminder, Nadia. A reminder that someone we love has died. But we will light these strands with maman's funeral pyre, won't we?"

The scene is gone in a puff of smoke. The world rattles as Nadia becomes Nadia once again. She is shaking, inhaling lungful after lungful of air. Her tears burn as they roll down her face.

When she blinks, she's back inside her bedroom. Simone sits across the circle from her, eyes indescribably dark. The room spins and spins and spins...

But then their hand is on her and all she can think about is how impossibly *good* it feels to have Simone touching her. How their touch cleaves through miles of flesh and burrows straight into her bones. More, more, *more*, she thinks, watching as the words take shape in the air around them. Give me more.

Fireworks dance behind her eyes when their hand settles on her thigh. She sends the image through the channels they've forged in her mind, hoping it arrives without issue. "This," she says without speaking, "This is how you make me feel."

The image darkens before vanishing entirely. Then, when she blinks, a new one. Simone sits at her side, hand crawling up her thigh still. The two of them are in the middle of a dense grove. Birds flit in the treetops overhead, shrieking to each other in their own languages. For a second, Nadia thinks she understands them, but the meaning is gone the moment she tries to conjure it.

A gentle breeze ruffles her hair. Simone's voice whistles through the trees. "This is what you do to me."

She doesn't register their fingers inside her at first, as consumed as she is by the overwhelming feeling of her and them colliding. So like the sweltering heat inside of stars, she thinks, a second before the flick of a thumb shatters her capacity for thought. How surreal it is, to know the feeling of Simone's hand as if it was her own.

She grips their wrist, feels the pressure of her own touch at the same time. When she blinks, she sees herself, mouth agape, lips the pink of Akalese cherry blossoms. Then she blinks again and Simone is hovering over her.

She's never had sex on Serenity before. The thought flows through her like a string being plucked, the vibrations centering at the base of her stomach. And yet, even in her detached state, their touch makes her pulse quicken. They're all she can focus on. Their soft orange-and-vanilla scent, the golden aura radiating from their skin, the soft flash of their teeth as they lean closer and attach themself to her neck.

Without much effort, Simone has her on the precipice of orgasm. She's so close, she could faint.

And then it hits her with the force of a tidal wave, so warm she's feverish. Her nails dig rivers into Simone's back, and she feels their pain in her peripheral, but it doesn't stop the scream that erupts from her, so quickly silenced by Simone's mouth on hers. Nadia clings to them, so sure if she lets go she will be washed away, riding them through the softer aftershocks with tears of joy and pain and everything in between streaming down her face.

In the sudden clarity that follows, a single thought floats to the surface of her mind: How could she ever think to leave them?

TWENTY-ONE

Simone Allard || After

Etienne's gaze flicks from the leafs of paper in their hand to their face, brows knitting together as he does so. "I had a feeling something of this sort would happen," he says, taking the pages from them to review one by one.

Simone's breath catches. Despite the impossibility, they allow themself a small kernel of hope. "What do you mean?"

With the jerk of his chin and the flash of his hand, Etienne's front door shuts. The figure painted on the back begins to speak, but it's muffled by Simone's sweater, reduced to an icy chill down their back. On instinct, they step closer to him, heart thudding.

"I still don't know who you are," he says. "And yet, all of this... it fills me with some semblance of pride, I think."

Tears swarm their eyes in an instant. "Enough with the pleasantries," they say through clenched teeth. "Can you work with these or not?"

"Oh, most certainly." Etienne shoves the pages into his breast pocket before raking wild eyes along his walls. Simone follows his gaze. Many of the photos he'd hung previously have been taken down.

One of the three white walls bears the faintest pencil marks across its surface. It's difficult to make out the details, but between the smudges of black and the cans of paint on the floor before it, Simone deduces he's preparing to paint another mural.

The realization gives them pause. He was impressive enough when they thought his pieces were elaborate enchantments, but he paints the whole image himself? How?

"Hours upon hours of work," Etienne says, as if he's read their mind. When they turn on him, incredulous, he takes a half-step back. "You were staring quite intently at my next project," is all he says in elaboration.

At this, they frown. "Aren't you graduating in a few weeks?"

"Hopefully," Etienne mutters, more to himself than to them. Then, with a snort, "Of course. And these murals are not just for my amusement."

Another wave of his hand. The river mural on the back wall ripples. Yellow and grey sigils flare to life at each corner of the wall. Illusion and Transmutation. Of course he would go for such deceptive forms of Casting.

As soon as the thought emerges, they stomp it down again. "Impressive," they say, fighting to sound like they mean it.

"I commissioned the spell from—Doesn't matter." With a cough, Etienne straightens, cheeks gaining a rosy hue. Simone knows the look on his face, though. It's the look of someone overwhelmingly excited about whatever they're talking about. Nadia has described the look to them before, how their eyes had gained a celestial glow when discussing historical sights with her.

Their chest tightens at the thought of her. *So close*, they remind themself as Etienne spins on his heel and surges for the back of the apartment. *So close to finding out the truth of it all.*

As soon as Simone makes to follow him, he whips around with a glare. They freeze where they stand.

"I have not forgotten that, the last time you were here, you tried to kill me." His voice is an unusual rumble in his throat. "I suggest you not forget, either."

They say nothing, letting him retreat into his bedroom with a deep-seated frown. How is it a man can lose access to the most important memories he has of himself and his best friend, but will cling so stubbornly to the misunderstanding he and Simone had?

Well, they suppose it hadn't *entirely* been a mistake. The memory of their pale-knuckled grip on his shirt collar, the way they had wanted to break his skull open like an egg if it meant obtaining his secrets, feels to them now like a phantom of their imagination. But, if it had been, Etienne wouldn't be this cautious with them now.

Simone examines the lines of their palms and tries not to think about how Nadia would take their hands and stare at them for minutes at a time. Sometimes, she would prattle on about their future. They trace the line forming a wide berth around their thumb. "You're a vivacious one," Nadia had told them once. "You're going to touch the lives of so many people. You already have."

They drop their hands with a snort. With every passing second, they felt the noose-like consequences of their actions further tighten. The coiling in their gut was sign enough; the end is coming, and soon.

Etienne re-emerges before too long, face half-hidden behind his tower of books. He sets them down on the back of one of the couches with a heavy sigh. "You'll have to help me cross-reference all of this, of course."

Their throat goes dry. "Do we really have the time for—"

His eyes are all green fire, hot enough to melt the tower around them to the ground. If not for the lack of a Casting glove on his hand,

Simone is sure he would fire off a volley of spells strong enough to immolate them. They half-expect him to lunge across the living room at them, and they brace themself accordingly. One second goes by, then another. Still, he doesn't move.

At last, every muscle in his body as taut as a bowstring, he flips open the top-most cover. "I think we have *plenty* of time." His voice drips acid with each syllable. "I am not fucking around with this. One errant line in our sigils and my mind is as useful to us as a scrambled egg. Do you understand the risks I am taking? That I've *been* taking already?"

With a hard swallow, they nod. Despite their own struggles, they know it will do no good to mention them now. Not when they're so painfully close.

Etienne lobs a book in their direction before they can blink. "Then get to reading."

***

As has happened each time Simone has made the attempt, they can't make sense of the Enchanting sigils Etienne has them flip through. At one point, bridge of his nose pinched, he stops their reading to go over the shapes particular to this realm of Casting, but his harried explanation enters one ear and out the other. Never before has Simone struggled so terribly to retain information.

"I don't know why you aren't understanding," Etienne groans at last before reviewing the notes Simone gave him again. "See this swirl? The direction of it and whether or not it's internal or external dictates the direction of the effect. I know the direction in these spells means the effect is supposed to be internal, and which way the tail is pointing means..."

Simone palms their eyes and sits back. "I don't fucking know what it means."

The pen groans in his hand. Straightening, Etienne sets it down. "Fine. How about this series of lines here?"

They glance at the runes they were given, then to the spellbook open at their side. Etienne's spidery handwriting suggests the glyph they're looking at, a series of overlapping curves, can dictate the range of the spell. Their gaze flicks back to the runes. Here, the curves are fewer and less complex. "It means..."

And then they trail off. They don't know the answer, for once. The revelation sets tears to their eyes and laughter bubbling within them. Rare is it they cannot comprehend something. They almost forgot how frustrating the sensation is.

His palm strikes the table like a thunderclap. Simone flinches at the suddenness of it, sure the next place his palm will land is their face, but it doesn't. His harsh breathing punctures the silence. At last, he drags the book back towards him.

"Each realm has its own language," he says through his teeth. "I can't expect you to be fluent in Enchanting." Though he says it aloud, it sounds more like a proclamation to himself, a recitation to ease his anger. Still, the motion does little to soothe their nerves.

Their lips form a thin line. Drumming their nails on the table between them, they watch as he thumbs through several pages, then several more. Dozens of sigils blur by, each as incomprehensible as the last.

Their stomach is a tightly-wadded ball by the time he's finished his note-taking. All too soon, they expect someone to come for them. They just hope there's still enough time to squeeze the answers out of him first.

"Seems solid enough," he says as he shoves the book aside. "Though you can never be too sure."

Simone's drumming stops. "I suppose this isn't the best time to ask, but what do these... do?"

Etienne's brow quirks before relaxing again. "Right," he mutters under his breath. Then, flapping one of the loose pages, he says, "This one will be our best bet."

"And it does...?"

"That's for me to understand and for you—hopefully—to never have to know."

They breathe deeply through their agitation. He's being pragmatic, they know. Perhaps for the first time all afternoon. *It's his life on the line, after all. Not mine.* Still, it doesn't stop the tick in their jaw.

He stretches his Caster's glove over his gnarled fingers. "I suppose you should wish me luck." Even as he speaks, his hands shake. Still, he sticks the scrap of paper to his sweat-slicked scalp without further preamble. A shudder rolls through Simone, but they don't dare stop him. Not now, when they're so close.

His glove glows green, so bright it blinds them. Then, as it dims, he slumps over in his seat. His eyes roll in his skull like skittering bugs, his pulse just as erratic when they press their fingers to his wrist to check it.

"E-Etienne?"

The blood drains from his face. With his newfound grey pallor, he looks to them the way he did within the hospital.

"No, no, no." Tentatively, they smack his cheek. Then again. "Wake up, Etienne."

With a strangled gasp, Etienne bolts upright. He blinks impossibly fast, eyes still rolling behind the lids. His pulse gallops beneath their fingers now. Their fingers are slick with his sweat.

Then, after several harsh breaths, Etienne pulls away. He plants a hand to his temple. "Lights," he bites out. "Turn off the lights."

The magicite lamps seem to flare in response to his newfound state. Simone jumps to obey his request. One by one, they extinguish the lamps, the magicite blistering their fingers as they do.

At last, darkness cloaks the two of them. Etienne releases a loud sigh. "Good, good," he says. Simone makes out his shadow as it flops against the couch. "Gods, my head hurts."

Simone approaches him with slow steps, hands extended like he's an animal ready to strike. They don't have time to handle any further complications. *Nadia. Ask him about Nadia.*

And yet, the moment their mouth opens, what comes out instead is, "Are you okay?"

His head tilts in their direction. "A strange question." His voice is thick with emotion. With a sniffle, he pats the couch cushion next to him. "Come and sit."

They perch themself on the edge of the seat. By the second, their eyes are adjusting to the gloom. They search for Etienne's form.

"Nadia is dead, Simone."

Somewhere deep down, they know it's the truth. They can't imagine any other reason why she wouldn't have shown her face. Surely, she would have known that nothing she did was terrible enough she couldn't come home to them.

And yet. Their fingers curl tight around their capelet collar. "How?" they ask, eyes squeezed shut. They almost can't bear the answer.

"I... I wish I could describe it." Etienne's hand cups their knee, the gesture simultaneously nausea-inducing and comforting. "One moment, she was fine." His voice catches.

"A-And then?"

He takes their hand and tugs them for the bedroom. Soft blue light floods the space at his provocation.

The room is the same as the last time Simone looked it over, as if Etienne couldn't bear to clean up the remnants of his attack. They cut a glance in his direction. Perhaps he can't. Even the bed lacks a human-shaped divot to it.

Their jaw sets. Begrudgingly, they allow themself a twinge of pity for him.

"This is where it happened," they say, hoping it will urge him to speak.

"It is." He doesn't elaborate for several moments, gazing instead to a blank corner of the room. Then, in a voice so unbearably small, he continues. "She came to my apartment in a panic, the day that she died. The day I almost went with her. She was having a hallucination—at least, that's what I assumed. It had happened to her before and we had blamed it on Serenity's influence. But she was completely sober this time."

"A hallucination?" Their breath flutters in their throat.

He nods. "When she came to see me, her hands were... disfigured. Black to the wrist and with daggers for nails. We'd seen this before, like I said. Or rather, she said she had. And then, while we were in the midst of trying to come to a solution..."

His voice breaks, and a part of them hates themself for prodding. "What happened next?"

Etienne points a trembling finger at the largest black stain on the carpet. "I can hardly make sense of it, even now. Have you ever seen a snake's jaw unhinge?" If he's expecting an answer, he doesn't wait for it. "Her mouth opened impossibly wide. She let out the most vile scream I've ever heard. The next thing I know, she lunged at me."

They take in the scene again, the puddles of pitch and the eviscerated pillows, the bloody handprint on his desk. It's all too much. Simone staggers, throat constricting, as the first tears prick their eyes and roll unfettered down their cheeks. All of their weeks of searching, reduced now to splotches of miasma on the carpet.

The sludge on the floor between them bubbles to life, forming the beginnings of some small avatar. In the other room, someone bangs hard at the front door.

"Mister LaChance, please let us in," comes a muffled voice.

Eyes wide, Etienne reaches for the magicite lamp, intent on plunging the both of them back into darkness. A formless spell crackles in Simone's palms. It wouldn't be enough to harm anyone, not without runes to focus the magic through.

The splintering of wood booms across the apartment. Several heavy footsteps march their way. From across the room comes a heavy thud, but Simone doesn't dare speak. Instead, they lunge for the source of the sound. If Etienne's been hurt again...

The light in the bedroom flashes on again the moment they crouch beside him. He's thrown himself prone, arms over his head and his eyes screwed shut.

"H-Help me!" he says, and at first they think it's a plea to them. The moment they reach for him, though, he flinches. "They're going to kill me!"

It's enough to make them recoil. Behind them comes the sound of metal gliding across metal.

"Step away from him, Mx. Allard."

They don't move. They almost don't dare to breathe. It's not until calloused hands close around their wrists and haul them upright that it dawns on them. They've been caught. After all this time, with everything they've done, it almost shocks them how long it's taken to come to a head.

"I-I don't know what happened." Etienne's lip trembles. "They came over and they were fine and then they just... lunged."

They thrash in the grip of their captors. "Liar!" Their fury burns holes in their throat. Their next words come out hoarse. "You fucking liar!"

Anything they could think to say next is clamped down their throat. When they try to scream, their lips fuse together. A rainbow of colors flashes on the wall in front of them. One moment, their rage threatens to boil them from the inside out. The next, their thoughts turn to mud in their brain.

"Just rest for a while, Mx. Allard, hmm?"

They've never heard a suggestion more reasonable before. Simone's eyelids flutter closed. The last sensation they recall is their utter weightlessness as they slump forward. Then, they remember nothing at all.

TWENTY-TWO

Nadia DuPont || Before

When Nadia's eyes flutter open the next morning, Simone is sleeping next to her, their warmth seeping into her skin. Flickers of last night play behind her eyes like the films she's heard are growing in popularity in the larger cities. Their hands roaming her body. The way they had sent supernovas through her blood.

Warmth fills her stomach at the thought, accompanied by a soft ache between her legs.

She considers waking them for a second, more sober roll in the bedsheets, but stops short. Their face is blank with peaceful sleep. It would be selfish of her to wake them.

As carefully as she can, Nadia slips out of Simone's grasp, rising on wobbling legs. A familiar discomfort floods her bones the instant her feet touch the floor. Someday, perhaps, they will have an answer to her woes, but not today. For now, she'll have to check her reserves for something to take the edge off.

Her gut tightens. Before her search, she should use the bathroom.

Nadia tiptoes through her apartment with unusual care. Dio materializes at her side, tail winding around her leg, and he lets out a soft mewl of greeting.

"Good morning, sweet boy." She stops to scratch behind his ears, but the instant she bends down, he darts away with a startled mewl. She shakes her head. Sometimes, it surprises her how skittish he can be.

She hums a soft tune as she relieves herself, then moves for the sink. The tune continues as she washes her hands. Some lullaby her mother used to sing to her, though she can't remember the words anymore. It soothes her nonetheless.

As she shuts off the faucet, it occurs to her: the pain isn't as bad today. At least, not the likes of which she's used to. It's enough to bring a soft smile to her face. Sure, a night of lengthy, drug-addled sex won't be enough to cure her, but if it's enough to wake her in good spirits the next day, she should do it more often.

As quickly as the thought comes to her, she shoves it away. Simone would tell her that isn't a healthy mindset to have. They hadn't had the best time with their return back to earth, by the sounds of it, and didn't seem the type of person to enjoy frequent ventures outside of themself.

She makes to splash her face with the excess water in the sink when the sight of her hands stops her dead. Blackened skin surges up to her elbows. Her fingers end in sharp, terrifying claws. Nadia springs back with a barely-repressed shriek, half a step from slamming into the door behind her.

The figure in the mirror is enough to elicit a whimper, though.

"No." She watches the disfigured mouth move, the way its jaw hangs loose to one side. Her panicked breaths are enough to make her head spin as it is, and she tries desperately to remember the breathing techniques her mother taught her as a child—in through the nose, out with the mouth puckered tight like a straw. As much as she runs monstrous hands over her face, desperate to disprove the vision she sees, it doesn't go away.

"No, no, no."

In a blink, the vision is gone. Her face is paler than it was moments before, undoubtedly due to the force of her fright, but it's... her. Not some sick warping of herself, like what she just saw suggests. Even her hands have returned to their dusty brown shade, the nails filed down like normal.

Simone is still sleeping in the next room. Maybe they will know what to do. This thought, too, she shoves away. If she's shifted in this manner, there's no telling what will happen to Simone if they see her. Would they think her a monster?

She grips the sink until thin cracks spiderweb across the surface. No. Simone can't help her.

No one can, the voice inside her goads, and it's almost enough to send her to her knees. *You could very well become a monster, as you fear. Kill everyone here. Everyone you love. Everything you've ever cherished.*

Now she does drop, hand over her mouth to muffle the scream. The tiles underneath shatter with the force. Iron hands grip her stomach and twist it tight. It's as though a chasm has opened up beneath her.

I can't stay here. Her gaze whips around the room. *I can't stay here. Where can I go?*

Etienne. He's an Enchanter, after all. There must be something he can do, some way he can pull the voice from within her, some way to pull the visions threatening to drive her mad.

Or perhaps not. But there's only one way to find out.

Nadia slinks through her apartment as quiet as her heavy footfalls will allow, stopping for her capelet and her Caster's glove on her way.

Dread flows through her veins with each step. Hood pulled low over her face, she takes one last lingering look at Simone's sleeping form before leaving.

***

It takes seconds for Etienne to answer when she makes it to his apartment. Her intestines still feel as though they're being twisted, no matter how many deep breaths she makes herself do. It's because of these breaths, she thinks as she raises her fist to knock, that she didn't collapse somewhere on the stairwell.

His pencil-thin brow arches at the sight of her. Were it anyone else, she would take the gesture as a sign of derision, but she knows better with Etienne. His concern couldn't be plainer if he tried. He doesn't ask if she's okay, doesn't stop her when she barges her way into his apartment and sits down. He closes the door with the click of the lock, hands buried deep in his pockets as he turns to face her. From over his shoulder, the portrait that resembles his mother mutters its greetings. The simpleness of it all is almost enough to make her start sobbing anew.

Instead, in an impossibly thin voice, she says, "I think I'm going to hurt someone."

He's nonplussed by her statement. They've had these sorts of talks before in undergrad, when she hadn't yet gained control of her agitation and anger at the world. Then, she had been a scared girl new at college and incapable of maintaining herself. Now, only their shared memories and the scars on her hips remind her of those days.

"Do you want to talk about it?" he asks.

Yes. No. Maybe. The words circle her brain, a torturous roulette. Finally, she forces out, "Do you remember the last time we took Serenity together?"

He rubs a hand over his face, shoving his glasses out of the way before straightening them again. "Vaguely."

"Do you remember the... vision I had?"

"A hallucination and nothing more, I suspect. Have you not gotten over it?"

She grips her skirt with paling fingers. "It happened again."

Etienne's lips flatten. His shoulders heave with the weight of his sigh. For several beats of her heart, he doesn't speak, doesn't move. Then he crosses for the kitchen. She watches as he turns on the burner on his stove and sets a tea kettle over top the blue flames. He ladles heaping spoonfuls of a substance she can't make out into his beverage press.

"Have..." He winces at whatever it is he's thinking of saying. "Have you considered telling someone?"

During undergrad, she had discussed her violent tendencies towards herself with the faculty. It'd been enough to cover her in warning labels to her peers. No one in her life had granted her enough compassion to do anything farther. No one, that is, except for Etienne.

Her grip tightens. "I think I would rather die than endure that again."

He doesn't argue. Instead, he cleans out two teacups with a sponge before setting them aside to dry. The water in the kettle starts to steam before too long.

"Truth be told, Etienne, I don't know what to do anymore." Heaving a sigh, Nadia pulls her knees to her chest and bites her lip until she tastes copper. "I just don't want to hurt anyone."

With this, the last of her strength crumbles away. She sobs hard enough to rattle her entire body, the sound so thick it's as though she's yanking it from the base of her chest. Thick rivers of tears pour down her face and soak the front of her skirt. She wants to claw herself to pieces, to scream until her throat gives out. Anything at all to soothe the vacuous hole forming in her chest. In her frustration, she beats her head against the top of the couch.

Etienne is on her in an instant. His hand cradles the back of her head. With some force, he pulls her against his chest. Her sobs begin anew.

"Am I going to die soon?" she asks when she has enough air. Her mind whirls her around all the while.

"I don't know. I sure hope not."

The whistle of the kettle is enough to drag her back to reality. From across the campus, a bell tolls. First bell. Nadia surveys his apartment with bleary eyes, gaze landing at last on the clock on his wall.

"Can..." She trails off when he returns to her with a cup of coffee. "Can I stay here for today?"

She knows it's a foolish question as soon as she's said it. The warning notes from the faculty have grown dust in the corner of her desk, but she remembers all the same. Too much more time outside of class and they'll expel her for truancy. And yet, she can't find it within her today to care. Not for the thought of Simone's reaction. Not for the risk of losing her home and degree from Voterique.

"Of course you can." Etienne's smile doesn't reach his eyes. He knows as well as her how precarious her position has become, but undoubtedly her emotional unraveling and compromised state of mind have been enough to sway him. "Stay as long as you need."

Neither of them move. To break the silence, Nadia takes a sip of her coffee, nose wrinkling at the bitter taste of the dark liquid, before setting the cup aside. Rising on unsteady legs, she makes for the bedroom.

"You don't mind if I go to bed?" she tosses over her shoulder.

"No." Still, the click of his heels draws closer behind her. "Never."

His bedroom is devoid of all illustration. She recalls the last time she gazed upon this room, how paint had stretched from wall to wall and even onto the windows. He must have gotten bored of the mural, given how it's all been wiped away now.

As she perches herself on the edge of the mattress, Etienne moves deeper into the room. "I just need a couple of things for classes," he explains, but he stops first to guide her backwards to the mattress. He doesn't tuck her in this time. She can't read the expression in his eyes as he stares at her.

Something within her stomach snaps. Nadia salivates at the sight of the human before her.

Meat. Hungry. Consume.

Her stomach rumbles at the thought. A sickly-sweet stench fills the air, originating from the human looming over her. His blood, she realizes as he frowns and leans closer. Will his blood taste as sweet as it smells?

"Nat? You okay?"

She doesn't know who this "Nat" is. Still, the confusion the question stirs is enough to make her being ripple in confusion. Clouds of red form in the corners of her vision. What the fuck is she doing?

"Nadia." The human—*Etienne! His name is Etienne!*—grips her by the shoulders and shakes her, concern blooming across his face now. "Can you hear me?"

Nadia snaps back to with a gasp. Gone is the redness. She can no longer hear Etienne's blood thrum through his veins—though a faint coppery stench lingers all the same. Despite herself, liquid pools in the back of her throat.

"Y-Yeah." She palms her temple, shaking her head in an effort to clear the fog consuming her. "I—"

Her bones warp as the two of them crash to the floor. She feels it in the popping of her spine, the sickening groan of her joints as her limbs grow too big, too big, too big. All at once, she towers over him, jaws dripping pitch. Puddles of it form on the floor around them.

The unmistakable burn of magic pierces the air, shifting the blood in her body and the miasma on the floor. How strange, to feel her lifeforce move with its own will.

The instant her jaws close around the human's torso, a blast of bright light from his hand shoves her away. She hits the side of the bed with enough force for the wood splinter and shower around her. A single thought consumes her as blood coats her tongue: *I want more.*

As she scrabbles to her feet, another blast from the human's gloved hand envelopes her. She's faintly aware of the smoke curling from her fur, of how her blood sings in response to the magic in the air. The room is thick with the scent of something rotten. Despite the pain bristling through her from nose to tail-tip, however, she's the calmest she's ever been.

Etienne...

The monster stamps the thought down at the same time that she brings down a massive furred paw on the human's shin.

Then there's another blast. Not from the human in front of her this time, but from the doorway and the human suddenly within it. A searing dart of magic, strong enough to tear through her end to end. The monster's limbs buckle with the impact. The red rim around her vision slowly fills with black.

Beneath her, the human claws at his blackened wounds and whim-pers.

"Etienne." Her new maw struggles to form the words, but the more human part of her forces it out, anyway. "I'm sorry."

With a last gasp and yet another bolt of magic, the monster crum-ples to the floor. Blackness consumes the rest of her vision. The last dredges of the human that was once Nadia DuPont lets out a terrible, warbled howl.

The monster's consciousness dims to a flicker. Then it is gone.

TWENTY-THREE

Etienne LaChance || After

Not many students are unfortunate enough to be aware of the dungeons lurking underneath the campus. Etienne was once one of them.

He keeps a hand to the wall as he creeps through the damp corridor, embers dancing on his open palm. Down here, the air is thick with mildew and waste. After the time he spent in these dungeons, the countless interrogations and torture, he's used to the scent. Still, cold prickling shoots down his spine at the memory. He almost can't believe he talked himself into coming back here.

But he has to. For her.

If he thinks too long about Nadia, their last moments flit across his mind's eye. The pitch-black jaws. The unspeakable pain. Even now, after his weeks spent recovering, the thought of her makes him flinch. It's worse than the limp in his step and the scars along most of his body, physical reminders she left behind. Not the sort of legacy she would be proud of, he knows, and his free hand clenches. More than anything, he wishes he could scrub this monstrous version of her from his memories. She deserved better than that.

In some ways, she deserved better than him.

He sighs. If she were still alive, he and Nadia would graduate in two weeks. But he knows better. Those last, haunting moments he has of her prove her death better than any corpse. Nadia won't see today, let alone graduation.

Shards, *he* won't see graduation himself if he's caught down here.

The bricks are slick with moisture. An uneven layer of moss forms a soft carpet under his touch. One leg lags behind the other, making his trek all the more treacherous, but he presses on with a clenched jaw. For once, he's grateful his injuries have forced him to forgo his beloved heeled boots.

Before long, the endless hallway opens into a wider corridor with lines of metal-and-glass cells. A rainbow of sigils light his way, revealing slumped shapes and ravenous shadows. The sigils prevent him from hearing the screams he knows are beyond, but it doesn't still the ghostly chorus in his mind. For a heart-shattering moment, he remembers his time behind the glass, the way the other denizens of this rotted hall had kept him awake at all hours, but then he shrugs it off with a shiver.

Focus, Etienne, he tells himself. Adjusting his crooked glasses, he scans the darkness for the cell he needs.

There. The cell at the end doesn't stand out from any of the others, but he knows it's the one he needs before he approaches. Like the rest, an array of sigils line the floor in front of it like a rug. He recognizes a sigil for emotional soothing, as well as another for raising alarm if someone—somehow—breaches the bars. The rest of the runes, however, are beyond his expertise.

The figure beyond the bars remains hunched in the corner, so still Etienne almost thinks them a statue. If not for the placard revealing their name, he would have thought himself mistaken in being here.

But no. He knows who sits inside, even if they don't take in his presence.

Simone Allard.

He grinds his teeth together at the sight of them. Even now, even at the end of all things, he can't let go of the lump of hatred burning within his breast like coal. He's here, though, weeks after their arrest. Not as a favor to them, but because it's the least he can do for her. For Nadia.

"Simone."

The name shakes them from their slumber. Simone scrabbles across the stone ground, gripping the bars so hard their knuckles pale. Rust—or maybe blood—smears their palms.

"Etienne." Their voice is harsh with disuse. "I didn't think I would see you."

"Nor did I think I would come."

Their stare turns sharp, dulled only by the strings of matted hair framing their face. "Then why are you here at all?"

I've asked myself the same thing. Stuffing his hands in his trouser pockets, he tips his chin and glowers. Neither of them speak for several moments.

The dripping of something—perhaps a leak from the sewers—brings him back to. "I don't know," he says, and for once it's the truth. "I should have left you here to rot like the pathetic thing you are."

Something not unlike dismay flits across Simone's features. "Then you can leave."

He considers it. It would be so easy to spin on his heel and let them seethe. It's as much as they deserve. But then, noting the way their brown fingers have sharpened at the tips, he shakes his head.

"The faculty will let you die here, you know."

Their gaze is all embers, but they don't respond.

"And if they don't," he continues, "they'll torture you."

"Are you going to say anything useful, or are you just here to gloat?"

Etienne shrugs, sheathing his hands in his pockets. "Both, I suppose. Let me see your hands."

At first, they don't release their grip on the bars, clenching until their knuckles pale. Then, slowly, they withdraw. He's relieved—that is, until they spin on their heel and slump down into the shabby cot in the corner. His jaw clenches, hard.

"Don't you care?" he says—perhaps too loudly—into the space between them.

"How can I?"

Though the runes on the bars keep him from touching them, he leans his temple against the buffer they form. "So you're giving up?"

Now, for but a moment, they regard him again. "Shouldn't I?"

"I never meant for you to be captured."

The proclamation burns his throat like acid. Simone recoils in place.

"Could have fooled me."

"I mean it." He strains for the bars and stops short. "It was a decision made in the heat of the moment. I... I couldn't let the Society try to warp me again. You have to understand."

It's the truth. Or rather, it's as close to the truth as he's willing to get. If he thinks too hard about his time down here, he remembers the sterile procedures and the cruel sneers of the Enchanters and the hours spent screaming himself hoarse. After all their torture, he was willing to say *anything*. A small mercy, then, Nadia was already dead. She wouldn't have forgiven him for selling her out otherwise.

Simone won't look at him. The dismissal burns through him, enough to turn him into a husk where he stands. What was he thinking, coming down here? He had already told them the truth of it all. His debt to them had been paid.

And yet.

The clinking of the bars signals their return in front of him. Simone extends a hand as far as the runes will allow, revealing fingers as black as Nadia's had become. The corruption is mild still, and their skin reverts under his stern gaze, but it won't be long before they join Nadia and her monstrous transformation.

He wipes his face with the back of one palm, surprised to find his cheeks are wet. When he closes his eyes, he sees her: Nadia, mouth unhinged like a snake's, sludge dripping from pointed canines.

"I could kill you," he says when the memory at last fades.

Simone snatches their hands back.

"It would be a mercy," Etienne continues. "Compared to what the faculty will do."

This, too, he remembers. Beneath the braying moans of the other denizens of the dungeons, scientists muttering to themselves and "experimenting". If Etienne is being honest with himself, he knew most of the anguished screams were because of them and their work. He'd been able to hear their conversations, on occasion. How students they'd imprisoned had shifted in the blink of an eye when injected. How monsters had been branded by magic like cattle.

If he thinks too hard about it, he can even recall the smell of it all, hot and acrid and utterly vile. Like animal fat set ablaze, the gristle left to rot under a brutal summer sun.

Simone brings themself to their full height, chin jutted out in defiance. He's almost proud of them and their damn stubbornness.

"Leave," they growl, shadows falling across their face and highlighting the fury within their amber eyes.

Damn stubborn, indeed. And a damn fool. Etienne buries his hands in his pockets again and shakes his head. "As you wish," he replies with the click of his tongue. Then he turns away, intent on turning his back on them for good.

A couple of steps later, he pauses again. "You have two weeks, Simone. Two weeks to change your mind, and then I will graduate and I will be far, far away from here. I can't do anything further for Nadia—Gods know how much I want to. But I can stop you before you end up like her all the same.

"Do not mistake me, though. I do not offer this out of kindness for you. It is a last favor for Nadia and nothing more."

Etienne resumes his uneven pace through the dungeons. This time, he doesn't stop.

EPILOGUE

In the dark, the shadow loses all sense of time and space.

It cannot remember being anything more than what it is. It had a name once, and a sense of being and personality and a grander purpose for its existence. Now, all it knows is hunger, consumption. It's a burning urge it has no means to sate.

The shadow has grown so terribly hungry.

In the scant moments of lucidity—the ones where something within it wrests control of the shapeless amalgamation—the shadow is able to stretch its consciousness to the edges of its cell. It assumes it's a cell, at least, given the concrete walls and rune-d bars framing it in. Even if it had the energy to, the shadow can not stretch its consciousness beyond the cell. Still, in those scant moments, it can listen.

Footfalls. Dripping mildew. The clicking of locks and the hiss of burning torches. All of this and more undulates in the darkness like waves on the shore, a crooning lullaby in its quietest moments. The tactile instability is enough to drive it mad.

A larger awareness trickles into the forefront of its mind. Formless shadows fill its vision. The scent of rot and despair burns its nostrils, so acrid all of its eyes water. Voices, soft as down and too muted to comprehend, float into its ears. All the while, the shadow's void-like hunger grows.

And then, blessedly, true sight. The world around it solidifies in increments each time it claws its way back to lucidity.

True to its assumptions, the shadow lingers within a cell, though it can't strain itself far enough to tell where. Something in the center of its being gurgles with recognition, a momentary split from itself attempting to gain its own sense of feeling.

She is here, she is human, she has a presence and her name is—

It has half a mind to spit. Whatever—whoever—it was before no longer matters. As quickly as the distortion comes, it is gone again, consumed by the hunger.

Still, its moments of lucidity extend. Now, without having to strain itself, it hears the piercing screams of other denizens of this dungeon, so loud it's as if they're in the same space. With the screaming, too, comes a growing awareness within itself, a sense of kinship with the beings it cannot see. Almost as if the shadow within the bars and the shadows without are all part of the same whole. The shadow's sense of self shifts, water in an overflowing bowl.

In a blink, it is somewhere else. Somewhere close. Its whole being stiffens, overwhelmed by the new sensations wrapping around it. In this cell, the torches shed warping light around the cramped space. The muffled warmth of voices down the hall is closer now.

"I could kill you," one voice says, so soft the shadow almost misses it. The shadow's being ripples again with that same aggravating familiarity. A single thought swims to the forefront of its mind.

Etienne?

The shadow returns to its original placement with a grunt. Or, what it imagines would be a grunt if it possessed vocal cords. How foolish, to think any familiarity they may feel matters.

With effort, it tamps down the part of itself so desperate to be something—some*one*—else. There is only the shadow now, pulsing and hungry.

***

In a wooded grove across the world, a woman claws her way out of muck and ruin. First one pale arm, then the other, then shocks of bone-white hair as she hauls herself upright with a gasp. Miasma sloughs from her and into the mass of black still encasing her lower body. Streams of it trickle from her mouth. All she can taste is bile.

One agonizing handhold after the next, she drags herself free and flops down on solid ground. A shotgun clatters beside her.

She remains still for a long while before her eyes flutter open to regard the sky. A smattering of stars twinkle above, pinpricks against an inkspill of black. The earth cradles her like a child to its bosom. A blanket of moss pushes its way through her fingers.

She takes her first moments of true, singular consciousness to give herself an appraisal. Nothing aches, as far as she can tell. She bears two arms and two legs and a head. Small wings flutter on her temples, catching in the nighttime breeze. All things in normal working order.

The miasma does not react when she stands. She isn't sure if she expected it to or not, but she can't help the mild sense of disappointment nonetheless. Naked as a newborn, she gives a sweeping look to her surroundings. Trees encase her on all sides. A stone structure's crumbled doorway yawns open, beckoning her.

The woman looks again at the sky. Amongst the pinpricks unfamiliar to her is one star, brighter than all the rest. The instant she catches sight of it, she feels its call within her, bones-deep. She can't explain the burning need within her to follow it, just that she must.

Arms wrapped tight around herself, the woman begins to walk.

Acknowledgements

This is the part where I start waxing poetic about all the help I had and how nothing I've done would have been possible otherwise. And truly, this book would not have been possible without the influence of these people, whether said influence was direct or not.

To start, special thanks goes to the litany of writing Discords I've found myself in, including Book Or Bust, Sapphic Writers Support Group, The Bluest Hour, and one aptly named Writers. I wouldn't have been able to do this all without the various minds I was able to bounce ideas off of from these servers. Even more specific thanks to Lottie, Lisa, Lina, and Aca, who encouraged my shenanigans in one form or another.

Thanks next goes to the first readers this story had—my beta readers. Special thanks go to Rose, Pax, and Andi in particular. Your work was greatly appreciated and getting to read through your comments was a delight. I humbly thank you for your time, effort, and overwhelming enthusiasm you all put into reading for me.

Thanks also to Quinton, my editor. Your time and effort was greatly appreciated as I put the final parts of this novel together, and your enthusiasm was the confirmation I needed to remind myself how important this book is.

And of course, a shout out to the members of my patreon members: Ceph, Hannah, and Larkspur. I appreciate your months of patience and support.

I also wouldn't have been able to talk about a lot of Nadia's struggles without struggles of my own. And so, to my body, the machine held together by wet paper and duct tape. We rarely see eye to eye, but I wouldn't have you any other way. We're carrying each other through this world, hand in unloveable hand.

A special shout-out as well to my best friends, Dory and Eva. I thought of you in Etienne's and Nadia's better moments, though not in their worst. Much love to the both of you.

None of this would have been possible without my darling partners. To Naota: The love I have for you knows no words. You've stood beside me through countless struggles, just as I have for you. The sweetest parts of Nadia's and Simone's fleeting relationship are distilled from the best parts of you and I. To Rhonnie: While our relationship is newer, I've greatly enjoyed getting to know you and hope I can continue to do so. You're a special person. Don't ever forget that.

Finally, thanks goes to you, the reader. You're one of the biggest reasons any of this was even possible. Sure, I could have just thrown this into the void and called it good, but a lot of what kept me going was the prospect of your eventual reactions. And if you liked what you've read, I greatly encourage you to leave a review. It's what keeps writers like me going.

REALMS OF CASTING

The following is an overview produced by the Academic Coalition for Arcane Study (A.C.A.S.) in relation to the eight realms of magic Casting.

Abjuration | Abjurors — Blocking, banishing, and protecting.

Conjuration | Conjurors — Pulling something from or through alternate planes of existence.

Divination | Diviners — Discernment, clear-knowing, and foresight.

Enchantment | Enchanters — Entrancing of others and modifying of memory.

Evocation | Evocators — Bending of natural forces, production of something from "nothingness".

Illusion | Illusors — Bending the rules of reality, or the art of smoke and mirrors.

Necromation | Necromancers — Bending the forces of the living and the dead.

Transmutation | Transmutors — Bending and transforming matter from one shape into another.

About the Author

Alex is a speculative fiction writer and mountain of indescribable goo living in the PNW. When they aren't gluing airplane parts together, they're reading from their arsenal of books, being a general menace, or playing video games. You can contact them via email at authoralexh arvey@gmail.com, or by howling into the woods when you're alone at night. Alternatively, a collection of their links and online denizens can be found at the QR code below.

9 798330 332700